EVIL ON THE HIGH SEAS

A Diana Daniels Mystery

DIANE DEMETRE

LUMINOSITY PUBLISHING LLP

EVIL ON THE HIGH SEAS
A Diana Daniels Mystery
Copyright © JULY 2020 DIANE DEMETRE

Paperback ISBN: 978-1-910397-99-2

Cover Art by Poppy Designs

ALL RIGHTS RESERVED

No part of this literary work may be reproduced in any form or by any means, including electronic or photographic reproduction, in whole or in part, without the written permission of the publisher.

This is a work of fiction. All characters and events in this book are fictitious. Any resemblance to actual persons living or dead is purely coincidental.

The author acknowledges the trademark status and the following trademark owners mentioned in this work of fiction:
Chanel No. 5 ™

DEDICATION

For Agatha Christie, the greatest mystery writer of all time, whose classic whodunnits filled my young imagination with mystery, murder, and mayhem.

In the struggle for survival,
the fittest win out at the
expense of their rivals
because they succeed in
adapting themselves best to
their environment.
—Charles Darwin, *On the
Origin of Species, 1859*

CHAPTER ONE

LONG BEFORE I PROMISED TO scatter my husband's ashes to the wind, a part of me knew trouble was coming. The obstinate knot in my shoulder that's been my constant traveling companion for the past twenty-four hours proves it. All my life it's acted like a portent of doom and today it's on high alert. I try to ignore its message by digging my fingers into the source of the pain, but relief is only temporary. Like Alice peering down the rabbit hole, I'm about to plunge head-first into a fantastic wonderland known as the Galapagos Islands. However, unlike Alice, my first solo adventure and final farewell to Tom aren't going to be just a curious dream. I have a feeling it'll be more than I bargained for, and not in a good way.

I stare out the coach window, hoping I'm wrong, but then again, I'm seldom wrong. Overhead, the translucent San Cristobal sky does its best to distract me, while the Pacific Ocean tries to soothe my apprehensions with its sparkling azure and turquoise palette. A day in all its glory and I'm missing it. *For goodness sake, Diana, you're fifty-five, not fifteen. Stop stressing. Everything'll be fine.*

When the coach eases to a stop at our port of debarkation, I breathe easier knowing that I've finally arrived. At first glance, Puerto Baquerizo Moreno is a quaint seaside settlement edged by a sweeping harbor. Without honking traffic and modern buildings, the town appears trapped in a romantic, maritime antiquity. However, the horrible smell that accosts me when I step off the coach into the sweltering Ecuadorian summer spoils my first rosy impression. Along with the other passengers bound for the exclusive *Silver Galapagos* expedition ship, I cover my nose at the putrid stench of decayed fish.

When the murmurs of disgust change to delight, I nudge forward to see what the fuss is about. There, no more than a couple of feet in front of me, surrounded by hordes of people, I find the cause of the commotion and the smell. A massive sea lion lounges on a bus bench like a reclining Buddha, oblivious to the overjoyed tourists taking photos and selfies.

"Okay, everyone, step back, please. Not so close to the sea lion." Like a football referee, a large man breaks up the scrum and then stands guard so that no one gets too close.

Looking past the dispersing crowd, I spot dozens of sea lions sprawled across pedestrian pathways, languishing on public benches and slumped across the rocky shoreline warming themselves with total disregard for the human inhabitants.

"Amazing . . ." I murmur to myself.

"Isn't it?" A man's honeyed voice drizzles over my right shoulder, taking me by surprise. I glance around with a frown, but his gaze is fixed firmly on the sea lions. "Look over there."

Clearly in awe of the spectacle as much as me, he points to the furthest wharf, where hundreds of the big, blubbery mammals lie side by side or atop each other, as if knowing their protected species status gives them absolute sovereignty over the harbor. *Tom would be in his element.*

"Terrific, isn't it?" The man's accent is unmistakably American. One of my favorites.

I swivel to face him and hold out my hand. "Diana Daniels."

"John Nash." He clasps it in a firm, but not too strong grip. "Are you Australian?" He tilts his head and his tanned face splits in a lopsided smile.

"I am. And you're from?"

"California. I haven't traveled as far as you though. You've done long haul. Are you traveling alone?" He looks around before returning his green-eyed gaze to me.

"Yes. My husband was to join me. Unfortunately, he died nearly a year ago."

"I'm sorry to hear that. But with a hundred passengers on the ship, I doubt any of us will be alone for long. I hear they've got our days filled with land and sea excursions. You weren't expecting a relaxing holiday, were you?"

"Well, I had thought I'd get some rest." *In fact, I'm looking forward to it.*

"This is an expedition vessel, not a cruise ship. No pools to laze around, no night clubs, or late-night cabaret shows. It's about getting up close and personal with nature. I think the only rest we'll get is when we drop into bed at night." He regards my sneakers. "I hope you brought waterproof walking shoes?"

Just as I'm about to confirm I've at least packed appropriate footwear, a thick-accented South American voice sounds over the megaphone. "All passengers for the *Silver Galapagos*, this way." The same man who protected the sea lion earlier waves us over.

"It looks like they want us down on the lower jetty." John glances at my bag. "Do you need help with your hand luggage?"

"No thanks, I can manage." I tug my wheelie cabin bag behind me and side-step the obstructing sea lions to join the chattering crowd moving down the wharf.

After a quick safety demonstration on how to wear our life belts, we wait to be grouped in lots of ten to board the zodiaks, the rubber inflatable boats which idle around the landing jetty that will transport us to the ship. With nothing else to do, I study the other passengers. I figure they're from Japan, Scandinavia, the UK, and America, mostly traveling in groups or couples. I notice some older women huddle together, probably widows. *Urgh! I hate that word.* But like it or not, I've now graduated into their ranks, and I must make the best of it.

Appearing from the shadows, a tall, willowy woman dressed in designer white slacks, white silk blouse, and white boat shoes, steps forward. She wears an enormous white picture hat strategically dipped over one eye, just like Carly Simon sang. Bug-eyed sunglasses cover most of her upper face under which a slash of tangerine lipstick curves upward in a blazing smile at the guide who helps her board. Like a celebrity, her striking presence quietens the crowd, and we watch spellbound as she glides gracefully onto the first zodiak. She ignores the guide's instruction to move to the back of the boat and instead sits in the middle on the zodiak's rounded rubber sidewall. She's not moving for anyone. The other nine, obviously disgruntled, passengers maneuver around her to find a seat. Like a queen bee, she remains enthroned—a glamazon in white splashed across nature's pristine backdrop.

John slips in beside me. "That's one for the record books." He sounds amused.

I nod in agreement but can't drag my eyes away from the woman in white. "I doubt they've had many passengers like her board a zodiak. I wonder who she is?"

"I guess we'll find out soon enough. Dressed like that, she won't be hard to miss on the ship."

Indeed, she won't. The knot in my shoulder twists in affirmation.

Filled with its quota of ten passengers, the zodiak slowly reverses, turns, and motors out toward the *Silver Galapagos*. With its imposing navy-blue hull and four passenger decks painted in arctic white, the ship's anchored in deep water on the ocean side of the harbor. Though considerably smaller than a cruise ship, she looks a magnificent vessel, stately, yet sturdy.

As the first zodiak picks up speed, I notice the woman in white remove her hat. With hair sculpted close to her head, she turns her face toward the ship. Master of her surroundings, she bears the same regal demeanor as the *Silver Galapagos*.

Who is she?

A surge of energy lifts the hairs on the back of my neck, and I can't decide whether my mounting excitement is because we're underway or my fascination with the mysterious woman in white.

★ ★ ★

"IF THERE'S ANYTHING ELSE YOU need, Mrs. Daniels, this is my card. Please call me." Dressed in an executive valet's uniform, Jimmy, the butler for deck four, bows and places his card on the countertop in my cabin. A tall, unassuming man, probably in his late thirties, he conducts himself in a polite, professional manner.

"Thank you." I shoot him a gracious smile, but it does nothing to soften his reserved expression. He bows again before making a humble exit.

After he leaves, I give my cabin a cursory inspection and nod with satisfaction. Suite 420 is spacious, well-appointed, and immaculately maintained. With a bespoke teak and marble en suite, a comfy king-size bed on which lies a throw rug emblazoned with the word "Welcome," and more space than I expected, the cabin exceeds my expectations.

Deck four boasts ten suites, five either side of the passageway, with mine at the starboard forward end. Next to it a Staff Only access door leads to the commanding bridge, which means I'm closest to the crew if the ship goes down. I find the thought reassuring, since my sea-legs are questionable at best.

Shifting bands of light bounce off the waves outside, drawing me out onto my cabin's narrow balcony. Eight-foot-high partitions divide each suite's balcony from its neighbors', giving plenty of visual, but little vocal privacy. The voices of other passengers travel on the breeze, and I try not to eavesdrop on their conversations. Still, I wonder if any of the voices belong to the woman in white? Before my mind becomes sidetracked, the balmy mid-afternoon breeze captures my full attention, cooling things down a little. "Perfect boating weather," as Tom would say.

Leaning on the timber railing, I inhale a deep breath of clean, salty air, in the hope it'll clear the familiar loneliness his memory brings. It helps a little, but not enough, so I grab my tourist pamphlet and study the nearby landmarks. In the distance, two towers of golden volcanic rock jut up from the ocean, impressive against the purplish sky. Named Kicker Rock, the monolithic monsters are remnants from a long-ago past and iconic to the Galapagos Islands. Overhead, the similarly prehistoric frigate birds with their two-meter wingspans swoop and cruise at high speeds on the air currents surging off the ship. Tom had booked many holidays for us before, but he'd excelled himself with this one. If the service and scenery over the next seven days match what I've experienced already, it's going to be a grand expedition. A shame he's not here to enjoy it.

I glance at my watch. "Damn. I better get a move on. The orientation lecture begins in thirty minutes."

Within no time, I store every item away, clothes on hangers, toiletries sorted by purpose on bathroom shelves, underwear in drawers, and my suitcase and cabin bag placed in the passageway for Jimmy to stow for the week.

With a few minutes to spare, I curl up for a quiet moment on the sofa. My most precious cargo—a silver canister, about the size of a jewelry box—rests in my hands. "Well, Tom, I've brought your ashes all this way to scatter them in the most pristine place on earth. Just as you wanted." I caress its smooth edges and sigh. "There's no rush though. I'm sure I'll know when the time's right." It's not going to be easy to cast him to the wind, but no matter how hard it is for me, I won't break the promise I made to him on his death bed.

"*Orientation in five minutes everyone.*" The crisp, clear voice of a man voice startles me.

My gaze shoots upwards to a speaker in the ceiling above my bed and then searches for a volume switch. None. "Urgh." John was right. There'll be little chance of rest and relaxation with the crew giving us updates and prompts over the cabin loudspeaker.

"*Remember to bring your life jacket and life belt for the emergency evacuation drill in the Explorer Room.*"

"I've got to go, Tom." I place the silver box safely in a bedside drawer and pop the lanyard with my room keycard around my neck. After gathering up my life jacket and life belt, I head to the internal staircase down to deck three.

Laughter and excited chatter greet me before I reach the bottom. No larger than a medium-sized conference room, the Explorer Room acts as a muster point for passenger briefings and activities. With its low ceiling and dim lighting, the venue's claustrophobic atmosphere is exacerbated by the hundred passengers, guides, and selected crew milling around. I angle through the crowd, chuckling to myself at those passengers who've already donned their cumbersome fluorescent life jackets. Like giant emperor penguins, they waddle from side to side, trying to keep their balance now that the ship's underway. Others jostle for the power positions in the front row of seats, while I slip into my preferred spot—the last aisle chair in the back row.

Tucked to one side of the room, away from prying eyes, hides the woman in white, minus her hat, but still hidden behind her glamorous sunglasses. Again, I watch her, intrigued by her incognito persona. She leans over and speaks to a dark-haired man beside her. He nods dutifully, but I notice he sneers when she looks away. *No love lost there.*

"Is that seat beside you taken?" John Nash stands grinning in the aisle, his arms wrapped around his safety gear.

My focus shifts and I swing my knees to let him pass. "No, that's fine."

He squeezes through and drops onto the chair, balancing his vest and belt on his lap. "I told you this wasn't going to be a relaxing cruise." He tags a good-natured laugh onto the end of his reminder.

"I guess not." I shrug while studying him a little closer. He's like one of those all-American heroes. Handsome, probably in his mid-forties, and a real lady killer, except there's nothing boastful about him. He's the sort of fellow who doesn't give much away. The type who keeps his cards close to his chest. Then it dawns on me that he's not offered any information about himself since we met on the bus landing. "Are you traveling alone, John?"

"Actually, I am. Looks like we're both orphans this trip." He pauses, his expression tightening. "I see you're still taken with the lady in white." He tips his head in her direction while arching a brow at me.

"She's very intriguing." My gaze strays to her once more.

"Let me guess. You're a journalist for a celebrity gossip magazine."

I stare at him and screw up my nose. "No."

"Okay. You're an author on the hunt for unusual characters?"

I shake my head.

"I give up. What line of work are you in? And what makes you so interested in our mystery woman over there?"

"I'm a high-level management consultant. Major organizations and government departments contract me, predominantly in human resources, recruitment, and training."

He gives a slow nod. "You're hired as an expert in human behavior and industrial relations to help companies select the right person for the job, so to speak."

"Yes. My role is to recruit, build, and train the right team, at the right time, for the right price. So, anything out of the ordinary always gets my attention."

"And the mystery lady is definitely out of the ordinary."

"That she is."

I follow his gaze to the corner of the room, but she's gone. In her place, an orange life jacket signals a missing passenger. I stiffen and scout the room. It's compulsory for everyone to attend this drill. Unable to see her anywhere, my eyes return to the inscrutable expression on John's face.

"Where did she go?" I ask.

"I don't know, but I'm sure she's here somewhere. She can't just disappear off the ship." He nods to the front of the room where the crew line up in single file.

"If I could have everyone's attention please …" I recognize the voice from my cabin's loudspeaker. "My name is Israel, and on behalf of the captain and crew, I want to welcome you …" As Israel continues in his well-rehearsed speech, my mind returns to the woman in white. *Where is she? Why did she leave?*

As if the knot in my shoulder isn't bad enough, a familiar feeling in the pit of my stomach begins to stir. I know the sensation well. It's one of my hunches. An unexplainable feeling that usually surfaces when I least expect it. Some call it intuition or a sixth sense about people or things. I don't know what it is, but I've had it since I was young. If I try to ignore it, its insistence grows, until I do what it tells me. Although I'm pragmatic by nature, my hunches have been fundamental to my professional success, because I intuitively know if a prospective candidate is right for the job or not, even if they shine in their interview.

And here it is, sending up distress flares about the woman in white. If Tom were here, he'd say that I'm being silly, I'm reading too much into things. But my hunch shouts in my head, loud and clear. There's something not quite right on the *Silver Galapagos*—and it has to do with the woman in white.

CHAPTER TWO

AFTER THE MUSTER DRILL, WE file back to our cabins confident that we won't go down with the ship if it sinks. In no time, I strip off and step into my shower cubicle, eager to wash off the day's grime. I often do my best thinking in the shower, so I treat myself to a long, slow drenching and debate with my nagging intuition. As usual, it wins, urging me to find out more about the mystery woman. While I blow-dry my hair and formulate my plan, someone knocks on my cabin door.

"Just a minute," I call, cinching my cabin robe and padding to the door.

"Good evening, madam, my name is Bruno. I'm the Butler Manager." A diminutive man, dressed in a crisp silver-gray three-piece suit which matches his precisely trimmed silver-gray hair, stands at attention at my door. Though his accent suggests Italian, rather than Ecuadorian descent, he exudes the same level of excellence as the rest of the crew. He bows and proffers his card.

"If you need anything and cannot get Jimmy, please feel free to contact me on this number."

"Thank you, Bruno. That's most kind." I accept his card and tuck it into my robe's pocket.

"Have you made your dinner reservation, Mrs. Daniels? If not, I can do that for you."

"That's fine, Bruno. All done."

"Well, if there's nothing else . . ."

"There is one other thing. I remember when my husband booked this trip, I was sure our suite was 430. But I'm now in 420?"

"I took the liberty of changing your suite, Mrs. Daniels. When I heard about the sad circumstances of your husband's death before being able to experience the magic of the *Silver Galapagos*, I thought you might appreciate more privacy at this end of the deck, rather than in the original suite closer to the piano bar."

"That's most considerate. Thank you."

"You're welcome. Good evening, Mrs. Daniels." After another well-executed bow, Bruno retreats in short, sharp steps down the empty passageway to the next cabin.

If the service gets any better, they'll be in here with me. Impressed and amused by the staff's efficiency, I close the door and continue dressing.

Having decided on an understated outfit of fitted black slacks, low-heeled black pumps, and a fine knit black sweater, I take my time dressing. I've always thought that a few, quality garments were better than buying flashy fashion items that go out of date once the trends change. On purpose, I keep my closet neatly arranged with conservative, well-cut clothes. But now as I review my outfit, I wonder if I did this more for Tom—than myself. I love color, but it doesn't feature much in my wardrobe. Deciding not to chase after this thought, I throw a lightweight wrap around my shoulders and leave my cabin.

I remove the itinerary of tomorrow's activities from the Perspex mail slot outside my cabin and pop it into my purse. That they still print off daily itineraries for their guests adds a touch of whimsy to the cruise and warms my heart as I stroll down the long, central passageway. Pools of soft light puddle on the cinnamon-colored carpet, while slanting shadows smudge the two-toned, beige walls. The effect is at once intimate, yet mysterious. *Or is it just me finding mystery everywhere I look now?* Considering the ship's full, I can't hear a sound from any of the other cabins, which means a good night's sleep looks promising.

Suddenly, the ship lurches. I grip the handrail and wait for my stomach to subside. The mad, keen seafarer had been Tom, with me as his loyal, but queasy companion. If he hadn't paid for this trip, and if I hadn't promised to scatter his ashes in the Galapagos Islands, I wouldn't have come. Although I loved being on the ocean, it didn't love me. Thankful for the seasickness pill I'd popped earlier, I straighten and continue toward the piano bar at the aft of deck four, with one hand skimming the handrail, just in case.

The doors are open, and the sound of happy revelers reaches me like a gentle breeze. I cross the sleek foyer and pause briefly before entering. With its private sweeping staircase leading down to deck three, the piano bar is reminiscent of an Englishman's private club of the 1940s. Glossy teak tub chairs and lounges swathed in soft, caramel-colored leather are grouped on the polished timber floor in clusters of two, four, six, or eight. Interspersed between them are glass-topped tables, gleaming under a variety of drinking glasses, each filled with colorful concoctions and dripping beads of condensation onto gold-embossed coasters.

At the bar, a handful of people sip pre-dinner drinks and chat. A few passengers are still dressed in their muster drill gear, with their life belts around their necks. Not taking any chances in case the ship goes down. Others have changed into smart casual clothes while a few wear evening attire. However, everyone wears expressions of delight.

From the wall sconces, warm, amber light bathes the art deco bar in an elegant glow, reminding me of an Agatha Christie novel. A dinner-suited pianist, who looks like the author's famous detective, Hercule Poirot, tinkles the baby grand piano, adding the final sophisticated touch. A symphony of voices, some resoundingly loud and enthusiastic while others muted and reserved, segue between the classic melodies he plays.

Tom would love this. Tonight is my first social occasion with strangers, without him. Although I enjoy meeting new people, I miss his guiding hand on my elbow and his strong presence beside me. I glance to my right, half-expecting him to be there. Instead, I catch my reflection in a mirror. "You look more like forty-five than fifty-five," my hairdresser had said to me last week when he cut and colored my hair in a short Marilyn Monroe style. But I'm not so sure. After giving it a quick fluff, I draw a deep breath and walk into the piano bar.

"Hey, Diana." A woman's voice laced with a distinctive Texan drawl reaches me before I spy the Pinkertons tucked together at the piano. "Would you like to join us?" Tippi is a big, horsey-looking woman with cropped, corn silk hair that floats around her head in a constant state of flux. This evening, the effect's amplified by the floating tent of a dress she wears. Her husband, Jim is even larger of stature but bald as a cue ball. They introduced themselves after the muster drill and took pity on me, the poor widow traveling on her own. They mean well, but they're one of those boisterous couples who talk non-stop. Nice people, but over-bearing.

"Thanks, Tippi. I'll just get a drink first and maybe join you shortly."

"Well, you know where we are." Jim adds a mighty guffaw, which seems to be a tagline to whatever he says as if auditioning for the role of Santa Claus at Macy's Thanksgiving Day Parade. Nevertheless, I can't help but laugh at their enthusiastic welcome.

"Vodka martini. Stirred, not shaken please," I say to the bartender. The antithesis to James Bond's martinis, but according to Tom, far better. "You never shake a martini, Diana. You bruise the vodka," he'd say whenever he made my favorite aperitif.

Once my martini arrives with its three olives, I sip a little and head back into the fray. That's when I spy her. The woman in white. Alone.

She's wearing a stunning, crystal-studded white caftan, with her long, chestnut hair draped artfully over one shoulder like a giant python. Her eyes are still hidden behind a pair of sunglasses. Not the big, Hollywood type from today, but a more subdued pair with gold rims. Straight-backed, she sits at a table for two with a martini in front of her. This is my chance. My sixth sense urges me on.

"Hello, my name is Diana Daniels. I'm traveling alone and noticed you sitting here by yourself. Would you like some company?" My heart skips a beat at my boldness.

She leans forward and clasps her drink with heavily bejeweled fingers. "I see you like martinis, too?" Her voice matches her presence, haughty and detached. She's a hard read behind those glasses.

"Yes, I like them stirred, not shaken. What about you?" I wait, giving her a friendly smile.

Her expression softens. "Me, too. I'm Celeste Constanzo. Please join me." With a flourish of her free hand, she motions to the spare chair.

Relieved, I lower into it. "Cheers." I raise my glass, and she returns my salute, and we each take a sip of our exceptionally good martinis. "Are you traveling alone?"

"No. I'm joined by my three grown stepchildren and their partners." Her nose crinkles as if an unpleasant odor passed under it. "My daughter, Emily, was supposed to be here. This whole trip was planned for her thirtieth birthday. But she canceled at the last minute because her daughter fell ill. Emily and I love cruising," she says, in a brighter tone. "But now she's not here to enjoy it, I'm terribly disappointed." Her perfectly lip-lined mouth pouts before she takes a sizeable slug of her martini.

"That's a shame." My mind flashes to the dark-haired man sitting beside her this afternoon in The Explorer Room—the one who sneered. He must be one of the stepchildren. I sip my martini while watching Celeste scull most of hers.

She leans toward me and I can just make out her eyes, behind her sunglasses, darting around the room. "They don't like me." Her hushed voice possesses the slightest of slurs. Obviously, this isn't her first martini of the evening. I angle closer and wait for her to continue. "Joe's children. They're his children by his first marriage. They've never liked me." She purses her lips and then drains the glass. When she lifts her gaze, a waiter rushes over, and she orders two more.

"You don't look old enough to have three grown stepchildren."

"Joey, the eldest, is only seven years younger than me. I'm sure that's why they hate me . . . because their father married a much younger woman. *Pfft*." A flick of her hand sends a wayward lock of hair from her cheek. A trophy wife is what she'd be called. She stiffens. "Here they come now. Up the stairs." From the corner of my eye, I notice five well-dressed people appear near the piano. "That's Joey, the narcissistic namesake and his wife, Clare. She's way too smart for him. Then there's poor Rose, the middle child. She plays the good wife to her politicking husband, Angelo. He's a defense attorney. The nicest of the three is Tony. He just broke up from his girlfriend, so he's here by himself."

The five of them pause and regroup. Imbued with the self-confidence of the first-born child, Joey remains in the lead, impeccable in his designer suit and expensive shoes. Angelo shunts in beside him and adjusts his cashmere sweater while casting gracious smiles around the room à la movie star. Like good wives, Clare and Rose settle behind the men. Though Rose assumes the role with subservience, Clare sets her jaw, hinting at a quiet strength. Young and handsome, Tony loiters to one side as if embarrassed by the stares of the other passengers. On Joey's mark, they step off together and head to our table, while Celeste resumes her sphinxlike demeanor.

Joey leans down and pretends to air kiss her cheek. The gesture is as cold as its delivery. "Evening, Celeste."

"Good evening, Joey." Her voice is clipped. *That's my cue.* I place my glass on the table ready to leave, but she waves me to stay. "Everyone, this is Diana Daniels. Diana, this is Joey, his wife Clare . . ."

As she proceeds with the introductions, I acknowledge each of them, trying my best to add a little warmth to the atmosphere. But they're a cool group, obviously used to their own company. Except for Angelo who's the ultimate networker. His effusive hello and hand-pumping diffuses the tension, causing them to visibly relax. But not Joey. His cold hostility doesn't thaw one bit. Angelo scans the room and in the voice of someone used to being heard says, "There's a group over there just leaving. How about I grab that big table for us?" Not interested in anyone approving his plan, he strides off to stake his claim. Rose scurries behind him, Joey and Clare follow, leaving Tony behind.

"Are you going to join us, Celeste?" He seems a personable young man, probably in his mid-thirties. Unlike his older brother, he speaks in a sympathetic tone.

She pats his hand resting on her shoulder. "I think I'll stay and chat with Diana a while longer. I'll join you shortly."

"Are you okay?"

"I'm fine. Now off you go." When he moves away, she reaches for her evening purse and extracts a crisp, white handkerchief. Lifting her sunglasses, she dabs it to her misting eyes.

I know that gesture. "Are you all right?"

"It's just hard at times . . ." She sniffs, and her nose reddens. In slow, deliberate movements, she reaches up, slides off her sunglasses, and folds them in her lap. When she lifts her gaze, I stare at her eyes—striking golden-flecked, hazel eyes that wing upwards on the outer corners, accentuated by luscious false eyelashes and glinting with emotion.

"Is there anything I can do?" I ask.

"Only if you know how to bring my dead husband back to life."

My breath hitches. That Celeste shares the same loss as me somehow brings us together, not as new acquaintances, but as old friends. We've both experienced the grief of losing our husbands and are trying to reinvent ourselves as single women. Perhaps that's why I've been fascinated by her. "My husband died nearly a year ago, and I know how hard it can be. Tom and I were married for over twenty-five years. He booked this holiday before he was diagnosed with cancer. But he died . . ."

"Joe died only six weeks ago. A terrible accident on his construction site. He fell to his death. Very strange. I mean, he's built skyscrapers for over twenty years. He was used to heights and walking along steel girders. I can't understand how it happened. No one can." She tucks her handkerchief back into her purse, spies the waiter who hasn't delivered her order, and flaps an impatient hand at him.

"No one witnessed his fall?"

"Not a soul. Or if they did, they haven't come forward. There are so many unanswered questions. I keep going over and over everything, but it's no use." She shakes her head. "It's got so bad; I can't sleep at night without taking sleeping pills." I meet her distress with sympathetic silence and an understanding nod. "When Emily couldn't join us to celebrate her birthday, I was devastated. I feel so alone stuck here with Joe's children without her." I glance over her shoulder and notice Joey watching us. His dark brows, eyes, and hair add a threatening intensity to the stony expression on his face. By the look of him, it's obvious he doesn't approve of Celeste talking to me, or probably anyone for that matter. He's not a man who hides his emotions.

"I'm sorry for the delay, madam. Your martinis." The young waiter places the drinks in front of us and retrieves Celeste's empty glass. Mine's still half full.

"Thank you." She gulps most of the martini in one determined swallow, barely wincing at the hit of alcohol. "Do you have any children?"

"Yes. A son. Harrison. He's doing his medical residency in psychiatry." The thought of my gentle-hearted, intelligent son makes me smile.

"No stepchildren?"

I shake my head.

"You're lucky. My life's been nothing but misery because of them." Leaning toward me, she teeters a little before her hand finds the table. "I bet Joey is watching us right now with that judgmental scowl on his face." I glance over her shoulder and nod. "You know he tried to kill me when I married his father?"

"What?"

"He poured petrol over my car and was going to set it alight when I got in it, but Joe caught him."

"That's terrible. What happened?"

"Nothing. He just got a dressing-down and that was it. He should've been sent for counseling, but Joe refused. He didn't want the Constanzo name associated with mental illness. I always thought Joey was somehow not right." She taps her finger to her temple. "And now that Joe is dead, I wouldn't be surprised if he's scheming to bump me off." She slurs her 'ss' more noticeably, before slumping back in the chair and draining every drop from her glass.

"Surely not?" I wonder if the alcohol contributes to exaggeration.

She shrugs. "Who knows? I'm stuck here on board with them for the next seven days. That, in itself, will be murderous."

"Is it really that bad?" I hope not, but the uneasy stirring in my stomach hints it is.

She leans forward again, this time closer. "The truth is, I don't know. I can't be sure of anything, anymore."

During the long moment which stretches between us, Celeste's beleaguered expression sends a brisk chill up my spine. I don't know what to say, but I sense she's in some sort of trouble, either real or imagined. She puffs out a breath, breaking the tension. "Anyway, since I've paid for their passage, I better do the right thing and host dinner." Despite her liberal consumption of alcohol, she rises in one fluid movement, reminding me of a Grecian goddess. Whether it's because of our shared widowhood or a deeper sense of concern for her safety, I'm drawn to help her.

Standing, I meet her gaze. "Perhaps we can do some of the walks together. Get you away from the family a bit. What about tomorrow?"

"I'd like that. Thanks for listening. I didn't mean to download like that."

"Perfectly all right. It's good to get things off your chest. I won't say anything."

"Lovely to meet you, Diana. See you tomorrow." She lifts her head high, gestures to her stepchildren, and floats from the piano bar toward the staircase, leading down to the restaurant.

Nearly every man's head turns and watches her pass. I understand why Joe Constanzo married her. She's striking, fragile, and enigmatic. Ultra-feminine. My professional recruitment brain switches on. Whenever I interview candidates for job placements, aside from tuning into my intuition, I use the Myer Briggs personality test as an indicator of a person's psychological framework. It categorizes sixteen different personality types based on the four principle functions of sensation, intuition, feeling, and thinking.

Even though Celeste and I spent only limited time together, I think she's an INFJ. Introverted, intuitive, feeling, and judging. A complex woman who appears gentle and acquiescent to the point of submissiveness, but she possesses an underlying strength. If she's sufficiently challenged, her inscrutable, delicate exterior will transform into that of a defiant, stoic survivor—which I suspect is what she did to survive in the Constanzo family.

Now, as I watch her float from the bar with her indifferent stepfamily in tow, I worry about how she's going to survive long term. Will she make it? Or will she, like many of the animals of the Galapagos Islands, become extinct? A sinking feeling in my gut tells me the answer is close at hand, and that I'm somehow involved.

CHAPTER THREE

AT THE BASE OF THE ramshackle, planked walkway winding up to the peak of Bartolome Island, I steel myself for the three hundred and seventy-four-step climb. Around me mill about fifty other passengers, each brave enough to test their fitness this morning as the sun treks upward into the powder blue sky. With its lava rock landscape blanketed in a layer of coarse ochre-colored sand, Bartolome Island is wind-swept of all vegetation except for a scattering of strange clumps of white plants, resembling bleached coral branches. The island's jagged terrain appears more alien than earthly. Desolate and dramatic, everything about it is at once beautiful, and yet forlorn. It reminds me of Celeste, who's obviously opted for a less strenuous start to the day. Probably nursing a raging hangover.

"Did you enjoy Israel's six-thirty wake-up call this morning?"

Startled, I swivel to find John beaming down at me. "You scared the daylights out of me." I nail him with an indignant pout. "Why is it that you creep up on people?"

"Sorry. Just habit, I guess." He pauses, his gaze drifting upward. "It's pretty steep. Are you ready?"

"I'll be fine." I jut my chin high, reassuring myself more than him.

"Well, if you need a helping hand, I'll be here."

"Yes, scaring me to death, I suppose." I snort.

He chuckles.

Marianna, our guide, calls us forward and we fall in side-by-side to begin the climb.

"How are you enjoying the cruise so far?" He hefts his backpack higher onto his shoulders and leans into the slope.

"So far, so good." I mirror his movement and step out stride for stride. Within ten steps, my hamstrings smart. This isn't going to be as easy as I thought. I make a mental note to get back into my gym program when I return home.

"Did you find out who your mystery woman in white is?" He flashes me a cheeky sideways glance.

"As a matter of fact, yes. I had a chat with her last night in the piano bar."

"And?"

"Her name is Celeste Constanzo . . ."

He slows and motions at the passengers behind us to pass while pulling me aside. "Are you sure?"

"Yes. Her husband died recently. He—"

"Fell to his death. I know. Joe Constanzo was a well-known crime boss. The investigation is still open, and his widow is under suspicion for his death."

"That can't be true . . ."

"If she hadn't been wearing those sunglasses yesterday, I probably would've recognized her. I don't think you should be getting involved with her."

"Come on you two. Keep up please." Marianna waves us forward. The main group had disappeared around a sharp corner up ahead, and we'd been left behind.

"We need to catch up." John takes off up the stairs as if on combat maneuvers.

I try to keep up but fail. "Can you slow down please?" He takes pity on me, and I fall in beside him, panting. "Thanks." I gulp a lungful of air and continue. "Celeste told me all about Joe's death, and I'm sure she had nothing to do with it."

"And what do you base that on?"

"Call it a hunch."

"A hunch?" The hint of sarcasm in his voice doesn't surprise me.

"Yes, a hunch." *Why is it that men find the idea of intuition so threatening?* "My hunches are normally right. In fact, I've built a successful business based on being able to read human behavior and on my hunches, so . . ."

He stops again and fixes me in a cold stare. "I'm sure that you're a smart, successful woman, Diana. It's just that this is a serious case. I really think you should leave it alone. You could be in danger."

"I appreciate your concern, but don't you think you're being a bit overdramatic?"

His tone hardens. "Listen, the Constanzo family is bad news. They're involved in shady deals, one way or the other. I know it's none of my business, but I really think you should keep your distance."

"Why are you so concerned about this? What are the Constanzos to you?" Then the obvious question dawns on me. "Who are you?"

Grim-faced, he deflates, before he answers with obvious reluctance. "I'm a detective in the Monterey County Sheriff's department."

"A police detective?" My heart skips a beat while my legs want to dance a little jig in delight. *Just the person I need, but I mustn't look too eager.* "Are you working on Joe Constanzo's case?"

"No. It's not in my jurisdiction, but I'm familiar with it. I'm telling you; you shouldn't be getting involved with Celeste Constanzo."

Too late. John couldn't possibly understand that the intrigue brewing on board was way beyond my not getting involved. Or that my hunches wouldn't be denied. Darwin wrote that the thirteen islands of the Galapagos were a little world within themselves. And I'd fallen smack-bang down the rabbit hole into this strange place. Alone, in a land that time forgot. No Tom. No anyone. Just me, my hunches, and as if by serendipitous design, an off-duty police detective.

"Come on, we better keep walking." I set the pace for the remainder of the hike and the conversation. "I understand your concern, but I can't shake this feeling that something is wrong."

"That's what I'm trying to tell you. There *is* something wrong—with the Constanzo family, with Joe's death, with Celeste, with all of it . . ."

"No, not that. Just hear me out . . ." While we tramp up the stairs, I explain my conversation from last night about Celeste's daughter and Joey, Rose, and Tony being on board to celebrate Emily's birthday. I tell him about Celeste's comments about her stepchildren hating her, of Joey's unveiled ominous looks in the piano bar and how, as a young man, he'd tried to kill her.

Perspiration trickles down my temples, but it isn't just due to the exercise and the day's rising temperature. Inside me, an intense gnawing continues. One I've learned to recognize and respect. My hunch of something being amiss is correct. The more I think about it, the surer I become. It's the same feeling as when Tom and I went to see his doctor about Tom's test results. On the trip to the clinic, a sinking feeling churned in my stomach. Although Tom thought there was nothing to worry about, my hunch told me otherwise. When Dr. Abraham delivered the diagnosis of inoperable cancer, Tom had reeled with the news. But not me. I knew. My sixth sense had foretold the horrible event. Not that I ever told Tom. That would've been too awful for him.

And now that feeling was back. There was something wrong on board the *Silver Galapagos* whether John believed me or not.

We round another corner and catch up with the group only a few meters in front of us. This time, I stop short. "As a detective, you know probably better than most, that if your gut instinct tells you something, it's usually right."

He nods, but his pursed lips indicate he's not happy with where the conversation is going.

"Well, my gut instinct tells me that something terrible is about to happen and it has to do with Celeste. I know you probably think I'm crazy, but I could use your help."

His eyes lower, and he shakes his head. "I hate it when women ask that. It usually ends up badly."

"What do you mean?"

"That's an entirely different topic." A sharp exhale passes his lips as he tugs his ear. "Go on. Tell me what you want, but I'm guessing I already know."

"With your police know-how, and my hunches and ability to read human behavior, maybe we can stop something bad from happening. Surely, it's better to prevent a crime than solve one?"

My nerves spark like kindling in a wildfire. The prospect of an adventure reawakens a long-forgotten, dormant energy; something I'd given up when I was twelve, and Mum died. I'd had no choice back then, but to give up the activities I loved and grow up fast. Though Tom loved adventure and took me on many of his, they weren't mine. Now, it's my turn. Like Jill from Enid Blyton's *The Adventurous Four*, my favorite childhood book, I'm ready for an extraordinary adventure of my own. And what better adventure could there be than protecting Celeste, a widow, like me.

"Diana, if I recall our first conversation on the bus landing in San Cristobal, we both came on this trip to relax, regroup, and enjoy the magic of the Galapagos Islands." John flourishes his arm, trying to impress his case upon me. "All you have to do is stay away from Celeste Constanzo and her family. Then nothing bad will happen. And if it does, it won't happen to you."

"But I can't. I promised Celeste to do things with her since Emily isn't here. To be her cruise buddy. I can't break that promise. Seriously, I can't just ignore her. Besides, my hunches are never wrong. Isn't your police motto . . . to serve and protect?" I cock a brow at him.

"Yeah. Yeah. Cheap shot." He tuts three times before a half-smile creases his face. "Okay. Count me in if you need a sounding board. But don't say I didn't warn you. You're treading where angels fear to go."

"Now you sound just like my late husband. Tom was a worry-wart as well."

"Geez. Why is it that women feel compelled to stick their nose in where it doesn't belong?" Before I answer his sexist question, his focus shifts up ahead to the last section of walkway. "Come on. Let's get to the top and at least take some pictures."

"Good idea."

With a renewed spring in my step, I pick up the pace. Pleased with myself, I stride the last fifty meters without effort. No longer hurting, my hamstrings loosen, and my quads strengthen, propelling me forward. Better still, the gnawing in my gut quietens. A good sign. The moment I act on my hunches, the visceral nagging eases, signaling I'm on the right track.

When we breach the crest of the six-hundred-meter plankway climb, the entire vista opens. An isthmus in the shape of a dinosaur's backbone reaches across the cerulean blue waters below, seemingly intent on touching the volcanic ranges of Santiago Island across Sullivan's Bay. From the water's edge, the monolithic blade of Pinnacle Rock juts upward, like a rusty nail poised to pierce a giant's unsuspecting foot. A grand design of structure and proportion that only nature could create.

I heave a breath of appreciation at the magnificent landscape before me, while my thoughts stray to a more serious landscape awaiting me on board ship.

★ ★ ★

AFTER SPECTACULAR SNORKELING IN THE warm waters at Pinnacle Rock that afternoon, I settle in for some overdue reading and an iced coffee on the deck outside the piano bar. Having taken a seasickness pill earlier, I find the cruising to nearby Buccaneer's Cove quite enjoyable. With the afternoon sun warming my shoulders, I lean back and close my eyes to capture its full effect until a pale shadow lands on my face. I open my eyes and peering down at me are two elderly women, their faces stretched in identical smiles, much like the Cheshire Cat's.

"Do you mind if we join you?" They sound in high spirits.

"Ah, no, not at all." Although surprised by such a direct request, I nod to the chairs on either side and introduce myself.

"Lovely to meet you, dear. I'm Judy Blum." The woman on the right extends her diminutive, liver-spotted hand, then introduces her sister, Nancy. Since I can barely tell them apart, I memorize that Judy's on the right and Nancy's on the left. "I see you're reading Tennyson?" Judy eyes off the little red book, which is one of my treasured traveling companions— *Select Poems of Tennyson.* A gift from Tom for our engagement.

"Yes, reading Tennyson always helps me think more clearly." My head swivels from side to side.

"We love Tennyson, too, don't we Nancy?" Judy smiles sweetly at her sister.

"Yes, we do." Nancy smiles sweetly in return. They remind me of two characters from a children's book, both living in blissful unison. "Which poem are you reading, my dear?"

"The Lady of Shallot." I sip my coffee, amused at the antics of the older women.

Both sisters titter and after a quick sideways glance, recite the last lines of the poem together. *"She has a lovely face; God in his mercy lend her grace, the Lady of Shallot."*

Almost a parody of sisterly love, their fondness with each other makes me giggle. I figure they're spinsters, probably in their seventies, though well-preserved, obviously as a result of a skillful surgeon's knife. And judging by the size of their ostentatious rings inlaid with gems the size of plump grapes, they're not short of money.

"You know who that poem reminds me of?" Nancy fidgets with her pearl necklace while directing the question at her sister.

"No. Who?" Judy strokes her pearl drop earrings.

"Celeste Constanzo." Much head nodding follows.

I barely manage to swallow my coffee rather than spitting it across the table. "How do you know Celeste?"

"Oh, her late husband, Joe, used to buy a lot of jewelry from us for her. His death was so sad. Poor Joe." Nancy's ruby-red lips pout in an insincere way.

"We're diamond merchants and jewelers, my dear." Judy smiles. "The best in Beverley Hills, actually." She lifts her chin and Nancy mirrors.

"So . . . you knew Celeste would be on this cruise?"

"Oh yes. Of course." Judy leans forward and raises her hand to her mouth. In a conspiratorial whisper, she says, "We're hoping to convince Celeste to let us buy back one of the pieces we sold to Joe not long before his death."

"We know it sounds terribly cold to be talking about money after such a tragic accident . . ." *That's an understatement.*

"But we thought if we approached her in a friendly, holiday setting she might be more conducive to our offer."

I scratch my head and reassess the two dears perched beside me. Despite their old-world persnickety charm, I suspect they're crafty, astute businesswomen, used to making deals in their favor. There's nothing fragile or innocent about them. But I wonder why they targeted me to discuss their proposed buy-back scheme.

"I see. And what's the piece you're hoping to buy back?" I ask.

"It's a rare and elaborate necklace with matching earrings." As Nancy's hand sweeps around her neck, tracing the design of the necklace, her voice rises to match her evangelical expression. "It features two rows of pearls, intersected with eight separate clusters of diamonds centered by cushion-cut fire rubies. In the center hangs a diamond and silver bail which is attached to a large pendant cluster of diamonds, then rubies and then pearls."

"But why do you think Celeste would consider selling it since it was a gift from Joe?"

Both women shuffle their chairs closer toward me. "Because she needs the money, dear."

My ears prick. "How do you know that?"

"Joey, her eldest stepson told us. He's the one who told us Celeste would be on this cruise and that we should come on it too. He thinks she'll sell it back for the right price."

Oh, he does, does he? The mention of Joey's collaboration irritates me. "And if she doesn't want to?"

"Joey said he'd make sure she did." They nod, like a pair of cunning witches.

"But why are you telling me all this?" A part of me doesn't want to hear the answer, but I'm hooked by their farcical routine and my concern for Celeste.

"Because we watched you last night in the piano bar, and we both agree that Celeste seems to like you. Perhaps you could convince her to consider our offer . . ."

What? I've met a few people who placed their own self-interest above all else, but none so blatantly audacious as the Blum sisters. That they asked me, a stranger, to convince a recently widowed woman and someone I'd just met, to sell her jewelry back to them leaves me speechless. I try scratching the disgust from my brow, while both women eagerly await my answer.

I keep my voice low and measured. "I'm not sure why you think I'd speak to Celeste on your behalf, but I won't." They blink at me, their flushed faces piqued. I lean closer. "A word of advice . . . I wouldn't believe everything Joey tells you." My lips clamp tight. I've no reason to say that or to even know it's true, but he's worried me from the moment I met him.

"We didn't mean to offend you . . . Joey thought you might be able to help. "

Of course, he would. Send you in to do his dirty work, more likely.

The poor dears talk over each other in frantic apology. They've obviously been misled in approaching me. *A sly one, that Joey Constanzo.*

I rise from the table, my book in hand. "I'll leave you with one of Tennyson's quotes, *'No man ever got very high by pulling other people down.'* Good afternoon, ladies."

★ ★ ★

THE LIGHTS DIM IN THE Explorer Room for the afternoon showing of Part One of *The Galapagos Affair*, a documentary about an unsolved murder mystery in the Galapagos. It tells the story of the early settlers on Floreana Island—lovers and proponents of Nietzsche's philosophy, Dore Strauch and Friedrich Ritter, a simple, God-fearing couple Margaret and Heinz Wittmer, and a flamboyant, Viennese Baroness, and her two lovers, Philippson and Lorenz. From the screen, in deteriorating black and white silent footage, this odd collection of people smile and wave, while a narrator tells of their arrival and life on Floreana in the early 1930s. Overdubbed actors' voices give the documentary an intensely personal glimpse into this strange new Garden of Eden.

My nose twitches at a familiar perfume. "They're a bizarre group, aren't they?" Celeste nods at the screen, as she slides into a chair beside me. Another pair of sunglasses shade her eyes. I wonder why she hides her beauty behind glass all the time. Or is she hiding from something or someone else? We exchange smiles and settle next to each other.

"Yes, they're all very peculiar in my opinion," I say. "Have you had a nice day?"

"I stayed on board while the others went ashore. Peace and quiet." She sighs.

Along with about thirty other people, we watch the remainder of the film in silence. At the end, the other passengers drift from the room, while Celeste and I remain. "So, what do you think will happen?" she asks.

"With what?"

"With the Baroness and her lovers and the rest of them . . ."

"Oh, that . . .With all the bickering and fighting among them, someone is sure to end up dead." I try for the casual tone of a friend critiquing a movie but suspect I fail. The story of the Baroness and the petty conflicts surrounding her bear an uncanny resemblance to Celeste and her stepchildren. Like the Baroness, Celeste is at the center of the drama while everyone else jostles for a power position or tries to topple her authority. In my view, both situations have disaster written all over them.

She removes her sunglasses. "And that's what I'm worried about . . ."

"What?"

"Murder."

She controls the undercurrent of panic in her voice well, I think. Her eyes dart around the room, while my heart beats faster. "What are you talking about?"

"Can I trust you?"

"Of course." I clasp her hands. They're cold and clammy.

"When we spoke last night, I could tell you were upset by your husband's death." I nod. "But I'm not upset that Joe is dead. I'm upset at the mess he's left. My husband was a wicked man, particularly when it came to money. He controlled everyone he could with it, but mainly his children. If they did as he wanted, they'd be favored with new cars, houses, and the like. If they refused to do his bidding, he'd cut them off." She slices a hand across her throat. "Joey got fed up with it and started his own business—Ricco Constructions—years ago. Joe never forgave him for it. Rose fell in love with Angelo and married him against her father's wishes. Joe refused to have them or their children in the house. Then, dear Tony . . . he's a successful stockbroker. For a while, he was his father's favorite because Joe made a lot of money investing in the stock market based on Tony's advice. But there was gossip about Tony being gay, so Joe disowned him as well."

Celeste's story of family dysfunction sends my intuition into overdrive. "And you? How have you coped with all this?"

"I just did what I was told. If I ever offered an opinion about smoothing things over with his kids, Joe got so angry I thought he'd kill me. And I had Emily to consider. She was ten when Joe and I married. Since he's not her real father, her safety was the most important thing to me. So, I kept my head down when it came to him and his kids."

"He sounds like a narcissistic sociopath." I'd encountered these personality types over the years in my business. Unpredictable, controlling, and abusive.

"He was a very difficult man to live with. But I loved him because when he was the Joe Constanzo I fell in love with, he was the most generous, loving man in the world." She gives a sad shrug. "So, I stood by him."

"But why this rift between you and his children since you're the one who's tried all along to bring them together?"

"It's Joe's fault, as usual." She rolls her eyes. "Last Thanksgiving, he brought the whole family together and told them he'd changed his will. I knew nothing about it. Because he was furious with Joey, Rose, and Tony and how they disobeyed him, he said he was leaving his entire estate to me with the three of them getting a small stipend of $500,000 each and the same for Emily. You can imagine how angry they were." She closes her eyes as if trying to rid her mind of the memory.

"Are they challenging his will?"

"I think it's worse than that. The will's provisional clause for this bequest was that I would only inherit his estate if I survived him by sixty days. Otherwise, it'll be split equally between Joey, Rose, and Tony, with the original half-a-million stipend going to Emily." She fixes me in a steely stare. "I think they're planning to kill me within the next two weeks." Her hands twist in her lap like a pot of boiling eels.

"You can't be serious." I study Celeste's face which carries the tell-tale signs of deep anxiety. I've seen this expression before on women who suffer domestic abuse . . . a terror of not knowing what will happen next, of not being in control. Whether rightly or wrongly, Celeste Constanzo feared for her life.

"Throughout our twenty-year marriage, Joe kept a lot of things from me. And there was a lot I didn't want to know. I'm scared, Diana. Joe could be a violent man and maybe the apple doesn't fall far from the tree."

"Death is a dark monster. It makes us imagine all sorts of terrible things. I know it's hard being here alone and especially because you were looking forward to celebrating your daughter's birthday on board, but you're safe here. No one can hurt you on the ship. When you get back home you need to get good legal advice."

"I've already done that. I've redrawn my will and left my home in Beverley Hills, my Ferrari, and all my jewelry to Emily. Joe's kids will have a tough time contesting that, even if they do kill me. And if anything does happen to me, at least Emily will end up with more than just half-a-million dollars." I marvel at her pragmaticism under such stressful circumstances. "I'm not like her, you know . . ."

"Like who?"

"The Baroness. I'm not conceited or boastful. Sure, I've made choices when I was younger, that I wish I hadn't. But everyone has. But I'm not like the Baroness, I don't pit people against each other and stoke hatred." Emotion chokes her voice.

A wave of sympathy washes over me. "I'm sure you don't. Come on. Let's go somewhere more private."

I help Celeste from her chair, and we walk to the small reference library nearby. Fortunately, no one's there. I sit her down, whisk a couple of tissues from a box on the shelf and close the door. "I'm a pretty good judge of character, Celeste. That's my job. And from what I've seen, you've taken on the role of whipping boy for the Constanzo family." She raises her face, her expression, pitiful. "First, your husband, Joe, and then his kids. In fact, your husband is still abusing you from his grave with his will. Tyrants inspire no love or loyalty. It's time to protect yourself."

She nods. "But what can I do?"

"We'll be off this ship in six days. Why not do what you did today? Don't have too much to do with the family. Let them do their own thing. The less contact you have the better."

She stares out the window for a few moments as if waiting for the sea to agree. A protracted silence fills the library while Celeste considers my advice, giving me time to consider John's. Am I getting involved with a dangerous woman? Is the Constanzo family capable of murder? I know money, status, and power make dangerous bedfellows, yet my sixth sense urges me on.

"It's a good idea." She stands and runs her fingers down the creases of her pale blue crepe trousers. "The less contact I have with them, the better. They can go off on their excursions, and I'll spend my time relaxing on board. We'll just keep out of each other's way."

"Yes. Take on the peacekeeper's role."

Her face draws into resigned compliance. "I've been doing that for years, so one more week won't be a push."

I hold her gaze. "Why have you confided in me? You don't know me, and yet you've told me your family's—"

"Ugliest secrets?" She finishes the sentence for me. "To be honest, I don't know. I've been desperate to tell someone. Someone I can trust, and you struck me as that someone. Unlike everyone else in my life, you've nothing to gain by my life—or death. I'm tired, Diana. I'm tired of being scared, of pretending, of being trapped. I'm sick and tired of it all." Her shoulders sag.

"It's okay." I understand how difficult it can be when the world caves in around you. I had friends and family to confide in when Tom died. Poor Celeste obviously had no one. "If you need anything at all, call me. We can hang out together if you like. I'm sure you'll feel safer if you weren't alone."

She steps forward and encircles me in her arms. "Thank you. You've saved my life."

I refrain from commenting on her last sentence. But inside, I hope it's true.

CHAPTER FOUR

BEFORE THE CAPTAIN'S COCKTAIL PARTY gets underway, I corner John at the bar and enlighten him of my conversation with the Blum sisters and Celeste. "What do you think?" I sip my martini, barely keeping my eagerness at bay.

He scratches his freshly shaved chin. "I think you've stumbled into where you don't belong. As I said this morning, the Constanzo family is bad news . . ."

"Perhaps, but I've worked with enough women, to know that Celeste is a victim of abuse. She's scared for her life. Whether she had anything to do with Joe's death is immaterial. She thinks her stepchildren are going to kill her . . ."

On the verge of elaborating, I sense an energy shift in the bar. I glance to the doorway where Celeste glides into the room, radiant in a floating Grecian-style Valentino red silk gown, identical to one I'd seen an actress wearing at the Oscars. Everyone draws a combined breath. She's captivating, as is the jewelry gracing her neck and ears. The same necklace and earrings that the Blum sisters described to me this afternoon. I grip John's arm, and he nods in understanding. When the crowd parts, I notice her stepchildren aren't with her. "Go and ask her if she'd like to join us," I whisper in his ear.

He slides from the barstool and offers Celeste his arm while nodding toward me at the bar. From the corner of my eye, I catch Nancy and Judy whispering to each other, their lips moving at lightning speed. No doubt it's about Celeste's jewelry. Nancy's eyes gleam as bright as Gollum's, and when she glances at me, I scowl and shake my head.

I stand when Celeste arrives. "You look stunning." She plants an air kiss to my cheek. "I believe John's introduced himself?"

"Yes." She flutters her lashes at him while slipping onto the barstool beside me.

After martinis are ordered, my gaze returns to her necklace. "That's magnificent."

Her hand flits across her neck. "Yes, it is beautiful. It was the last gift Joe gave to me before he died. I planned on giving it to Emily for her birthday, here on the cruise. But since she couldn't be here, I'll have to give it to her when I get home."

John and I exchange glances. There's no way Celeste will sell the necklace and earrings if she's planning on gifting them to her daughter. Joey purposely lied to the Blum sisters. For what reason is anyone's guess, but I suspect it'll only benefit him.

The pianist ends his set on a grand crescendo.

"Good evening, ladies and gentlemen." Israel's distinctive voice fills the room as he introduces the senior crew—Captain Rodriguez; Lizzardo, the Hotel Director; Bruno, the Butler Manager, and Nicholas, the Head Chef. In his white naval dress uniform, the captain cuts an impressive figure during his speech, while the senior crew strikes me as an experienced team who work well under his command. After the formalities, the party continues and the four of them mingle among the passengers. While Celeste staves off Lizzardo's amorous advances by sculling another martini, my sixth sense prickles until I spy a young man wedged in at the other end of the bar. Every now and then, he tilts back and glances in our direction. Whenever I catch his eye, he turns away.

"Do you know that young man at the end of the bar?" I ask Celeste.

She shifts forward and back on her stool. "I don't know who you mean. Unless he's one of the family, I doubt it."

"He seems most interested in you. He keeps looking this way."

"Maybe it's the jewelry." She shrugs and orders another martini.

By the time I look back, he's walking toward the aft deck. I note what he's wearing and decide to track him down later. Just then, Joey hurtles into the bar like a thunderstorm and shoulders him out of his way. Both shoot daggers at each other, but Joey's ferocity outstrips that of the young man's.

"Watch where you're going," Joey barks.

His threatening tone quells all conversation in the room. Even the pianist's playing changes to *sotto voce*. He storms toward us and pulls up short in front of Celeste. All eyes watch the stunning woman in Valentino red face off against the bad-tempered man in the designer suit.

Celeste doesn't flinch. Her liquid hazel eyes meet his dark blistering stare. "Good evening, Joey . . ."

"We're all waiting." His voice is low and menacing.

With the stealth of a cat, John steps behind him.

An inscrutable expression graces Celeste's face as she regards her watch, then back to Joey. "I'm sorry. I'll be along shortly."

The woman's got nerves of steel.

"You're thirty minutes late."

"Start dinner without me." She holds her composure, but I notice a fine sheen of perspiration gloss her temples.

Joey leans in, like a dog primed to attack. "You may have been able to get away with this empress routine when father was alive, but not anymore. We're all sick of it. You've got sixty days. After that, Rose, Tony, and I will contest the will. We're through." His black eyes glower. "I always said you were a bitch, and I was right." He finishes his insult with a final snarl, then whips a turn and bumps into John. "Get out of my way . . ."

John's hand moves fast. He grabs Joey's forearm and drags him closer. I can barely hear him. "Are you threatening Mrs. Constanzo?"

"What's it to you?" Joey tries to snatch his arm free, but John holds firm.

"I suggest for everyone's sake; you stay away from her."

Joey's lip curls. "As I said, what's it to you?" With a fierce tug, he frees his arm and storms back through the piano bar, glowering at anyone who meets his gaze.

The Captain strides up and clasps Celeste's hand. "Madam, are you okay?" Beside him flinches a burly man with bulging muscles. "This is Patrizio. He's head of security. If you need anything, you call him."

Patrizio hands his card to Celeste.

"Can I have one of those too?" John palms Patrizio's card with a nod.

After a few minutes, the drama dies down and the festive atmosphere returns with the pianist playing happy Broadway tunes.

I edge closer to Celeste. "Are you sure you're all right?" Although her expression remains impassive, I notice the fright in her blinking eyes.

With a trembling hand, she slugs back the last mouthful of her third martini. The hit of alcohol seems to help, and she regains her poise. "I'm not sure anymore. Joey's got the temper of his father. He frightens me." She casts a quick glance over her shoulder. "Will you come back to my suite for a moment before you go to dinner?"

"Of course." I slide from the stool. "I'll see you later, John."

"Okay. I'll be here if you need me." He lifts his beer in salute before resuming his chat with the bartender.

Whether it's because of her striking presence or the scene Joey made, leaving the piano bar with Celeste is like walking the red carpet with a famous movie star. Every eye is upon her. I've often wondered what it must feel like to be the center of that much attention. I remember when I was a young ballet dancer in my pre-teen years, I loved the end-of-year recitals and being on the stage. But when Mum died, I had to give it up, and a part of me died too. I missed the performance, missed the spotlight. But not like this. Not like what Celeste must've endured being Joe's wife and a woman of extraordinary beauty. Like a deer in the headlights just before the moment of impact.

We cross the marbled foyer on deck four, our heels clicking softly.

"I'm just here on the right. In suite 430."

"That's the suite Tom originally booked for us. I'm at the other end of the passageway now, in suite 420."

When Celeste lifts the itinerary for the next day's activities from her mail slot, a piece of paper slides out. She unfolds it, and as her eyes scan the page, her body stiffens, while an ashen pall blanches her olive complexion.

"What is it? What's wrong?"

Without a word, she hands the paper to me, her hand trembling:

Bitch!
You think you could keep this a secret?
Well you can't.
And now you're going to pay.

"I think I'm going to be sick." She thrusts her evening bag at me, and I fumble out her keycard lanyard. After I swipe open the door, she stumbles inside and collapses on the sofa in a flurry of red silk chiffon.

"See. I told you. They're trying to kill me." She lies on the sofa with one hand to her forehead and the other to her heaving bosom.

"Here, let me put this cushion behind your head. Take a few deep breaths." I fuss around getting her comfortable. Once she calms down, I study the note again, before placing it on her cabin counter. Such hateful words. "Any idea what this secret is?"

"I've no idea." She moans. "I can't think of a secret I have to pay for."

"Well, whatever it is, the person who wrote this thinks it's important enough to make threats." The uneven formation of the letters reminds me of a right-handed person trying to write with their left. They're clumsy and misshapen. "You have to report this, Celeste. You must tell the captain."

"Even if I do, what's he going to do?" The panic in her voice drops a notch to frustrated resignation.

"I expect, he'll investigate. Maybe he'll attach Patrizio to you as a body-guard?" I do my best to convince her while I pour her some bottled water. "You have to do something. This is proof that someone on this ship wants to harm you." I hand her the glass and sit on the end of the bed, opposite her. "You must do something, especially after the scene Joey caused."

She swivels her legs around, flicking the layers of red chiffon out of the way and springs to her feet. "You're right. I will."

I watch her open her closet and activate her safe's keypad with four sharp beeps. She returns with a deep red velvet jewelry box, unclasps her necklace and earrings, and carefully lays them in the box and shuts the lid. "You're the only one I can trust, Diana. You take these and keep them safe."

I thrust the box back at her. "I can't do that."

"You must." She pushes the box toward me.

"Have the captain lock them in the ship's safe. That's where they belong."

"Don't you see. You're the only person who was with me all night. You're the only person who couldn't have placed that note in my mail slot."

Celeste's fear of the family trying to kill her has now escalated to a paranoia which includes everyone on board the ship except me. Mentally, she's sinking. "Celeste, please. Sit beside me." I clasp her hands and stare into her beautiful, yet frightened face. "I don't know what's happening or who's behind all this, but you need to report it."

Her shoulders shudder and big, fat tears break the brims of her eyes. "Please take the jewelry. You put it in the ship's safe. If anything happens to me, I know I can trust you to give it to Emily. Please . . ."

Her fingers clench mine so hard, my hands hurt. I feel so sorry for her. "But if the worst does happen, I don't know Emily. I don't even know what she looks like."

"What's your cell number?" She rummages for her phone. "I'll send you Emily's contact details and AirDrop you some pictures. No matter what happens to me, I need to know that Emily will get everything I've planned for her." Her fingers tremble as she forwards me her daughter's details. The urgency with which she works sends pinpricks up my arms.

"Okay," I say, checking my phone. "Everything's come through. I've got them."

I stare at the images. Emily possesses the same striking Mediterranean beauty, a heart-shaped face with wide-set eyes, classic nose, and generous mouth. A youthful, mirror image of her mother. I'll have little trouble recognizing her if something does happen to Celeste.

"Good. Now, all that's left is for you to take the jewelry." Determined, she shoves the box at me once more. "In this box sits a portion of Emily's inheritance. Five-million-dollars-worth to be exact."

You've got to be kidding. Palming my hands toward her, I shake my head. "I can't be responsible for that."

"Please . . ." The box hovers in mid-air.

"How do you know it's worth that much?"

"That's what those wretched Blum sisters offered me today. On board the ship." I say nothing about my encounter with them, but I'd like to give the old dears a thorough dressing-down. "They sold the jewelry to Joe and now they want to buy it back. How dare they?" The dark flints in her hazel eyes, flash. Once more, her tone reverts to entreaty. "Please, you must help me. Take the box. Keep it safe for me . . . and Emily."

"Listen, why don't we go to the captain—together? Take him the note and give him the jewelry to keep in the ship's safe."

"I suppose that would work." She looks uncertain.

"Come on. Let's go." I rise to leave, but she pulls me back down.

"I can't go now."

"Why not?"

"I can't. I'm too upset." Celeste's brown eyes swim in pools of tears that stream down her face in muddy streaks of makeup. "Look at me. I can't go out now."

She's so overwrought, her appearance matters more than the jewelry being placed in the ship's safe. I rush to the bathroom and return with a handful of tissues, dabbing at her cheeks in a motherly fashion. After handing her some clean tissues, I sit back on the bed. "Okay, we don't have to go now to the captain. How about I pop in after breakfast tomorrow, and we can arrange everything? We can even call Patrizio to walk us to the bridge. He can carry the jewelry if you like. What do you think?"

"I guess so." She slumps, wringing the tissues in her hands. "This whole thing with Joe's death, the wills, Joey's outburst, that hideous note and . . ." She hesitates as if she's going to say something else but decides against it. "I'm distraught." She drags the tissues across her nose, smearing her red lipstick in an ugly smudge. Not even that can detract from her inherent loveliness. She stands and squares her shoulders. "I'll just put this away, then." She lifts the box and places it back in the cabin safe.

I rise to leave. "I'm sure you'll feel much better, after a good night's sleep."

"Yes, you're right. I'll take a sleeping pill. That'll help me sleep right through." The panic lifts from her expression. "Thank you." Her smeared lips curve in a forced smile.

"Now you get some sleep."

"I will. I'm exhausted. I'll get a message to the family and let them know I'm not joining them for dinner."

When she opens the door, we stop and trade a sisterly hug.

"I'll see you tomorrow." I slip out into the passageway.

"Tomorrow. Thanks again." She raises a hand before disappearing back into her cabin.

Like Celeste, I've lost my appetite, so I turn in the direction of my cabin and head down the passageway. *That poor woman.* It's bad enough that she lived with an abusive husband whose children she suspects are plotting to murder her, now she's on the receiving end of hate mail. I reach my cabin, and as unlock my door, I instinctively glance back to Celeste's cabin. I send up a silent prayer that she gets a good night's sleep and that tomorrow things will calm down. *What an adventure you've booked me on this time, Tom.*

CHAPTER FIVE

WHILE JOHN AND I SETTLE in for breakfast in the restaurant on deck two, the place buzzes with chatter about the forthcoming day's activities, and no doubt, about the Captain's cocktail party last night. I scope the room but can't see any of the Constanzo family. At least Joey has enough decency to keep a low profile after his outburst last night.

"How did everything go with Celeste?" A hint of concern laces John's voice.

"Were you worried about me, Detective Nash?" I tease.

"I've been worried since you became interested in Celeste Constanzo. But hey, what would I know?" He laps his napkin with an indignant flick.

"I'm sorry. I don't mean to be flippant."

He cuts me a terse glance, which I avoid by unfolding my napkin. I dig my phone out, scroll, and slide it across the table. "Here. Look what we found in Celeste's mail slot when we got back to her cabin last night."

He enlarges the image and reads it. Then, reads it again. "I did warn you." He arches a disapproving brow. "You better tell me about it while we order."

By the time John's bacon and eggs and my Bircher muesli arrive, he's caught up with last night's events.

"Once we finish here, you should find Celeste. We need to have a serious conversation about this," he says, over the sound of crunching bacon.

"I hoped you'd say that. I'm sure if you spoke to her in your official capacity as a detective, she'd feel safer reporting everything to the captain." I dip into my gooey delight made from oats, yogurt, fruit, and nuts. I never eat it as a rule because of the hidden sugar content, but since I'm on holidays I indulge.

John swirls a mouthful of black coffee. "You know I've got no jurisdiction here?"

"Yes. On a ship, all authority lies with the captain." A shame though. Between the detective or the captain, my money's on John to stop a villain.

"Good. Because unlike you, I'm not going to step on anyone's toes. Understand?" While he swipes the last of his breakfast with a piece of toast, his steely gaze remains fixed on me.

"I understand." I spoon the last of the muesli it into my mouth. *Pity, though.*

By the time we stand to leave, the knot in my shoulder and the gnawing in my stomach return. Helping Celeste no longer seems like an adventure. "To be honest, I can't believe this is happening."

"From the little amount of time I've spent with you, I can." Although he grumbles, a smile lurks on his lips.

★ ★ ★

"I'M SORRY, MRS. DANIELS. I haven't seen Mrs. Constanzo at all this morning," Jimmy says. On my return from breakfast, and unable to rouse Celeste so we could take her jewelry to the Captain, I corralled him in my cabin while he was servicing my suite. Now, his back is against the wall, literally. Visibly uncomfortable with my questioning, his training obviously prevents him from divulging information about other passengers.

"I understand, but I was supposed to meet Celeste and then go deep water snorkeling at Isabela Island this morning." Zipped into my wetsuit, I fling my life belt over my shoulders. "I've been knocking on her door, but there's no response."

He shrugs, unable or unwilling to answer my question.

I huff. "Very well then. If you happen to see her, please tell her I've gone on the excursion and will catch up with her when I return."

A relieved smile brightens his face. "Of course, Mrs. Daniels. I'll tell her." Pivoting, he makes a hasty retreat. The six-star service is of no help to me this morning.

Grabbing my flippers, snorkel, and backpack, I rush off to the Explorer Room, hoping I haven't missed the excursion. Earlier, in his pre-activity presentation, Israel inspired us with the promise of swimming up-close-and-personal with sea turtles, the Galapagos penguins, and even the marine iguanas. "Expect the water to be chilly, but the experience will be worth it." I know what that means. The water will be freezing.

As luck would have it, I manage to clamber on board the last zodiak destined for Punta Vincente Roca. Perched like obedient schoolchildren, nine other passengers have already taken their seats. On spying Celeste's stepdaughter Rose, and her husband, Angelo, I squeeze in next to them. With a sharp tingle, the hairs on my arms lift. I glance sideways and notice the sullen expression of a warring couple etched on their faces. Despite their obvious friction, this is my chance.

"Good morning." I flash them a cheery smile. "We met on Saturday night. With Celeste. I'm Diana Daniels."

"Hello, Diana. Good to see you again." Angelo leans across his wife and thrusts out his hand, an ingratiating smile on his face. Rose slants him a withering look. Her husband's display of gushing magnanimity clearly annoys her. I grasp his hand and give it a quick pump.

She eyes me up and down. "Yes. I remember. Nice to see you again."

"How're you enjoying the expedition so far?" Talkative tourist is my new persona.

"It's terrific," Angelo says. "Lots to do. Good food, great wine list. What's there not to enjoy?" A devilishly good-looking man, he's tall, handsome and rugged, and oozes sex appeal like melted chocolate. I wonder why he married Rose, who could be best described as domestic and mousey. But the answer is obvious. She probably plays compliant servant to his autocratic king.

"Celeste told me how you're all here to celebrate her daughter's thirtieth birthday, but, at the last minute, Emily couldn't make it." An air of tension returns.

"Yes." Rose's icy glance leaves little doubt as to my unwelcome intrusion.

"Such a shame." While the other passengers murmur happily, a strained silence stretches between Rose and me. Instead of doing the polite thing and leaving the topic alone, I grit my teeth and plunge in. "Your stepmother seems a lovely woman." A gracious compliment most people would accept.

She turns on me, her dark eyes flashing. "Celeste pretends to play the good stepmother to Joey, Tony, and me, but her favorite has always been Emily."

"I guess that's only natural since Emily is her biological child." I try to sound unbiased, but, by Rose's unguarded reaction, I know I've opened a deep emotional wound.

"Perhaps . . . But it was our father who saved Celeste from a mundane life and welcomed Emily into the family. He even gave Emily the Constanzo name." A flaming rouge blush befitting her name flashes up Rose's neck. But it isn't one of natural beauty like the flower. Deep-seated resentment colors her skin. Like her older brother, she won't, or can't hide her dislike of Celeste.

"Blended families can be tough," I soothe. "When my father remarried, I got a younger brother and that didn't work out so good." It was true. Soon after Mum died, Dad remarried and Andrew steam-rolled into our house. An eight-year-old bully, with a chip on his shoulder which grew bigger over time. At twelve, I could keep out of his way, but life for Dad and me changed forever. I understand why Rose blames Celeste for stealing her father's affection and upsetting the family's status quo.

Along with another eight boats, we slow down to idle in a wide cove bordered by steep, craggy cliffs of volcanic rock on adjacent sides.

Our naturalist guide, Juan Carlos raises his voice. "All right everyone. This is where you'll go deep water snorkeling. Here you'll find many sea turtles. We call them the Buddhists of the sea." The Dalai Lama's serene, smiling face springs to mind. "Perhaps the Galapagos penguins, sea lions, and marine iguanas will also make an appearance. They love the cold-water currents around Isabela Island, which is one of the most volcanically active places in the world. When you're ready, put on your snorkeling gear and slip in. We'll keep an eye on you. We'll be here for about an hour."

As I pull off my life belt, I turn to Rose. "Are you coming in?"

"Oh, no. I don't like deep water. I came because Angelo wanted me too." She hurries to add, "And because I wanted to get off the ship, see the scenery . . ."

"I'll meet you in there, Diana." Throwing himself backward, Angelo splashes into the water and disappears.

"Please excuse my husband. He can be such a boor." She sneers at the bubbles rising from his snorkel underwater. I get the distinct feeling she'd rather not see him surface ever again.

"No need to apologize. He strikes me as a man who enjoys life." Adjusting my mask, I pause, wondering if she'll say anything else.

"Yes, a little too much for my liking." She stares off into the distance as if she's forgotten I'm here. "Father was right. I never should've married him."

Without a word, I slip over the side into the searing cold. Even with a wetsuit, my body shrieks. The fast-moving current hijacks me, propelling me toward the edge of the submerged cliffs. After narrowly avoiding the rock face, I change course and swim on a calmer current toward the cul-de-sac of sandy beach.

From the undulating patterns of sand under the shallow water rises a mossy-green shape, and I come face-to-face with my first sea turtle. While I hold my breath in amazement, it gazes at me, unafraid of my presence, before gracefully banking to its left and vanishing.

As it brushes me with its leathery flipper, I paddle around, ready to follow it. Then a dozen other turtles hover upward from the depths, like a swarm of giant jellyfish. Suspended in the ebb and flow of the current, I become the maypole around which they dance. No matter how I try to stay out of their way, my hands and feet invariably make reluctant contact. With no give-way rules in the sea, they swim straight at me oblivious of an impending collision. An unforgettable encounter.

Out of the corner of my eye, I glimpse something whiz past at high speed. A Galapagos penguin. There's no chance of catching the tiny speedster because he's gone in a flash. For the next thirty minutes, I'm at one with the fascinating underwater world of Isabela, until the numbness in my hands and feet force me back onto the zodiak.

"How was it?" Rose appears calmer than before. Her tone is less combative.

"Indescribable." After stripping off my wetsuit, I towel the blue tinge from my skin. Once a pink glow returns, I zip on my windcheater and resume my seat. Since Juan Carlos is snorkeling with the others, Rose and I are the only ones on the zodiak except for the non-English-speaking driver.

She appears lost in her thoughts, her gaze fixed on a distant point. "I don't want to leave here. It's so beautiful, so peaceful."

"Yes, there's magic and mystery here."

She swivels to face me. "I saw the way Celeste spoke to you the other night. She likes you." Her expression darkens. "She never liked me. She saw me as competition from the start. Competition for my father's love."

Although startled by her sudden outburst, I want to help. "But it's not too late to heal the relationship . . ." Though I doubt Rose possesses the 'forgive and forget' gene.

"Of course, it is. With Dad gone, there's all this drama over his death and the estate, which I'm sure Celeste told you about." Contempt clips her words. "The family's torn apart. She and Emily will draw battle lines against us. Joey's ready for the fight. Tony doesn't care, and I'm caught in the middle. As always. I wish Dad never married that woman . . . Bitch!"

I blink at her ferocity, while my mind races. That's twice the B-word has been spoken by the Constanzo family. It appears to be a favorite of Joey's and Rose's when referring to their stepmother. And it's the first word on Celeste's anonymous letter from last night. Rose strikes me as an ISTJ personality type from the Myer Briggs test—introverted, sensing, thinking, and judging. A practical, no-nonsense woman, who likes to know the rules of the game and where her role fits in. When Celeste first arrived on the scene, the game changed. The role of a doting daughter that Rose previously played no longer existed. Try as she might, her logic and compliance with her father's wishes couldn't bring order to her world. I suspect she's normally a quiet, private person, but the viciousness with which she'd just spoken demonstrated a deep judgmental streak. Probably inherited from her father, based on what Celeste told me about Joe. Rose was the classic damaged middle child, ready to erupt. No wonder she doesn't want to leave the most volcanically active place in the world. She's a kindred spirit of the Galapagos.

"Hey, Rose." Angelo's masked face peers up out of the water. "You should've come in. It's terrific." With a splash, he nose-dives under.

"He's such an idiot." She tuts a vicious sound while he swims away. "He thinks I don't know what he gets up to. Him and his women, and his secret meetings."

I expect her to recoil on revealing her husband's illicit activities, but she doesn't. When she faces me, her brown, doe eyes, glitter with malice. "This worm is about to turn. Mark my words. My father's death changed everything. I'm not putting up with anyone's crap any longer."

My lips purse in a grim line. I'm speechless that she's unburdened her innermost feelings to me. It's as if I'm wearing a sign proclaiming, 'Here's a friendly widow. Download all your shit on her.'

Tom's sister, Mimi, often says I don't know how to say no. That I let people corner me and tell me all their troubles. Now more than ever, she's right, particularly since I don't have Tom beside me. I wonder if the rest of the Constanzo family will be as forthcoming as Celeste and Rose.

By the time our zodiak's passengers board and we set off for the ship, a frosty chill silences Rose and Angelo once more. When we arrive, Rose nods a perfunctory good-bye and then stalks up the ship-side stairs. I'm in no rush, so I wait for the other passengers to disembark and sense Angelo's powerful body close behind me.

"You really shouldn't get involved with the Constanzos." I spin around, but before I have a chance to speak, he continues, "You seem a very nice lady, but you're getting mixed up in something that doesn't concern you."

"Thanks for the advice. But Celeste asked me to be her ship-board buddy. She's grieving the loss of her husband, as am I, and we have things in common. I don't see how my being Celeste's friend can cause any harm."

He guides me off the zodiak and follows me up the narrow stairway in silence. Although his comments unnerve me, I hope he'll say more. When we reach the top and queue to swipe our lanyards for embarkation, he edges in beside me. "Take it from me, getting involved in this family isn't worth it."

I glance up at his rugged jaw and chiseled features which no longer exude the handsome, playboy image. If I didn't know better, an undercurrent of fear clouds Angelo's expression. Fear not just for me, but for himself.

★ ★ ★

AFTER LUNCH, THE DAY SUDDENLY shifts gears. Dark, pendulous clouds peel open and drench us when we land on Punta Espinoza for the afternoon excursion.

"Did you end up seeing Celeste?" John drips beside me in his plastic poncho.

"No. There's a do-not-disturb sign on her door now. I knocked, but there was no response. I even circumnavigated the entire ship during lunch. None of the staff has seen her. I don't know where she is." I push strands of wet hair from my forehead and pull the hood tighter around my jaw. The drizzling rain adds to the uneasiness gathering momentum in my stomach. "I'm starting to get concerned. Where is she?"

He holds out his hand to help me cross the rickety timber landing onto the island. "Don't get too worried. She must be somewhere. Maybe she's just keeping a low profile after that letter last night. Careful. These rocks are slippery."

When I step onto the black lava terrain, my feet squelch in my walking shoes. *Waterproof! Yeah, sure.* I'm about to complain about my soggy feet when my nostrils pinch closed. "What's that smell?"

John points to a black moving mass only a meter away from us. "Marine iguanas."

I huddle beside him, staring at the ugly creatures. They're not the gentle, lumbering iridescent green and yellow iguanas of Guayaquil on the mainland. But rather their cousins, the slightly smaller lava-black marine iguana, as thick as a man's forearm and twice as long. Their pointy, misshapen faces have no redeeming features, least of all the crown of sharp spines that continue down their back. Irrespective of each other and especially of us, they spit random sprays of stinky, saltwater, secreting the bitter, revolting smell. My gaze travels up the path, and I shudder. The ground squirms as if alive. "There are thousands of them."

"Tens, maybe hundreds of thousands, I expect. Watch your step. They're easy to miss against this black rock. Particularly if they're still."

Here I was expecting another glorious excursion, but I've landed in a horror movie. It gives me the creeps. When we round the ridge, the pathway widens, and I move as far from the spitting, obnoxious lizards as possible.

Virtually all the passengers opted for this bleak afternoon excursion, and because of the iguanas, stay close to their guides, except for John and I who loiter by ourselves. When Marianna finally gives up waiting for us, we wander the gloomy landscape at our own pace. Through the drizzling rain, I study the other groups, looking for Celeste, but she's not here. Last night, she wanted to catch up this morning after breakfast, see the captain, and lock her jewelry in the ship's safe. For her to change her mind and not tell me, doesn't feel right.

In the distance, a blonde-haired woman catches my attention. I strain to see who she is, but the heavy mist makes it difficult. Still, I can tell by her body language that she's distressed by the man beside her. "Is that Clare Constanzo? Joey's wife?" I draw John behind a man-sized boulder out of view.

"It looks like her. But who's that with her?"

"It's definitely not Joey." The man is taller, bigger, fairer, and most insistent about something. Overhead a hawk screeches, and when Clare looks up, the man draws her into the nearby scrub. "What's he doing?" I glance back to John, who pulls a face.

"Look." He nods in their direction. With the shrubbery offering limited camouflage, Clare attempts to halt the man's advances, before melting into his arms.

"Oh my God." Wide-eyed, I stare at the illicit liaison. "If Joey finds out, he'll kill him."

"He'll kill them both."

"What the hell's going on?" I rub my eyes and curse. Like my shoes, my mascara isn't waterproof.

"Beats me. Are you sure you're not some kind of witch? Seriously, in all my time in the force, I've never seen anyone who attracts so much trouble. It's like the entire Constanzo family is hurtling toward oblivion because you happen to be on board the ship."

Snapping around, I scowl.

John laughs. "I take it back. You look too much like a panda to be a witch."

I rub where I know the smudged mascara rims my eyes. "You're a barrel of laughs, John Nash. Are you really a police detective? Because you certainly don't seem too concerned about this." My head jolts back toward Clare and the mystery man.

"Hey, I'm interested in facts, not people's emotional lives or affairs."

"I think that's a cover for your own repressed emotions."

He flinches. *Damn it.* I've said too much. Men hate having a woman expose their emotional shortcomings. Tom lectured me on that point many times. Alienating John wasn't what I meant to do.

"I'm sorry, that was out of line."

"Forget it." He strides off, leaving me caught between a rock and a hard place, figuratively and literally.

★ ★ ★

FOLLOWING THE AFTERNOON'S SHOWERS, THE sea settles with the sheen of polished glass. Without the need for a seasickness pill, I wander up to deck six, hoping to get a bird's-eye view from the top of the ship and gain a better perspective of my current situation.

Once on the ship's uppermost deck, I'm irresistibly drawn to the spot immortalized by Leonardo DiCaprio in *Titanic*. Spreading my arms like the wings of the frigate birds overhead, I too feel like the king of the world. From this vantage point, the isolation and insignificance of the *Silver Galapagos* in the vast ocean becomes only too apparent.

For a moment, the melancholy of Tom's absence rears its ugly head. Even with the distraction of the events surrounding Celeste and her family, I miss him. In my hand rests the *Select Poems of Tennyson*. Its tattered red leather cover and yellowed pages hold fond memories of Tom and our engagement. I clutch it to my chest and sigh. My thoughts go to his ashes waiting patiently in my cabin. I haven't forgotten, but I'm not ready yet. Despite my pragmaticism, the thought of throwing my husband's remains to the wind hurts.

With still an hour of light before the pre-dinner briefings in the Explorer Room, I stroll back up to the hot tub, intent on relaxing on a sun lounge to read. When I round the corner, a tall, bespectacled young man meets my gaze. In his late twenties or early thirties, his lanky limbs indicate he hasn't yet reached full maturity. A precise side-part divides his slicked-back dark hair, adding severity to an otherwise youthful face. He looks the studious, bookish type, not the least because he clasps a large pictorial volume in his hand. All of this I register in an instant because I've seen him before. He's the young man at the bar during the Captain's cocktail party.

"Hello," I say.

"Hello," he mumbles and flops onto a sun lounge.

With three sun lounges on either side of the hot tub, polite etiquette deems I should sit on a lounge on the other side. But I abandoned normal protocol the day I met Celeste. Stretching out on the lounge next to him, I glance at the book in his hands.

"I see you like reading. Do you read poetry?" I wave Tennyson in the air.

"Not really." His scowl answers my interruption. But if I'd been polite enough to talk to the dreaded Blum sisters when I wanted to read, I figured he could do the same for me.

"I'm Diana Daniels, and you're . . ."

"Jason Denham." He cocks an irritable brow over his black horn-rimmed glasses.

"What brings you on the cruise, Jason?"

"I'm a photojournalist."

I eye the book laid open in his hands. "That's why you're reading that book?"

"Yes. Not only is the photography top rate, it tells the story of the Galapagos in a unique way."

"And that's what you're hoping to do on this trip? Tell the story of the islands in your own unique way through imagery?

"You could say that?" For the first time, his lips curve upward, not so much in a smile as a smirk.

"Are you traveling with anyone?"

"No." He lays the book on his lap, obviously resigned to the fact that I'm going to keep talking.

"I'm alone, too. But I've met lots of new people. There's this wonderful woman, Celeste. Have you met her?"

He shoots me a nervous glance and his expression hardens. "No. I haven't."

I press on. "Oh, I thought you might have? I'm sure I saw you the other day chatting to her?" This was a blatant lie on my part. Baiting someone in this manner isn't something I'd normally do, but I want to see his reaction. His intense interest in Celeste at the bar on Monday night signaled more than mild curiosity, as did the suspicious way in which he hurried out after I caught him staring at her.

"You must be mistaken." He pushes his glasses up the bridge of his nose and avoids my gaze.

I scratch my head. "Perhaps. But wasn't it you taking photos at the muster drill on Saturday? I'm sure I saw you." This was true. I noticed him in the Explorer Room randomly taking pictures of everyone. Except his lens was predominantly focused in the direction where Celeste sat.

He curses under his breath. "I most certainly was not. And this Constanzo woman you refer to . . . I wouldn't know her if I ran into her."

There it is. I called her Celeste and he referred to her as Constanzo. If the anger in his voice didn't confirm my suspicion, his slip-up did. He may not have met Celeste, but he knew of her and wanted to keep it a secret. An uncomfortable silence descends, which, because of his annoyance, I suspect he'll break.

With less vehemence, he says, "What if I was taking photos? It's a free country. Well, it is back home."

"And where's home for you?"

His chest heaves with impatience. "California."

"Is that where your family lives?" I watch his mouth contort and wonder just how much more of my syrupy interrogation he'll take.

He inhales and sets his jaw. "Yes, my family lives in California. And you?"

"I'm from Australia . . ." I proceed to regale him with the 'poor widow' story in the hope of garnering sympathy and building a rapport with him. He listens, adding condolences where required.

"Well, nice to meet you, Mrs. Daniels." He makes to leave.

"Please call me, Diana."

"Nice to meet you . . . Diana. I'm sure we'll run into each other over the next few days." Sarcasm tinges his smile.

I reach out and touch his forearm. "You know, Jason. Many years ago, when my brother was about your age, he found himself in trouble through no real fault of his own. He lost his way and made some rash decisions."

He gives a baleful look. "What's that got to do with me?"

"Because you remind me of Andrew. You're intelligent, good looking, and you feel things deeply." His mouth draws into a thin line. "Whatever's happened to you isn't worth losing your way over." My heart goes out to him, he seems so disenfranchised, so embittered.

He leans over, his face close to mine. "You don't know anything about me. So, keep your nose out of my business." With a final glower, he turns and stalks off.

I seem to be pissing off all the men today. First, I upset Jimmy, then John, and now Jason. Must be the day for men whose name starts with 'J.'

I open my little red book of Tennyson, my lips tilting in a smile. While I flick through the pages, I ponder on how many other men on board have a name starting with 'J.' A metaphorical lightbulb glows above my head. Joey—Joey Constanzo. What a delightful coincidence. Inside my head, Tom's voice scolds me for being so reckless as to even consider approaching Joey. But damn it, I'm sick of playing it safe. If that's what it's going to take to find Celeste, then I'll do it.

CHAPTER SIX

"CELESTE, ARE YOU IN THERE?" I rap on her cabin door, but there's no answer. "Celeste, are you all right?"

"Excuse me, Mrs. Daniels…"

I jump at the nearby voice. "Jimmy, you startled me."

"I'm sorry, but Mrs. Constanzo isn't feeling well. She's asked not to be disturbed." His curt tone and downward glance to the do-not-disturb sign makes his opinion of my actions clear.

Straightening, I eyeball him. "Did Celeste tell you that herself?"

"No. Mr. Bellassai did."

"Who's Mr. Bellassai?" The last thing I need is another person in this unfolding drama.

"The Butler Manager, madam."

"Oh, you mean Bruno." Jimmy nods. "When did he see her?"

"That I couldn't say for sure, Mrs. Daniels. After you asked me this morning about seeing Mrs. Constanzo, I mentioned your concerns to Mr. Bellassai. He told me he'd seen her earlier. She said she wasn't feeling well and wanted to rest for a day or so. He put the do-not-disturb sign on the door at her request." Jimmy sounds pleased at having found the answer to my earlier question.

"But you never saw her?"

"No . . ."

"And you haven't been in her cabin to make up the room?"

"No, Mr. Bellassai took care of it."

"Thank you, Jimmy. I guess I'll just have to speak to Bruno."

"Will that be all, Mrs. Daniels?" He shuffles, obviously eager to be on his way.

"Yes. But please . . ." I lock eyes with him. "If you do see Mrs. Constanzo, come and get me immediately."

"Of course, madam." He nods and departs.

Disheartened, I lean on Celeste's cabin door and sigh. *What's going on?*

* * *

GIVING JOHN A LITTLE TIME to recover from my indiscreet comment about his guarded emotions, I find myself trapped between Jim and Tippi Pinkerton at an open-air 'hot rocks' dinner on deck five. On the arrival of our meat and seafood main course, we proceed to cook our meals to our desired taste at the table.

"Tippi and I have long wanted to go to Australia." Jim turns his slices of beef over and over until they're at their carcinogenic, well-done best.

Mirroring his barbeque technique, she says, "It looks a wonderful place."

I wince at their burning meat, flip my plump, pink prawn, dip it in the chili Asian sauce, and pop it in my mouth.

The Pinkertons' continue in their effusive compliments about my home country, and the conversation flows easily while they're in control. I don't mind. Aimless chit-chat suits me this evening.

A man's voice erupts up the external stairs from the deck below, "You know what, I'm tired of all this shit!" Sweeping his gaze left to right, Joey Constanzo breaches the deck like a wild animal, hushing everyone's dinner chatter.

"He doesn't seem very happy with the cruise," Tippi whispers, before devouring another piece of burnt beef. "Hey, wasn't he the fella from the Captain's cocktail party who barged into the piano bar?"

Jim grunts. "Yes. He made a right ass of himself."

"Do you know who he is?" Tippi asks me.

"I met him the other night, only briefly. He's Celeste Constanzo's stepson."

Her fork clatters to the table. "You mean the mobster's son? The one who fell off a building recently?"

"Yes. He's Joe Constanzo's son . . . Joey." I flip, dip, and eat another prawn.

"What's he doing here?" Jim burns more beef.

"The whole Constanzo family is on board for Celeste's daughter's thirtieth birthday. Unfortunately, her daughter, Emily, canceled at the last moment."

"Oh, that's a shame." Tippi's mouth droops.

Jim cocks his head in their direction. "Arrogant sort of guy."

I glance at the nearby table where a wary waiter seats them. "Yes, he is." I notice Clare glance over her menu, an embarrassed expression on her face. For a moment our eyes meet. I offer a sympathetic smile, but she looks away.

"Do you know Celeste Constanzo?" Jim asks, with more than a conversational interest in his voice, I notice.

"Not really. I just met her on board. We chatted a couple of times. She seems a lovely lady."

Tippi leans over, her eyes glinting. "You know there's talk about her murdering her husband for the money . . ."

I bristle. *Whatever happened to innocent until proven guilty?* "Yes, she told me about her husband's death, but from the little I know of her, I doubt she had anything to do with it."

"It's all very scandalous, isn't it?" Tippi's words quicken as does the breeze through her hair, giving her a golden halo. Angelic, she isn't. She strikes me as one of those women whose interest in others stems from a need to gossip. All sweet-as-pie to your face and then whamo! A knife in the back at the next dinner party. I turn my attention to the last sizzling prawns, leaving the Pinkertons to their speculation about the Constanzo case.

"You should be careful, Diana," Jim warns. "These mobster types are ruthless. I know—"

"What do you mean?"

"I invested in a hotel project and lost a lot of money. Nothing I could do to get it back. They screwed me, totally."

"Was it a Constanzo project?" I ask.

"I'd rather not say . . ." He forks more meat into his mouth, biting down harder than needed. "But a word of advice, don't get involved with them or any of their type. Assholes, the lot of them." With a sad shake of his head, he returns to his food.

We finish our meals in silence, which gives me time to think. Unlike the Blum sisters who planned to be on board, the Pinkertons couldn't have possibly known about Celeste or her family being on this cruise. Surely, it's a coincidence. But the gnawing in my stomach tells me otherwise. My hunch insists that the Pinkertons engineered to be on this cruise with the Constanzos. How, was anyone's guess. Maybe since Joe was dead, Jim planned to confront Celeste over his lost money. Maybe he planned on doing more than that. Or maybe my imagination was getting the better of me. With my head pounding from dissecting the endless possibilities, I scull the last of my white wine and nod to a nearby waiter to clear my plate.

"Thank you for allowing me to join you this evening. If you'll excuse me, I'm very tired. I'm off for an early night." I rise and tuck my bag under my arm.

Their surprised faces gaze up at me. "So soon," Tippi says. "We were hoping you might join us in the bar for a game of cards."

"Sorry, not tonight. I'm feeling quite worn out." I'm sure they scare many a prospective player away with their bombastic, busybody behavior. They do, me.

"Maybe tomorrow then?" Jim's barrel chest reverberates with his trademark chuckle.

"Yes, maybe tomorrow. Have a lovely evening." I twitch a smile and depart.

When I stop to chat with Paulette, the maître D, I glance back across the deck. Jim and Tippi are deep in animated conversation, with not a familiar Pinkerton characteristic between them. *Odd.* Neither is there a familiar face among the other diners. If the fair-haired man I saw earlier with Clare was here, I might have introduced myself. But since he isn't, I say good night to Paulette, deciding on a circuit of the deck.

Despite the dramas, it's a glorious night. Overhead, the sky resembles soft, crushed velvet. Its blackness folds back on itself with the brightest pinpricks of stars sprinkled across it like billions of Swarovski crystals. For lovers, it's the quintessential night for romance. But for those with evil intent, the night's inkiness provides the perfect cloak for their dark deeds. I detour into the nearest toilet to freshen my lipstick and tame my hair, without much success. When I turn to leave, soft sobbing echoes from the second cubicle. I go to the door. "Are you okay? Is there anything I can do?" The sobbing quietens.

After a few moments, the latch unlocks, and the door opens. Out steps Clare, eyes and nose red from emotion, with a tissue clutched in her hand. On seeing me, she blinks twice and squeezes past. "No. I'm fine."

I follow her to the vanity, mindful to keep a polite distance. Based on her secret liaison today and Joey's outburst on their arrival, I choose my words to cover all bases. "Men can be such bastards."

Our eyes meet in the mirror. "Yes, they can." She forces a smile and dabs the tissue to the smoky rim of mascara around her eyes.

"We met the other night, with Celeste. I'm Diana Daniels . . ."

She studies my reflection for a moment longer before remembering me. "Oh, that's right. I'm Clare." She discards the tissue and offers her hand.

"Pleased to meet you again. Are you sure you're all right?"

"Yes. Thanks." She rifles through her purse and drags out a lipstick. "Are you married, Diana?"

"Widowed."

She hesitates, lipstick in hand. "Sometimes I wish I was widowed."

I watch her reapply the soft, baby-pink gloss. She reminds me of the famous Hollywood movie star, the regal and enchanting, Grace Kelly who married into European royalty. Like the Princess of Monaco, she appears trapped in a life she never expected, but unlike the princess, Clare married mafia royalty.

"Have you seen Celeste?" She pops her lipstick back into her purse.

"No. Have you?"

She shakes her head. "I wanted to talk to her about something . . ."

"The deck butler told me she's not feeling well. It's odd we haven't seen her though." My mind nags at Celeste's continued absence. "Perhaps I can help until you speak with Celeste?"

She lowers her eyes and fidgets with the clasp on her purse.

With nothing to lose, I press on. "Is it about that handsome man on Punta Espinoza this afternoon?"

Her cornflower-blue eyes widen. "You saw?"

"Yes, but I don't think anyone else did."

She slumps onto the vanity stool, head in hands. "Oh, God, what am I going to do?"

"Sometimes talking about it with someone can help."

Her head lifts. "His name is Robert. We met at the opening of one of the hotels Joey built. He's the general manager. We didn't mean to fall in love, it just happened. We've been seeing each other for over a year."

"If you'll forgive me for asking, but why on earth would he come on this cruise?"

"I didn't know he was coming." Tears pool in her eyes. "He wants to confront Joey and demand he gives me a divorce. Robert thought if he did this on the ship, in public, it might improve his chances."

"Of what? Being thrown overboard by your mobster husband?" My hand flies across my mouth. Too late. "I'm sorry. That was out of line."

"That's fine." She waves away my comment. "I'm sure that's what Celeste will say. She's known Joey longer than me. I've no doubt she knows what he's capable of."

"But how do you think Celeste can help?"

She shrugs. "I don't know exactly. But out of everyone, she's the one who understands the Constanzo men. She's always been kind and understanding to me. I thought she might tell me how to handle this. I've got three children to consider. It's all too awful." She slumps and sniffles.

"Particularly since your husband appears so volatile."

"That's why I wanted to talk to Celeste. She lived with Joe all those years. I don't know how she did it. I often think that Joey and Rose went out of their way to make her life difficult from the very start."

"Why would they do that?"

"Because of what happened to their mother."

"What happened?"

She avoids eye contact for a moment, probably deciding whether to reveal the family history.

"Maria married Joe when they were both young. They had three kids, and Maria became the stay-at-home wife and mother. Not long after having Tony, she became depressed and developed mental health issues. Little wonder." She snorts. "From what I understand, her husband was a classic domestic abuser. Anyway, Maria got worse. Eventually, Joe had her committed. She was only forty-three years old. Joey had just turned twenty, Rose was eighteen and Tony, fifteen. Not long after he sent their mother away, Joe started dating Celeste. She worked as a dental assistant at the family's dentist's clinic for years, since the kids were young. Maybe they'd been having an affair for a while. Who knows?" She shrugs.

"So that's why Joey hates her?" The pieces fit together. The antagonism among them grew from a darker space than the usual blended family scenario.

"Yes, he blames Celeste for seducing his father and for killing his mother."

"What?"

"Maria died soon after she was committed, probably from a broken heart. Joe refused to divulge the name of the institution where he'd sent her, so the kids never visited her. A wicked thing to do to them."

"Did they ever find out the name of the institution?"

"Not until years later. Someplace called All Saints State Hospital. For Joey, the next time he saw his mother was at her funeral. While he stood beside Maria's coffin, Celeste stood next to his father. I don't think he's ever recovered from it."

"How awful . . . for everyone." The knot in my shoulder burrows deeper. Perhaps, like me, it wants to dig its way out of this twisted mess.

"I can't tell you how many times I've heard Joey talk about killing his father or Celeste. He's crazy. They say mental illness can be genetic. I think Joey's inherited his mother's predisposition to mania and his father's chronic manipulation."

My mind reels. The dysfunction goes deeper than I suspected. "That certainly explains Rose's dislike for her stepmother. In her eyes, Celeste was the reason she lost her mother, and the affection of her father." I drop a comforting hand to Clare's shoulder. "But what about you? What are you going to do about Robert? And Joey?"

"I don't know. I've told Robert to stay away from me. I'm terrified Joey will kill him. He's capable of anything now Joe's dead and left the fortune to Celeste. It wouldn't surprise me if Joey tried to kill her within the sixty-day period before she inherits the lot."

The same thought crossed my mind more than once. I pat her shoulder. "You need to reach out for professional help on this."

"I can't while I'm stuck on this ship. All I can do is keep Joey happy and hope Robert doesn't do anything stupid." Tears spill from her eyes. "God, I wish I'd never married him. If only he was dead, I could marry Robert." Swiping at her wet cheeks, she stands and composes herself. "Thank you for listening. I assume this will stay confidential?"

"Of course. If you want to talk again, I'm in suite 420."

"I doubt I'll be able to get away from Joey for more than a few minutes." She glances at her watch. "I better get back; he'll wonder where I've got to." She wedges her purse under her arm.

I reach out with a gentle touch to her arm. "If you happen to see Celeste, please tell her to pop in on me. I'm quite concerned about her."

"Of course." She manages a tight smile, opens the door, and leaves.

★ ★ ★

AFTER GIVING CLARE A FEW minutes' grace, I amble from the ladies' room, careful not to be seen. My plan of taking a peaceful stroll around the ship no longer matters. With more questions than answers swirling in my head, I skirt along a deserted deck, hopeful of getting to my cabin without an interception. The wind picks up, whipping my hair into a frenzy and shifting my equilibrium. *Time for another seasickness pill.*

I cut through the foyer of deck four and head toward the passageway. On my approach to Celeste's suite, I consider knocking and calling out once more. Instead a breathy gasp trembles between my lips. *It can't be.* Another piece of paper in the mail slot. I pause at the door and tap three times. No answer. I scan the passageway left and right. Empty. So, I slip the paper from the slot, slide it under my purse, and walk briskly to my cabin. My heart pounds. Not only am I embroiled in a dangerous, dysfunctional family drama, but I'm also a thief. Tom would be rolling over in his grave, if his ashes weren't in my suite.

CHAPTER SEVEN

MY EYELIDS SPRING OPEN, LONG before Israel's early morning wake-up call. I dress in a flash, find John, and convince him to join me on the first zodiak to Caleta Tagus, a protected cove on the largest of the Galapagos Islands. Isabela Island is where Charles Darwin formulated his theory of natural selection through his study of finches, so this excursion is a must-do.

In the distance, the morning mist hangs damp and thick over the island, shrouding it in a Macbethean fog befitting the mystery plaguing the ship. Along the craggy foreshore rocks, Galapagos penguins, blue-footed boobies, brown pelicans, and flightless cormorants spread their wings, trying to catch the first rays of sun. This is the adventure Tom imagined. Being up close and personal with wildlife in its untouched environment and enjoying life's special moments. A pang of regret touches my heart.

Once ashore, our guide, Horhay regales us about the island's natural and human history, reciting tales of pirates and whalers, while I finish whispering a quick update on last night's events into John's ear.

He shakes his head in what has become a familiar gesture whenever I speak to him. "You stole the letter?"

"I had to."

"Why?"

"Because I think something awful has happened to Celeste. As much as I tried to ignore it, the gnawing in my stomach kept me awake most of the night. My hunches aren't wrong, and the letter may be our only lead."

"Let's say you're right. Let's say foul play has befallen Celeste. If the letter is a lead, you've contaminated the evidence."

I lower my head. "I know. But there's nothing we can do about that now."

Another shake of his head. "What does the letter say this time?"

I shimmy off my backpack, pull out my phone, and open the image. "Can you read it?" My eyes dart to the other passengers. Luckily, they're more interested in Horhay's presentation rather than eavesdropping on our conversation.

"Time to own up to the secret, bitch. I'm here, and you're going to pay." He scrolls to the previous letter and then back, before handing me my phone. "I think you're right. It certainly looks like someone is serious about doing Celeste harm."

On Horhay's booming command, we scurry into line for the hike up the one hundred and fifty-five steps chiseled into the slope. Either side of us, the tangled scrub bursts in a canvas of leafy green, stretching toward the peak of the extinct volcano. Mimicking mockingbirds and fast-flying Darwin finches, no bigger than a chicken's egg, flutter and perch, teasing us to take a photo. Only those with the fastest aim capture their cheeky antics.

Because of its primal, unspoiled beauty, I understand how intrigued Darwin must've been when he first landed here. I picture Tom hiking beside me, warning me against my impetuousness. "And it'll be your love of intrigue that'll bring you unstuck if you're not careful, Diana." But Tom's not here. Instead, I glance at John. If I didn't know better, I'd say Tom brought me John as a protector in his absence. Dear Tom, he's with me always, just as he promised before he died.

We traipse on. "I haven't seen Celeste since Sunday night," I say. "Today is Tuesday. How does someone just disappear on a ship?"

"Procedurally, Celeste hasn't disappeared or is considered missing."

Of course, she is, I want to say, but decide to stay quiet.

He continues, "Bruno said she's not feeling well, and he's attended to her in her cabin. When Clare spoke to you last night, she didn't seem too concerned that she hadn't seen Celeste, did she?"

"No, I guess not . . ."

"It's normally up to the family to lodge a missing person's report. From a police perspective, the current situation with Celeste would be assessed as a low risk missing person's case . . . if that."

"But if she's in her cabin, why doesn't she answer the door? Unless she's been . . ." I don't want to say the word.

Suddenly, someone shoves between us. Head down and back hunched, he jostles past.

"Jason is that you?"

The young man slows and half-turns. A nervous expression pinches his face.

"Mrs. Daniels . . ." His lips pull into a stiff smile.

"Diana," I remind him.

"Yes, of course." He fidgets, keen to be on his way.

"This is John Nash."

"Pleased to meet you, Jason." When he offers his hand, Jason has no other choice but to accept.

"I need to get up ahead. For the finches, you know . . ." He lifts his camera in explanation, gives a curt nod, and pushes onward up the hill.

John studies him as he shoulders through the group. "He's in a hurry."

"Do you think he heard us?"

"Hard to tell. I doubt it."

Jason disappears into the crowd, and I frown. "He's terribly troubled about something, don't you think?"

"Acting like a guilty man in my opinion." John steps off and we resume our hike up the stairs.

"He's not the only one. I had dinner with Tippi and Jim Pinkerton last night. You know the ones—loud and obnoxious."

John nods with a groan.

"Jim said he lost money in an investment and intimated it was a Constanzo property."

"Really?"

"But that's not the interesting bit. When I was leaving, I glanced back, and they looked like two completely different people, having an intense tête-à-tête over something. Huddled over, like . . . I don't know, conspirators. Anyway, I got the impression that the persona they show to everyone else, is not who they are. All very odd."

"If they aren't the rambunctious Pinkertons from Texas, who are they?"

"I don't know, but they're also acting guilty in my opinion."

"Boy, those hunches of yours are working overtime at the moment." He lets out a good-natured chuckle. "Do you want to see my badge? Maybe you don't believe I'm a cop either?"

John's having fun at my expense, but I don't mind. I remember when Tom and I first met, he thought I was loopy. The idea of acting on hunches was absurd to him. But over the years, he came to appreciate the efficacy of them. He changed his mind, and John will too. I've no doubt. I flash him a smile. "Well if you're offering, I wouldn't mind seeing that badge of yours, detective. One can't be too careful nowadays."

He laughs. A joyous, open-throated sound fills the air, scaring off the birds. Disgruntled faces turn toward us. "Oops, now I've done it," he mutters. "Ruined everyone's photos."

Although John tries for the strong, silent, Alpha-male role, I think he's more spontaneous than he allows others to see. I waver only for a moment. Now or never.

"The other day you said you didn't like it when women asked for your help. It usually ends up badly. What did you mean?" I hope I haven't overstepped the mark again.

This time his laugh is short, sharp, and soft while we tramp off the steps onto a well-worn dirt track winding its way through the Palo Santo trees. "You'd make one helluva detective. You want the John Nash story?"

"If you don't mind." I flutter my lashes in an exaggerated fashion.

"Here's the abridged version. I grew up in Del Roy Oaks on the outskirts of Monterey county. I'm the eldest of three boys. My mother and father are salt-of-the-earth people. I went to college on a sports scholarship. I did well academically. I joined the police force straight out of college. I love my job, and that's why helping women ends up badly."

I shake my head. "I don't understand."

"I met my wife Bethany helping her when she dropped her groceries in the market. Love at first sight for me. We married in 2008 and at the beginning, everything was fine. Until my job got in the way. Bethany wanted me to give up the force, but I couldn't. It's in my blood. The more time I spent at my job, the more time she spent with her lovers." He drags in a tight breath. "We divorced in 2013. And here I am, a guy who's gun-shy of helping women."

"I'm sorry. But just because your marriage didn't work out, doesn't mean there's no second chance—"

"That's what Sharon keeps telling me. We've been seeing each other for a few years now. It's serious. But I'm wary of making a wrong decision."

"Perhaps you should've brought Sharon on this trip. Told her how you feel."

He stops and gives me one of his steely stares. "If I remember correctly, you're the one who said I have repressed emotions."

My hand covers my mouth in embarrassment. Seems I'm not the only one who remembers our conversations. "Sorry about that."

He waves away my apology, and we continue up the slope. "Doesn't matter. You were right. I find it hard talking about how I feel. That's what happened with Bethany. And I can see it's happening with Sharon. I came on this cruise to try and get my head together, sort out my shit. Sharon's a good woman, and I do love her. But she's not going to wait forever . . ."

He falls silent and pensive, so I leave him to his thoughts. He reminds me of Tom, an ISTP personality type—introverted, sensing, thinking, and perceiving. Independent, practical men. They like to focus on facts, make decisions based on logic, and prefer action to conversation, particularly if it means talking about the complexity of their emotions. If Sharon understood that John wasn't avoiding her as much as avoiding himself, I'm sure they'd develop a loving, communicative relationship. Just like Tom and me.

The warm sunlight dissipates the last of the mist just as we breach the top of the volcanic core. In the distance behind us, the *Silver Galapagos* lays anchored on the glassy, royal-blue sea. It cuts a fine, mid-frame profile, flanked by the ribs of ranges curving toward the cove. I take in the flawless view on an appreciative breath. Phones and cameras click madly as everyone takes advantage of the perfect picture. When Horhay calls us over to the edge of the core, I dart across the track in front of a few tardy photographers.

"Mind where you're going," a familiar gruff voice growls in my ear. "Oh, it's you." Joey Constanzo's lifeless eyes stare down at me. "Diana Daniels, isn't it?" Sarcasm drips in his tone.

"Yes, it is." I match his contempt with brusqueness. "How's Celeste?"

"I haven't seen her since Sunday night when you and your friend there" —he casts a scathing glare at John who edges in beside me— "decided to stick your noses into our family business."

I ignore his insult. "Neither have I. I'm starting to worry about her."

"Who cares? If I never see her again it'll be too soon." With a final glower, he pushes past us and sets off up the track. He shoulders through the line, and like Jason, seems hellbent on getting to the top.

I knuckle my hands on my hips. "In my opinion, that man needs serious help."

"Crap. He needs to be locked up. I've seen that type before. He's a loaded gun waiting to go off."

"That's what worries me. His hatred for Celeste has taken on a life of its own, and you know what they say?" I cock a brow at John.

"What?"

"An eye for an eye, a life for a life."

John and I exchange worried stares.

Horhay's cheery voice breaks the tension, directing everyone's attention to the crater below where a circular lake of brilliant blue-green water shimmers. He explains that Darwin Lake is a saltwater lagoon and because it has twice the salinity of the ocean, no life can survive in it. *How apt. No life.*

★ ★ ★

AFTER THE HIKE TO THE summit of Isabela Island and an hour of extraordinary deep-water snorkeling, my stomach grumbles. The past days' exercise has not only been good for my muscles but for my appetite too. The choice between a sumptuous buffet lunch served on deck five, or an a la carte service in the restaurant proves difficult. My stomach wants me to be on my way to either venue, but I wait for an expected knock at my cabin door.

"Hello, Mrs. Daniels. You wanted to see me?" Looking his cultured best, Bruno stands at attention, wearing an expression of six-star deference.

"Yes. I've been concerned about Mrs. Constanzo in suite 430. I haven't seen her since Sunday evening. Jimmy tells me that you've been attending to her. How is she?"

"She's feeling much better today." His heavy-lidded eyes hold mine.

"What's wrong with her?"

"She's been feeling seasick. Though I believe she's up and about today."

"Oh?" My brows lift. "I'm sure her do-not-disturb sign was still on her door when I got back from snorkeling an hour ago?"

"It's not there now, Mrs. Daniels. Perhaps she's gone to lunch."

"Thank you. I'll go and see if I can find her."

After Bruno bows and retreats, I grab my keycard lanyard and scurry down the passageway. He's right. The do-not-disturb sign's gone. Relief washes over me. Taking the steps two at a time, I dash up the internal staircase to deck five.

Wait staff rush around, serving the hungry, happy passengers filling the deck, while the pianist plays a selection of melodies on his portable piano keyboard. My eyes search for Celeste. *She'll be easy to spot.* I spy the Pinkertons bailing up some unsuspecting Japanese tourists who are too polite to retreat. The Blum sisters sit at a table for two, looking a picture of innocence. Though when they see me, their demeanor changes to one of suspicion.

I can't see any of the Constanzo family, although I spot Robert, Clare's lover, sitting by himself looking forlorn. If I wasn't looking for Celeste, I'd join him.

Slowing down my gaze, I focus on each table and the line at the buffet until I'm sure she's not here. *Must be in the restaurant.* I sprint down two flights of stairs and barrel into the restaurant. The narrow room bustles with staff and passengers, while a huddle of guests gathers at the juice station. When I spy Jason and Tony chatting, my mind goes into overdrive. Am I witnessing polite, passenger behavior or is there something else going on? I shake away my suspicions. I don't have time for that. Another quick scan of the restaurant reconfirms Celeste isn't there. I race into the ladies' toilets, but still no sign of her. When I dash out the door, the ship pitches.

I clutch the poor waiter carrying plates to the kitchen, and he nearly loses them. "Are you all right, madam?"

"I'm fine," I lie, steadying myself. "Have you seen Mrs. Constanzo, tall, exotic lady from Suite 430?"

The waiter considers for a moment, then smiles. "Yes. I think she was here earlier."

"Really?"

He nods and smiles.

"Oh, thank you. Thank you." Though I'm thrilled with the news, my stomach is still doing backflips. I make for the restaurant door in desperate need of fresh air, before my empty stomach makes a fool of me.

I swallow hard and plod up the staircase, hand over hand on the railing. Every gentle roll of the ship forces me to stop and wait until I recover my equilibrium while other passengers swan past without a care in the world. I envy their sea legs. Struggling to ignore my lurching stomach, I trudge up to the passageway of deck four. And that's when I see it, hanging from suite 430's door:

Do Not Disturb

My heart sinks. I want to pound on Celeste's door, shout out her name, but I'm too seasick to stop. I labor on, clinging to the railing like a drunk and cursing my super sensitive inner ear. Once inside my cabin, I grab my seasickness pills and pop one, dry, while filling a glass with water. After a hasty gulp, I head to my balcony and pin a hapless gaze on the horizon.

If Tom were here, he'd be mansplaining how calm the waters are, and that there's no reason for me to feel sick. But my fine-tuned biology disagrees. I gulp a couple of deep breaths until the worse passes. Lunch is out of the question now. Instead, a good lie-down. Random voices drift up from the deck below and on recognizing the woman's, I pause and listen.

"I need your help, Tony. I can't do this without you." Rose sounds desperate.

"I really don't know if I can . . ."

"But we've always had each other's back. We could do it together. What do you say? Please . . ."

"I can't . . ." By the sound of his voice, he's uncomfortable with Rose's request, whatever it is.

"Why not? When this is all over, we can each start a new life. You'll meet a new girl, settle down."

"I won't be meeting any new girls and settling down."

"Why not? Just because things haven't worked out this time—"

"God, don't you get it?" I can hear the exasperation in his voice. "I'm gay."

"What?"

"I never told anyone because father would've disowned me forever."

"I had no idea."

"It doesn't matter. I don't have to keep it a secret anymore now that he's dead. Thank God. I hated him."

"Don't say that."

"Why not? He was an asshole. The way he's treated us. Joey, you, and me . . . it was appalling." The venom in his voice contradicts the circumspect, cultured young man I met in the piano bar.

"No, he wasn't. It was that bitch's fault. Once she got her talons into him, he changed. She's the one who should've got shoved off a building."

"What do you mean? Shoved off a building. Dad fell."

"Who knows? Maybe he did, maybe he didn't? Celeste probably paid someone to kill him. I don't know."

"Don't be silly. Dad had plenty of enemies who wanted him dead. I don't think Celeste had anything to do with it. Anyway, it's all in the past. Now I can live my life, my way."

"And me? What about helping me?" She sounds frantic.

"When do you need an answer?"

"The sooner the better. If we're going through with this, I need to get everything sorted."

"Okay. Give me twenty-four hours."

"Twenty-four hours."

"But I'm not promising anything. Clear?"

"Crystal."

My head spins, matching the whirlpool in my stomach. I stumble inside my cabin and flop on the bed. What on earth was Rose trying to talk her younger brother into? And what the hell was with the do-not-disturb sign back on Celeste's door? I rub my face hard and pray that the ceiling speaker above me remains mute. The last thing I need is another of Israel's muster-time messages.

While the heaving sensation in my stomach persists, self-pity grabs its opportunity. If Tom were here, he'd have stopped me from the beginning. I'd have never met Celeste or got involved with the Constanzo's. But no, he's dead. And I'm alone and seasick, in the middle of nowhere, on a ship with more than its fair share of lunatics. "Why, Tom? You know I'm not good at cruising?"

CHAPTER EIGHT

THE CLATTER OF THE DESCENDING anchor wakes me. Fortunately, I've slept while the ship cruised through unprotected waters to the eastern side of Isabela Island and into the tranquility of Elizabeth Bay. Israel's sing-song voice croons from my cabin's speaker. "*All those going to the red mangroves for this afternoon's expedition, please come to the Explorer Room. The zodiaks will be leaving shortly.*"

The pill worked, and with the ship now anchored in calm waters, I'm ready to go. Ignoring my stomach's demand for food, I collect my life belt, backpack, and raincoat, and head off. Striding up to Celeste's cabin, I stop and lift my hand to knock. But what's the point?

My previous concerns about her welfare are now replaced by a disturbing resignation. My hunch of something bad about to happen has changed. It no longer speaks to me in the future tense. Something bad *has* happened. Although I've not directly witnessed what that was, every fiber of my being knows that my original fears for Celeste's safety were well-founded. I lower my hand, knowing she'll never answer the door again. But how I'm going to prove that, I've no idea.

Behind other groups of passengers heading off to the red mangroves, I file along the ship's port-side deck and scan my keycard before disembarking. With a crew member overseeing the process, the ship's electronic system checks passengers getting off and on the ship every time an excursion takes place. Lost in my thoughts, I almost miss it. But the metaphoric lightbulb above my head switches on. Of course, Celeste's keycard. If she disembarked on any excursion, she'd have swiped out. If the system shows she swiped out, but not back in, that would at least give us a timeline. The hard part will be convincing the captain to take my concerns seriously.

While I wait to descend the steep exterior stairway to the zodiak landing platform, I watch those behind me swipe out with their keycards. My idea will only be of help if Celeste left the ship of her own free will. If she didn't, the system will prove nothing, except that she's still on board. And just because I haven't seen her, doesn't mean she's officially missing.

"Next, please." Horhay's authoritative voice calls me forward.

"Sorry." I walk down the twenty or so steps, edge to the aft of the zodiak, and wait while others board.

A solid afternoon drizzle falls against the chilly, pewter gray background. *Another miserable afternoon.* Pulling my rain hood higher, I hunker down trying to keep warm and dry. Nine pairs of feet shuffle into place as the other passengers take their seats before the driver reverses the zodiak and sets course.

My raincoat protects my upper body, but not my lower legs. With only one pair of walking shoes, now sodden from the rain, I wonder how I'm going to get them dry for tomorrow. My gaze roams the other passengers' feet, who likewise try to shield them from the rain. Except for two pairs at the bow of the boat which remain steadfast in place.

Intrigued as to who they belong to, I glance up to see Jason and Tony, sitting side by side and ramrod straight. Staring staunchly toward our destination, they seem oblivious to the weather. I pull my hood tighter so only my eyes can be seen and study the two young men. While other passengers lower their heads against the biting rain, they lift theirs, reminding me of a couple who's had a tiff. Or perhaps, an unwanted advance was made and caused offense. Being the last passengers to board, they'd no other option but to sit beside each other, and by their body language, they're uncomfortable with the arrangement.

"We're coming up to the red mangroves now." Horhay points ahead to a sprawling, low-lying forest of green sliced open by inlets of shallow, clear water. We motor along the craggy coastline and through ornate, basalt gateways, formed over millions of years. Sea lions lounge in the afternoon rain, unconcerned by the sharp black lava surface, while hundreds of scurrying orange crabs, larger than a man's hand, glow against the rock as if illuminated.

"The red mangrove plant provides shelter for both the green sea turtles and hawksbill turtles as a resting area. When we go further into the mangroves, you'll see lots of turtles between the mangrove roots. We ask that you keep noise to a minimum, so we don't disturb them," Horhay says.

We cruise up the shallow inlet into the mangroves, watching the turtles and stingrays hover over the sandy bottom below. The unhurried rise and fall of their flippers and wings produces a sedative effect. Like meditating in a spiritual temple, the energy settles and the knot in my shoulder loosens. I peer over the side of the zodiak wishing my life was as peaceful as the turtles in Elizabeth Bay.

"Keep your eyes off my wife!" The voice shatters the stillness like a bomb blast.

All eyes turn toward the zodiak about ten meters to our right. In one swift move, Joey grabs Robert and hurls him overboard, causing their boat to rock fiercely. An almighty splash sounds as Robert hits the water. Women scream, and men still. Apparently, no one's brave or stupid enough to confront Joey, who stands in the middle of the boat, his hands clenched into fists. Blinking and spluttering, Robert rises in the waist-deep water, shooting daggers at him. "If you look at my wife again, I'm warning you, I'll kill you."

On Horhay's instruction, our driver motors closer to the commotion, and I spy poor Clare. Her pallid face and terrified expression say everything. She clutches at Joey's forearm, trying to get him to calm down. He spins his bad temper onto her, and she cowers under his vicious gaze. She retreats further into her allotted seat while Joey shoves in next to her.

As their guide and the other passengers haul Robert on board, I notice his face is a mixture of seething humiliation and vengeful intention. He shakes off the water as best he can and wedges himself as far from Joey as possible. No one speaks. Most keep their eyes downturned. Except for Robert. He exchanges Joey's malevolent glare with one of his own.

Horhay tuts and instructs our driver to resume the excursion.

"That's not going to end well." The exquisite lilt of a Scottish accent strokes my ear. I turn to the voice's owner and am met by glacial blue eyes and a shrewd smile sparkling with humor.

"No, it's not," I reply, matching his smile.

"I'm Derek Stewart." The man wrangles his hand out from under his raincoat.

"Diana Daniels." I do likewise, and we shake hello.

"What brings you to the Galapagos Islands on your own?"

I slant him a suspicious glance.

Mischief dances in his eyes. "You'll have to forgive me, but I've an eye for the ladies. Particularly those with style, grace, intelligence, and dare I say it, beauty, like yours."

What is it about Scottish accents and good-looking men? With a trimmed salt-and-pepper beard, arched brows, and well-proportioned face, I figure Derek's in his sixties. He possesses a Hollywood-style charisma, and he knows how to wield it, like a Scottish Outlander.

"How very astute of you, Derek. I am traveling alone . . ." I proceed with my widow story, hoping it'll diffuse his interest. It doesn't.

"Perhaps we could have dinner together?"

"Perhaps, but . . ." I hesitate at saying any more. He's almost too charming, too premeditated.

"Not to worry. I'm sure that whatever you're onto, you'll sort out the mystery."

Now he's got my attention. "What do you mean?"

"Over the past few days, I've been watching you while you've been watching everyone else."

"I've no idea what you're talking about." I try for righteous innocence, but I can't help but smirk.

"Don't play coy with me, Diana. You know very well what I mean. I've seen you . . ." He raises my smirk with a beguiling smile of his own.

"Why on earth would you be watching me?"

"I'm a retired theatre producer from London. Producing mysteries was my niche. I can sniff out a good mystery anywhere, particularly if I'm investing money in it." He chuckles low and soft, sounding a lot like Sean Connery. "You're onto something. I know it. I can feel it in my producer's bones. I've no idea what it is, but I'm hooked." His eyes narrow.

I laugh out loud and catch a dirty look from Horhay. "Perhaps I will have dinner with you after all," I tease in a whisper.

"Your place or mine?"

"The restaurant. At eight. Now, back to the turtles."

I spin around, ending the conversation. But I can feel his gaze boring a hole in my back.

★ ★ ★

WITH A BOWL OF BUTTERY popcorn on my lap, I settle into the Explorer Room for the late afternoon screening of Part Two of *The Galapagos Affair* which begins with a quick recap of the Baroness, her two lovers, the Wittmers and the Ritters. I enjoy being alone, although I get a twinge of sadness for Celeste. I intended on speaking with John after the red mangroves excursion, but since I couldn't find him, I slipped in here, expecting some quiet time to consider our approach to the captain. When someone slides onto the chair beside me, I half-turn expecting to see John, but it's Robert, Clare's lover.

"Diana?" He sounds nervous.

"Yes."

"Can I speak with you?" His anxious stare scans the room.

"Of course." I offer him some popcorn, but he declines.

He lets out a ragged breath. "Clare told me she spoke to you about us . . ."

"Yes, she did." I stop eating and give him my attention.

"I've got to get her away from that madman," he says, while on the screen, one of the Baroness's lovers, Philippson has disappeared. Vanished from the island without a trace, leaving six possible suspects of foul play. A shiver skids down my spine. "Joey's unhinged, I swear."

"I tend to agree with you. As I told Clare, your plan of confronting him on board the ship wasn't the smartest."

"Yeah. It was impulsive and stupid. But I thought that at least here, they'd be security on hand. Or at the very least, there'd be witnesses if he tried anything."

"But after this afternoon's episode at the red mangroves, I doubt Joey Constanzo cares about being seen. He cares only for himself. His propensity to aggressive, abusive, and even sadistic behavior isn't to be underestimated."

Robert curls his lips. "You're right. But I came because Clare can't go back with him . . ."

"Why?"

His grave expression deepens. "Clare doesn't know, but I think Joey had something to do with his father's death."

The hairs on the back of my neck bristle. "Do you have any proof?"

"I've had a private investigator on his tail for a few months now—for Clare's safety. And he's got some *pretty damning evidence* about Joey Constanzo." He air quotes with his fingers.

"So, why not tell her? Or better yet, go to the police?"

"I've gone to the police. I'm hoping they'll arrest him when we return to the U.S. But I'm worried about Clare. She can't return with him. He's likely to use her as a hostage if the cops turn up at the wrong time. The man's crazy."

"But why are you telling me this?"

"Because I know you've been asking about Celeste."

"Have you seen her?"

"No, but I did see Joey come out of her cabin at around one-thirty Monday morning."

A fist forms in my stomach. "Are you sure?"

"Positive. After he caused that scene with Celeste at the Captain's cocktail party, I kept an eye on him. He and Clare had dinner with the rest of his crazy family, then they went back to their cabins. I walked the decks for an hour or so, trying to work out what the hell I was going to do about this mess. When I was about to go to my cabin, I saw someone walk through the piano bar. I thought it was him, so I followed. He knocked on Celeste's door and when she didn't answer, he picked the lock and disappeared into her cabin. A few minutes later, he sticks his head out and slips down the internal staircase. Gone. Like the wind." He clicks his fingers.

Robert's news stuns me into shifting my gaze back to the screen. Phillippson's disappearance pits the six people living on Floreana against each other as suspicions of secret liaisons and murder escalate. Uncannily like the current situation on the *Silver Galapagos*.

I return a grave look to Robert. "Are you *sure* it was Joey?"

"Yes. He broke into Celeste's cabin and then left a few minutes later."

"Does Clare know you saw him?"

"No. I didn't tell her because I don't want her to panic."

"I suggest you stay well away from anyone in the family for the time being. I intend on going to the captain about Celeste's absence. What you've told me should be enough for him to take my concerns seriously."

He stares at me. "Be careful. Don't go confronting Joey or anything."

"I've no intention of doing that. I just want to find Celeste."

"Good. Because Joey has his eye on you."

Panic rises in my throat, but I manage to swallow it. "On me? Why?"

"He thinks you're a busy-body. Sticking your nose into the family's affairs."

My gaze reverts to the screen where I discover, Lorenz, the Baroness's other lover has also disappeared. The suspects on Floreana now number five. At that rate, they'll be no one left on the island by the end of the film. A vice squeezes my temples. Was the Galapagos cursed? Have I stumbled into some strange time warp? People disappeared in the past and now, the present. I hope I'm not one of them in the future.

I pin Robert in a sharp gaze. "Trust me. I won't be confronting Joey. In fact, I'll be doing everything I can to keep out of his way. Like you."

"Good." For the first time, he attempts a smile. A mere uplift of his lips, incongruent with his expression of concern. "I better get out of here. I don't want Joey to see us together. You take care."

"You too."

He slips from the chair as quietly as he arrived. I regard the lukewarm popcorn, my appetite gone. On the screen, black and white images flicker past. Each of the suspects looks more guilty than innocent. Then it dawns on me. The baroness, the Ritters, and the Wittmers didn't care about the disappearance of Phillippson or Lorenz. They only cared about themselves. Perhaps they were all in it together and hiding a shared secret.

While the 1930s real-life mystery plays out on screen, I mull over the current mystery. Like a spider's gossamer web, numerous threads radiate out from the center, which is Celeste. Though none of these threads seem to interconnect in an obvious pattern, I know that's not true. There's usually one thread, that if you tug it hard enough, collapses the web. I must find that thread.

My attention drifts to the screen as *The Galapagos Affair* comes to an unsatisfactory end. The mystery was never solved. As a post note, the wrinkled face of Margaret Wittmer stares down the barrel of the camera and says, "A closed mouth admits no flies."

It was time to speak to the captain.

CHAPTER NINE

WITH THE STAFF BUSTLING BEHIND us doing pre-dinner setup, John and I recline on deck five's aft railing and admire the muted reds, oranges, and golds of the sun's farewell. Despite the deepening tones of night's approach, a giant moon glimmers low over the now-familiar alien landscape, and I'm struck once more by the surreal beauty of these islands. For most passengers, this is aperitif hour. Time to debrief after the day's activities, relax, and unwind with a drink. But I need a clear head, especially since I took a seasickness pill when the ship pulled anchor thirty minutes ago. Sipping an iced coffee, I retell Robert's story of witnessing Joey coming out of Celeste's cabin in the early hours of Monday morning. It has the desired effect on John. His demeanor turns police professional.

"Now that we have a witness and not just your hunches, it changes everything."

Under an indignant brow, I lift my gaze over the rim of the glass.

"Sorry. But an eyewitness trumps your hunches when it comes to police procedure. Leave it with me. I'll give the head of security a call. I've got Patrizio's card back in my cabin. I'll set up a meeting and see if we can't find out what's going on."

"Thanks. I'm sure if you speak with him, it'll have more impact than an eccentric widow." I slant him a sarcastic look.

"Yeah, yeah. Be as smart as you want. But it is what it is." He snorts. "Now, what are you doing for dinner tonight?"

"I have a date." I play it for all it's worth. Again, it has the desired effect.

John's eyebrows fly upward only to draw together in a tight frown. "With who?"

"Derek Stewart," I proclaim as if he's a celebrity, which, for all I know, he could be in Britain.

"Who's that?"

I stop teasing and explain how Derek approached me on the zodiak, made comment about the scene between Joey and Robert, and invited me to dinner. "It's not a date, of course. I was just joking."

"Nevertheless, don't go walking along a dark deck alone together, otherwise you might find yourself swimming with the fishes." He barks a good-humored laugh, though I suspect he's concerned about my being alone with a stranger under the current circumstances.

"I've no intention of being alone with Mr. Stewart. I'm a recently widowed woman and a shipboard romance isn't something I want." I pout and add a curt nod for good measure.

"It mightn't be what you want, but it might be what you need." He holds up his hands, feigning protection.

"Now who's the one giving relationship advice." I smack his shoulder with a playful slap and laugh. Ribbing each other like siblings, our friendly banter breaks the seriousness which has become the standard for our conversations. A perfect way to enjoy the last of another pristine Galapagos day.

★ ★ ★

WHEN I WALK INTO THE restaurant a little before eight, the nervous fluttering in my chest surprises me. Perhaps I'd been fooling myself when I told John this wasn't a date? I reflect on how long it took me to choose what to wear tonight. I'd strewn clothes everywhere before finally settling on a navy-blue, silk crepe-de-chine wrap-dress, and nude pumps. Throwing the rejects back into my closet, I'd rushed from my suite before changing my mind, and clothes, again. Despite my melancholy over Tom, it seems the transition to singledom is happening whether I consciously accept it or not.

"Diana." Derek's lilting voice drifts across the room like a bonnie Scottish song. No longer looking bedraggled from the rain, he stands tall and trim in a black polo neck sweater, scrunched to the elbows, black trousers, and I suspect black shoes. A sophisticated, casual look. *My favorite.* On my approach, his face opens into a wide smile which I reciprocate without hesitation.

"Hello, Derek."

He maneuvers the chair and when he slides it in for me, his warm breath tickles my ear. "You look ravishing." The way he rolls his 'r' sends a warm shiver up my neck.

I glance up and meet his artic blue gaze. "Thank you, but there's no need for flattery. Remember, this isn't a date."

He slips into the chair opposite. "But that doesn't mean I can't compliment you." His eyes dance with such fondness, I've no reply. It's been a while since a man's been so forthcoming in his admiration. I fidget, feeling a little foolish as a blush warms my cheeks.

"I've taken the liberty of ordering champagne. I hope you don't mind." On spying the accomplice to his plan, he signals the waiter to bring the ice bucket and champagne.

"I'll have a glass, but I suffer from seasickness. I mustn't drink too much."

His lips tip in a charming smile. "One glass won't hurt you . . ."

The young waiter corks and pours, while I wait, demure and controlled. As the bubbles explode up the glass, I release a series of staccato sighs to match, as if I've been holding my breath for days. Derek's eyes lock mine. His long elegant fingers stroke the perfectly trimmed salt and pepper whiskers that grace his face, giving him the look of a sea-faring captain. His intense scrutiny reminds me of the wolf in the nursery rhyme. *All the better to eat you, my dear.* I suppress a girlish giggle. Who am I fooling? I long for some male company, and wolf or not, Derek fits the bill nicely.

He reaches for his glass and I, mine. "To you, Diana. Lovely to meet you."

I nod and give a soft smile. "And you."

The first sip tastes sweeter than it has in a long time. In fact, since before Tom died. I take another. Something rouses inside me. Perhaps it's hope that life can be good even if Tom has gone.

"Tell me a little more about yourself? You strike me as a woman who can take care of herself."

While we finish our first glass of champagne and order our meals, we share snippets from our lives. We start with the customary topic of family, speaking about our grown children, my son Harrison and his two daughters, Imogene and Alison. I tell him of Tom's death, and he speaks of his divorce a few years earlier. During our conversation, the waiter delivers our entrees, pours fresh glasses of champagne, and departs without interruption.

Dipping his spoon into the creamy seafood chowder, he lowers his eyes. "And what do you plan to do now?"

"Well, I'm not looking for romance if that's what you are referring to?" My flirty tone sounds quite the opposite to my statement.

His spoon pauses mid-air. "A shipboard romance? I hadn't meant that, but it does sound a fine idea." He raises his eyes in a blast of blue and winks.

"Oh, I'm sorry. I didn't mean to . . . It's just that . . ." I bite my tongue. *What am I doing?* Just because a handsome, successful man invites me to dinner is no reason for me to act like a silly high school girl. I cringe. If only the chair would swallow me whole. Concentrating on my spoon, I resolve to finish my soup, feign seasickness, and leave with a shred of dignity.

He reaches over and touches my hand, stopping it's relentless up and down between the bowl and my mouth. "Diana…"

I lift my head, a hot blush of embarrassment staining my cheeks, and try to avoid his gaze.

"I'd very much like a ship-board romance with you." He pauses. "But you've made it clear you're not interested. Despite how other men might behave, I'll respect your wishes. However . . ." His eyes twinkle. "If you change your mind, don't hesitate to inform me as I'm only too willing to oblige." He raises my hand to his whiskered lips and plants a soft kiss to it. My skin flames at his touch. I might be a novice at this singles game, but Derek's a master.

My shoulders drop on a sigh. "Thank you."

"You're welcome." He returns my hand.

"I mean, thank you for rescuing me from making a fool of myself."

"I doubt you could ever do that. You're too intelligent to be a fool."

Not based on current events and opinions. We finish our chowder and the bottle of champagne in casual conversation without double entendre.

"Do you like red wine?"

"Yes, but I don't think I should drink anymore."

"I'll order a bottle of the *Casillero del Diablo.* It's a Chilean shiraz and quite good. In case you change your mind." He casts me another of his melting smiles.

Feminist or not, I enjoy having a man order the wine, particularly if he knows good ones. Being single means, I can only order wines by the glass which invariably leaves me with little choice. To have a glass of decent wine means ordering a bottle. A bottle of wine and a widow drinking it alone isn't a scene in which I want to star. When our main courses of beef bourguignon arrive with their rich deliciousness steaming from our plates, I relent and sip the shiraz.

I hold the glass in front of me and lick my lips. "This *is* good."

"Yes. It's one of the better wines they have on board. *Bon appétit.*"

We each fork a cube of meat into our mouths and moan with delight. After the first impressive mouthful, Derek repeats, "And what do you plan to do now?"

Unwilling to be caught a second time, I remain silent and lift an inquiring brow.

He laughs a soft, throaty sound. "What do you plan to do now about this mystery you're embroiled in?"

I lower my fork and tear apart a dinner roll. "Why do you think I'm embroiled in a mystery?" I reach for the butter. "Just because you're a retired theatre producer from London who used to produce mysteries, doesn't mean there are mysteries wherever you go?" I spread on a thick layer as a reward for all the hiking I've done. My taste buds rejoice.

"Very well then." He reclines and raises his glass, swirling the ruby liquid before taking a mouthful. "For a start, there's that woman I've seen you with. Celeste Constanzo."

"How do you know her name?"

"I asked." He angles me an incredulous look. "It's easy to find out other passengers' names. After all, the crew wants us all to mingle, to have a good time. It's an expedition cruise, not an MI6 training maneuver."

I giggle and return to my meal. "Go on."

"Anyway, this Constanzo woman intrigued me from the start. She wanted to be seen. With that bloody big hat and dressed all in white. I suspect she intrigued you too since I saw you befriend her on the first night in the bar."

"My, you are the observant one," I tease.

"Then there was the ruckus that fellow made at the Captain's cocktail party. Threatening her at the bar. Who's he?"

"That's Joey, her stepson."

"I figured he was family of some sort."

"Why do you say that?"

"Not only did I produce mysteries, but I'm also good friends with Mathew Prichard . . ." I shrug. "He's the chairman of Agatha Christie Limited, the company that manages her estate. He's also her grandson."

I almost drop my fork. "You're kidding me?"

"Not at all. The plays I produced during my career in the West End were hers. You could say I have an intimate understanding of a good mystery." He salutes his glass accompanied by an undisguised self-congratulatory smirk.

"Derek Stewart. You're a man of many surprises."

"As was the greatest mystery writer of all time. That's why I know you're onto something. Now, spill it."

Perhaps it's the alcohol or because I suspect him to be an ENTP personality type—extroverted, intuitive, thinking, and perceiving, which complements my personality type, I decide to trust him. Over the next fifteen minutes, while we finish one of the best beef bourguignon I've eaten, I walk him through the events of the past four days.

"My word, you've stumbled into a hornet's nest." Not waiting for service, he tops up our glasses.

"That's what John says." I dab my napkin to my lips before reclining to savor my second glass of wine.

"Who's he?"

I explain my friendship with John, that he's a detective with the Monterey County Sheriff's department, his offer to help, and how he's someone I can trust.

"And are you and this John fellow romantically involved?"

I pout. "Of course not."

"That's good to hear. I don't want any competition if you change your mind."

My girlish giggle rings out, causing a few heads in the restaurant to turn in our direction. I don't care. I've probably drunk too much, but I deserve to relax. After all, that's why Tom booked this trip.

"Has anyone told you, you have an enchanting laugh?" Tilting forward, he reaches his hand across the table and encircles mine.

"I can't remember. It's been so long since I laughed like that." I squeeze his hand in gratitude.

"Well then. Let's see if I can't make you laugh more often over these next few days."

I remove my hand, once more returning to more serious matters. "But if I'm right and something has happened to Celeste, there'll be little time for laughter despite your best efforts."

"Maybe so, but we still have a few days."

"So, Mister Mystery Producer, do you have any words of wisdom regarding the mystery onboard the *Silver Galapagos*?" I speak in the dramatic tone of an old-fashioned radio narrator.

He leans on his elbows and steeples his fingers under his chin. Twisting his mouth, he glances upward to his left. A response to finding something from his memory. Despite the alcohol, my neuro-linguistic training still switches on.

"If I recall . . . the grand dame of mystery writing said, 'Every murderer is probably somebody's old friend.' If Celeste's been murdered, maybe you should follow Agatha's words of wisdom."

I push my glass away. The word I hadn't wanted to say falls from his lips with such ease, it unnerves me. There's a part of me, that voice of my sensible, level-headed Tom, that's told me I'm exaggerating. Reading too much into things. But here, a virtual stranger utters what my hunches have hinted for days. *Murder.* The knot in my shoulder reappears, twisting like taut rope. "I think I need to get back to my suite. Thank you for a charming evening, but I did what I said I wouldn't do. I've drunk too much."

In an instant, he folds his napkin and rises from his chair. "Let me walk you to your cabin."

"Thank you."

He captures my arm and guides me from the restaurant. My legs wobble as we climb the staircase to my deck. Whether it's from the increasing pitch of the ship, the effect of the alcohol, Derek's flattering attention, or from the thought of murder, I can't tell. I just need to get to my suite. When we breach the staircase to deck four, the chill in the central foyer sends shivers up my arms.

"Are you cold?" He wraps his arm around my shoulders.

"Just a little." I lean into him.

Crossing the foyer, I point to the nearest cabin. "That's Celeste's suite. 430." A hot lump of emotion wedges in my throat.

"I see." He squeezes me tighter, and I'm thankful for his support, physical and emotional.

"Oh, God." My knees buckle.

"What is it?"

"There. There." I point a trembling finger toward the suite's mail slot. "I think it's another letter."

CHAPTER TEN

DESPITE MY FRIGHT, I SCRAMBLE from Derek's arms and make a beeline to the mail slot. Glancing right and left, I check we're alone in the passageway before taking the paper.

"What are you doing?" He stands close behind me.

"I'm checking to see if I'm right." I unfold it. "It's a third anonymous letter." I hand it to him.

He reads aloud. "Time's running out. I'll find you and make you pay for what you did. Bitch!"

"Celeste! Are you in there?" My frustration grows as I pound the door. *Where the hell is she?*

He grabs my wrist. "Don't. You'll attract too much attention."

Hot tears prick my eyes. "Where is she? What's happened to her? Why isn't she answering her door?"

"I don't know, but it's not up to you to find out. Leave it with Detective Nash and Patrizio. Come on. Let's get you back to your cabin before someone comes."

"I'm taking the letter." I snatch it from his hand.

"Are you sure?"

"Absolutely. I took the second one, and I'm taking this one. If Celeste isn't here, these may be all we have to track a killer." There I'd said it. The thought that's haunted me. Celeste is dead.

Steamrolling down the passageway, we reach my cabin within moments. I swipe my keycard and step inside with Derek close behind. Before closing the door, I stick my head into the passageway to see if anyone's there. Deserted, like a ghost town, which makes the entire episode even more surreal.

"I'm having water. Do you want one?" I kick off my shoes and reach for the minibar.

"Thanks." He waits, watching me.

"Take a seat. I'll just nip to the bathroom." I hand him a bottle before dashing into the en suite. With the door shut behind me, I grip the basin, take three deep breaths, and rein in my emotions. For goodness sake, I'm a successful businesswoman experienced in dealing with difficult staff and situations. If Celeste's been murdered, I have the wherewithal to find out who did it. Gritting my teeth, I straighten, regain control, and join Derek on the sofa, where I scull half a bottle of water.

Concern etches his face. "What now?"

"I'll speak to John in the morning. Give him this letter and find out when we're meeting Patrizio. I think we've got enough evidence about Celeste to take to the captain." I set my jaw.

"Is there anything I can do?"

I soften. "No. I'll be fine. I just need a good night's sleep."

He clasps both of my hands in his. "If you need anything, call me. I'm in suite 515."

"Thanks . . ."

"Don't go being a hero, okay?"

"Trust me. I'm no hero." I force a smile, trying to lighten the mood. It doesn't work.

"And don't be one of those TSTL heroines, either."

"What's that?"

"It stands for Too Stupid To Live. You know the ones, the heroines who follow the killer into a dark alley and expect not to get into trouble. Don't go doing things like that."

"I promise, I won't be a TSTL heroine." I raise my hand and swear the oath.

"Good. This isn't a play or one of Christie's stories. This is real. There's someone dangerous on board this ship, and I'm worried you might cross paths with him . . . or her. Be careful."

"I will." I lead him to the door. "I'll see you tomorrow, no doubt."

"It's a date." He gives a small laugh before kissing my cheek. "Slide the safety chain across when I leave. Okay?"

"Of course." I gaze into his eyes and a part of me wants him to stay. To comfort and protect me, since I don't have Tom. But I ignore it. "Thanks again." I gently close the door, slide the chain across, and stare blankly at the evacuation map on the back of the door. *All routes lead overboard.* I shudder at the prospect.

After a few moments, I retrieve the silver box containing Tom's ashes and place it in the middle of the bed. In the past, whenever we had a disagreement, he'd lie on the bed, while I paced back and forth. That's how we sorted it out. He did his best thinking when he was still. I did mine when I moved. With only four steps one way, pivot, and four steps the other, my cabin offers limited pacing space, but it'll have to do.

"What can I say, Tom? You've got me into a fine mess this time." I stop and scowl at the filigree box, then resume pacing. "Of all the holidays on your bucket list, you had to book this one. Then you up and die on me, leaving me on a ship in the middle of the Pacific Ocean with some crazed stalker or worse, killer. What am I supposed to do now?" My hands knuckle on my hips. "I know. I know. I have John and now there's Derek who wants to help. But don't you see that's not the point. They're not you . . ." My pacing stops. "They're. Not. You."

I slump onto the sofa, eyes brimming with tears. "Oh, Tom, I don't have you as a sounding board anymore. Although we disagreed on some things, your opinion mattered to me. Now that you're not here, I'm at a loss." My chin drops into my hands. "And to make matters worse, I'm talking to a box on a bed." I sigh and shake my head. "I know . . . everything will look better in the morning. But I'm not so sure

. . ." I shuffle over, kiss the box, and return it to the drawer. "Good night, darling."

As Tom's ashes slide from view, the first of many tears land on the back of my hand.

★ ★ ★

I STIR FROM A FITFUL sleep and glance at my phone. Two in the morning. It'll take me ages to get back to sleep now. Eventually, after doing a relaxation exercise, my eyelids droop, but my ears prick to a sound. A noise in the passageway. I listen harder. Damn it!

After throwing back the covers, I tip-toe to the door and press my ear against it. Nothing. As quietly as possible, I slide the chain and crack open the door. A shadowy figure in a dark hoody and sweatpants retreats up the passageway, sure-footed and fast. I can't tell whether it's a man or a woman. On reaching the marbled foyer, it turns and flees down the staircase, head down, face covered.

Derek's words filter through my mind . . . Too Stupid to Live.

Even if I am TSTL and want to follow the mystery figure, they'll be gone by now. The *thud, thud, thud* of my racing heart echoes in my head. *Too little, too late.*

Just as I close the door, something on the floor catches my eye. An envelope. When I pick it up, I recognize the ship's embossed stationery. The same as in my cabin. A rush of panic prickles my skin. Although there's no name on the envelope, I know that whoever's been lurking in the passageway left it for me. I withdraw, locking the door behind me.

Once seated on the sofa, I carefully peel open the back of it and slide out its contents. I waver for a moment before unfolding the paper which has three neat crease lines in it. Holding it between my fingers like a set of pincers so as not to damage or contaminate it, I read aloud, "This does not concern you. Mind your own business."

A strange numbness creeps over me while I reread the thinly veiled warning. "This does not concern you. Mind your own business." *Or what?* I return the letter to its envelope, push off the sofa, and walk outside onto my balcony. The ship clips through the water on its overnight voyage, and gripping the railing, I stare down at the churning water below. It must be at least a seventy-foot drop. If I fall overboard, no one would know. I'd just disappear forever. Without a trace. Perhaps whoever left me that letter, has no qualms in tossing me overboard if I don't stop interfering. The thought makes me tremble. Yet, deep within me, a slumbering giant stirs my emotions, transforming my apprehensions into single-minded resolve.

Forty-four years ago, when my mother died, it'd been me who supported Dad, rather than the other way around. I'd stood strong for both of us at the funeral. I'd sacrificed my teenage years and taken over managing the house while he worked. I'd become *his* rock. Then when he remarried, I'd focused on my future rather than getting caught in the web spun by my stepmother and her unruly son, Andrew. Throughout my career, it'd been me championing problems and disputes to find agreement and resolution, to get the job done. Even when Tom died last year, and I thought all was lost, I'd dug deep and not given up. Now, I'm under threat from some unknown nefarious person. Someone who doesn't know me at all. Someone unfamiliar with the central tenet to my personality . . . an unwavering determination, true grit. "You're like a terrier with a bone," Tom often said.

My knuckles whiten on the railing. "Nobody tells me to mind my own business. Enough is enough."

★ ★ ★

I HARDLY SLEEP AFTER THAT. I lie awake fluctuating between anger that somebody dared tell me to mind my own business and concern that I've attracted the attention of someone that sinister. After a few hours of tossing and turning, I decide to get up and use the skills I've honed over my career—scrutinize, strategize, and solve problems. The past days of waiting for Celeste to show, in my opinion, have been pointless. Time to act. Though an ungodly time for normal passengers to be up and about, by six A.M., I exit my cabin and head down the passageway which still resembles a ghost town.

As I approach Celeste's cabin, I notice the do-not-disturb sign still hangs on the door. "That'll be coming off soon." Nothing or no one is going to stop me from gaining access to suite 430 any longer. After that, I'll move forward with solving Celeste's continued absence, or murder. Whatever the case may be.

Up ahead, I notice someone leaving the staff office behind the reception counter in the central foyer. I press my back against the wall and tip forward to see who it is. A male passenger by the clothes. But I can't see who, because his attention is on the papers he carries in his hands. He shuffles and studies them one after the other in a deliberate fashion.

"Shit." He misjudges his exit and hits the reception counter with such force the papers fly into the air.

I hurry toward them as they float to the floor, while he curses and clutches his foot. At my feet lie six or more A4 photos of Celeste, taken at different times, in different locations. I bend to collect them. One is of her in her white outfit obviously taken the first day in the Explorer Room at the beginning of muster drill. Another shows her dressed in her white caftan which timestamps it as Saturday night. She's dining in the restaurant with her stepchildren. The others are a collection of images of her on board the ship during lunch, having a drink on the aft deck, and leaving the day spa on deck six. Stunned that Celeste stars in each of them, I freeze.

"Those are mine."

I recognize the voice's affronted, petulant tone. "Why do you have photos of Celeste, Jason?"

"Give them to me."

I hug them to my chest. "I asked you a question. Why do you have these photos?"

He glowers. "They don't belong to you. They're mine, and I want them back." He steps toward me, his hand outstretched.

I step back. "When did you take these?" I fan open the images that I know weren't taken on Saturday. "Jason, it's important. What day did you take these?"

His eyes roam the images. "Sunday."

"Are you sure?"

"Of course, I'm sure."

"Do you have any others taken after then?"

I notice his brow crease. "No."

"Right. I'm keeping these." I wave them in the air before wedging them under my arm. He tries to interrupt, but I shut down his protests. "I'm not sure what you're up to or why you're so interested in Celeste, but—"

"Fine. Keep them. I don't care."

I study his face, watching a mixture of fear and fury cloud his expression. I soften. "Jason, please. Tell me . . ."

"I don't have anything to tell. Forget it." Although he waves a flippant hand at me, he hesitates for an instant, anguish on his face. He's scared, I'm sure of it. But of what? It's an expression I've seen on any number of faces over the recent days. But his seems familiar. "Do what you want with them. I can always print off another set." With a final sneer, he snaps a pivot and marches off.

My heart pounds like a quarter-horse after winning the sprint. A stand-up altercation isn't my favorite way to start the day. Riveted to the spot, I exhale and glance around to see if anyone has witnessed our face-off. Assured we went unseen; I piece together what just happened.

Jason obviously used the ship's printer to print off the images. That he's done so this early in the morning means he wanted to keep it secret. My unexpected appearance certainly caught him off guard.

I stroll across the foyer and bend over the reception counter for a better view into the office. A crew member is perched behind a computer, engrossed in his work. He must've allowed Jason to print off the images, probably straight from the SD card in his camera. Since he doesn't notice me, I spread out the images on the countertop.

Jason has a good eye. He's captured Celeste at every angle, highlighting her extraordinary beauty, symmetrical features, and various expressions. While I study each image, a familiar nagging tugs at my gut. There's something important here, in these photos. What is it? What am I missing? Why is Jason so intrigued with Celeste when he previously denied knowing her?

"Good morning, my name is Nathaniel, can I be of assistance?" Startled, I blink at the young crew member who now stands smiling in front of me.

I bundle up the photos. "No, I'm fine thanks, Nathaniel. I'm just off for an early morning coffee." Pasting a sweet smile on my face, I head toward the bar as he wishes me a good day. When I reach the threshold, I glance back. He's disappeared, so I backtrack and dash down the stairs before anyone else spots me.

* * *

"JOHN, ARE YOU AWAKE?" I speak in a loud whisper while knocking at the door of cabin 342 just loud enough to be heard. "John?" This time my voice's louder, more urgent. When I pull my fist back to rap louder, the door cracks open.

"For God's sake, Diana. It's six-thirty in the morning. What are you doing here?"

"Can I come in?"

He grumbles, opens the door, and allows me into his cabin. Tight and cramped, it has no balcony, only a small porthole. Without a horizon line to focus on, my tolerance to the pitch of the ship wanes. Fortunately, the seasickness pill I took earlier saves me.

I do a quick scan of the room and notice John's clothes folded on the chair and his personal items arranged side by side on his counter. A good sign. His neatness confirms what I suspected about his methodical thinking processes. After closing the door, he re-wraps the robe around himself, giving me an unintended glimpse of his well-toned, athletic physique clothed only in boxer shorts. Another good sign. If we're chasing a killer, I need a physically fit, strong partner.

"What in God's name are you doing here?" The tone in his voice grates me as much as my presence clearly grates him.

"I found another letter in Celeste's mail slot?" I swivel around watching him stride past me and throw himself on the bed. I smile and think about how much he reminds me of Tom.

"Sit down." He nods to the chair where his clothes hang. I pick them up and hesitate. "Just put them on the end of the bed." He punches his pillows behind his back. "What's so important it couldn't wait until a reasonable hour?" Folding his arms, he scowls, although I glimpse a slight upturn of his lips.

"This . . ." I spring up and hand him Celeste's third letter, which he reads, refolds, and places beside him.

He rubs a hand across his bristled chin. "Three letters in the same number of days . . . Sunday, Monday, and Tuesday."

"Correct."

"Yesterday afternoon, Clare's lover, Robert tells you he saw Joey coming out of Celeste's cabin at one-thirty Monday morning, but we've no idea whether what he told you is the truth." He angles me a look. "After all, he's screwing Joey's wife."

"I guess so." With no corroborating evidence to Robert's story, John's got a point.

"The do-not-disturb sign has been on Celeste's door since Monday except for that brief time during lunch yesterday when you went looking for her and a waiter told you he'd seen her."

"Yes." He's got a memory like a steel trap. Another good sign. I perch on the edge of the chair and force myself to wait. I can all but see his mind piecing together a puzzle he's determined to solve. Like me, he's hooked on getting to the bottom of this. After a few moments, I interrupt his thinking. "Did you speak to Patrizio?"

"I did. We didn't meet up until late last night . . ."

"And?"

"He said he'd look into it."

"That's all?" I'm shocked that the head of security didn't act with more urgency.

"I did say this is *their* ship. I can't force them to act against their protocols. I can ask, but that's all I can do."

"But surely, he's concerned that one of his passengers" — I pause for effect— "who he witnessed being threatened by her stepson, hasn't been seen since Sunday night?"

"He said he'd investigate it, today. He'll speak with the staff, and he'll check the ship's system to see if Celeste has left the ship since embarkation."

I begin to pace, barely managing two steps and a pivot. "But that's not good enough. Don't the threatening letters in Celeste's mail slot warrant a search?"

"Listen. I stressed all the points you just made. I can't do any more than that. But I'll take this to him this morning." He waves the recent letter in the air.

"You can take this one with you as well." Shoving my hand into my jacket, I retrieve the letter left for me and thrust it toward him. Scanning the page, he swings off the bed and blocks me.

His face hardens. "When did you get this?"

"About two-thirty this morning. Something woke me up and when I opened my door, I saw someone rushing along the passageway and down the stairs. When I looked down, I found that."

"Shit." He turns away. "I told you not to go meddling in other people's affairs, particularly the Constanzo's. I've worked homicide long enough to see innocent, well-meaning people, like you" —he glances back at me— "end up in all sorts of trouble."

I stand firm. "I know what you told me, and I don't expect you to look after me. But it is what it is." I skip a beat.

"What's that phrase I'm looking for?" Wagging my finger in the air, I recite, "'Evil flourishes while good people stand by and do nothing.' I won't stand by and do nothing while evil flourishes on this ship."

John shakes his head, a strained expression on his face. "You're one determined woman, Diana Daniels."

"It's one of my most endearing yet frustrating traits, as Tom used to say. And look what else I've got." I edge past him and lay out the A4 images at the foot of his bed.

"Where did these come from?" He studies each one in turn.

"Jason Denham . . ." I explain what just happened upstairs. "So, what do you think?"

"I think you better let me get dressed." He guides me to the door. "I'll meet you for breakfast in thirty minutes. In the meantime, try to stay out of trouble. Okay?"

"Okay. I'll see you in the restaurant."

In high spirits, I head to the piano bar for a well-deserved cappuccino before breakfast. But, when the thought of bumping into the shadowy figure in sweatpants and hoody at the blind corner on the staircase pops into my head, my confidence slides from me like an oversized coat.

CHAPTER ELEVEN

ON ENTERING THE BAR, THE subdued chatter of a few other passengers greets me, for which I'm grateful. This entire affair has mushroomed, leaving me alternating between anxiety and anger. At least being with other people gives me some sense of safety. But as I watch the other passengers watching me, my discomfort grows. Could any of them be the person who left the letter at my door? Could whoever it was be following me now? I've no idea, but I'll have to keep my wits about me from now on.

Like an unexpected visit from an old friend, the morning light streaming in through the windows cheers me up. Outside, another glorious day dawns in a blaze of golds and yellows, besting my apprehensions. Not wanting to miss the tail-end of the sunrise, I order my coffee and stroll outside to the aft deck to admire the new day. The ship's anchored in the middle of the ocean, with the largest of the islands, Isabela behind us and one of the smallest islands, Floreana before us. After soaking in the vivid hues, I close my eyes and take a deep breath. I surrender to the Galapagos' energy to enrich me, to heighten my senses. If there wasn't so much going on, this trip would be the perfect escape.

"Good morning, dear." Lyrical, twin voices float toward me, disturbing my peace.

I grit my teeth, wishing I could escape an early morning chat with the dreaded Blum sisters. Still, I manage a polite grin. "Good morning, Judy, Nancy."

Although surprised by their presence at this early hour, I'm less so by their appearance. They wear matching navy and white nautical garb including designer jackets with faux naval insignia. Their hair is coiffured and sprayed to within an inch of its blonde-dyed roots' life, and their jewelry sparkles like the crystal prisms in Mr. Pendergast's lamp from the movie, *Pollyanna*. And like Pollyanna, I'm mesmerized when their diamonds refract the morning light into dancing rainbows.

"Glorious day, isn't it?" Nancy's eyes twinkle, matching her garish diamond earrings.

"Yes, it is." I direct my gaze back to sea in the hope the sisters will leave me alone. By the ensuing pause, I think luck is with me. It isn't.

"Are you enjoying your cruise?" Judy asks.

Resigned, I smile. "Yes, I am. And you?" I eye them with a vague air of suspicion.

"Oh, yes," they chime.

"Your coffee's ready, madam," interrupts the waiter. I motion for him to place it on a nearby table. Both women blink at me as if waiting for an invitation, just like Berty, my ten-year-old cocker spaniel, when he wants attention. My lips curve upward, and I relent.

"Would you like to join me?"

"Oh, yes. That's so kind of you, dear." They titter their appreciation and perch on either side of me. Trapped between the Beverley Hills hubble, bubble, toil, and trouble witches again, I sip my coffee, bemused, yet cautious. The waiter returns with their pots of tea which they make a great display of setting in precise pouring alignment with their teacups. Cups to their right handles aligned to the right, pots to the left with their handles aligned left. After fussing with the arrangement, both women leave the tea to steep.

"Have you seen Celeste?" Nancy asks.

I stop mid-sip. "No, I haven't. Have you?" I keep my voice light and casual.

"No. We haven't. We thought it a bit strange, but it doesn't matter . . ."

I notice Judy send a testy glance in her sister's direction. I jump on her obvious *faux pas*.

"What doesn't matter?"

Nancy purses her lips so hard, her red lipstick bleeds into the fine lines around her mouth. Her eyes dart sideways, and Judy says, "Oh, nothing. Everything's just dandy." The grin creasing her face strikes me as gleefully sinister. Surely, these two elderly ladies have nothing to do with Celeste's absence. They couldn't overpower a kitten, let alone a woman. I watch them both lift their pots and pour their tea in time. When they replace them, they sip in silence, their eyes lowered to avoid my gaze.

Time to rattle their defenses. "I understand you ended up approaching Celeste to buy back the jewelry."

"Yes, we took your advice and spoke directly to her about it," Judy says in a matter-of-fact tone.

"Celeste tells me she turned down your offer?"

"Yes, she did, but let's just say—"

Nancy hisses, and Judy clamps down on the rest of the sentence. It's like watching a pair of cutthroat bridge players vying for the highest points. Each warns the other of her potential wrong move which could cost them the game.

"It seems you two share some good news that no one else is supposed to know?" I arch my brow, hoping they'll let me in on their secret.

They lower their teacups and lean toward me, eyes darting. "We do have some good news, but we're not at liberty to tell anyone yet," Nancy says.

"Oh, I see." I tip forward. "I can only assume it's extremely good news." I know the ground rules to this game . . . cheer and compliment if I want to join the conspiracy. "Since you're such astute businesswomen, I can only guess you've done some wonderful deal?"

Their mouths twitch, clearly desperate to divulge the juicy details.

"We have." Judy pours more tea.

"Yes, we have." Nancy upends her pot as well.

"And could it be the deal you hoped to make while on board the ship?"

Both women blush the prettiest shade of pink. "We can't say." But their expressions suggest I've hit the proverbial nail on its head.

Had they bought Celeste's jewelry? But when could they have done that? And why would Celeste change her mind and sell it to them? I wondered if I'd read Celeste wrong. Maybe I'm being played for a patsy. My head throbs.

I glance at my watch. "If you'll excuse me, ladies. I'm meeting someone for breakfast. Perhaps we'll catch up later?"

I shove from my chair and make my escape, while the Blum sisters' delicate good-byes jab like razor-sharp daggers into my back.

★ ★ ★

JOHN TAKES MY ARM AND steers me back up the staircase from the restaurant. "Where're we going? Aren't we having breakfast?"

"I just spoke to Patrizio, and we're to meet him outside your cabin. Come on." Together we rush up the stairs, across the foyer, and past Celeste's cabin. At the end of the passageway, just beyond my cabin waits Patrizio, looking somber and official. We exchange stilted hellos on our approach.

"The captain's waiting on the bridge. Follow me." He spins a smooth turn and opens the Staff Only access door through which we enter. Down the deck and then to our left, we march through another door onto the bridge. Across the one-hundred-and-eighty-degree glass panels wrapping the front of the bridge, a vista of uninterrupted ocean and occasional plots of land sweep before us. The half a dozen crew execute their tasks with barely a glimpse in our direction. Screens glow, instruments beep, and activity buzzes.

We trail behind Patrizio to the back of the bridge where he knocks and then opens another door.

"Good morning, Mrs. Daniels, Mr. Nash. Please come in." Captain Rodriguez rises from behind a polished woodgrain desk and motions us to the three vacant office chairs, me in the middle with John to my right, Patrizio to my left. Seated in front of the captain, in his well-ordered, though small executive office, the whole situation with Celeste suddenly comes crashing home, like a runaway train. The clinical, white walls, and sterile expressions of the captain and head of security, make me wonder if this is such a good idea. Perhaps I've overreacted to Celeste's absence. I cast a quick sideways glance at John who must've read my thoughts and gives me a reassuring smile.

"Thank you for seeing us, Captain," he says in a respectful, yet authoritative tone. "I assume Patrizio has filled you in on our concerns about Celeste Constanzo?"

"Yes, he has. It's most distressing to think that someone on board my ship has sent anonymous letters to Mrs. Constanzo."

"And neither I nor her family have seen her since Sunday night after Joey threatened her at your cocktail party." My interjection is met by three pairs of cool eyes. I purse my lips and wait.

"Yes, Patrizio has passed on your comments and concerns to me." The captain remains impassive.

"As you're probably aware, Captain Rodriguez, I'm a police detective with the Monterey County Sheriff's department, and although Celeste mightn't be officially missing, it's concerning that Diana also received a similar letter . . ." He nods at the culprit on the captain's desk. "And that the Constanzo family on board ship hasn't raised a missing person's alarm, despite also not seeing her."

A stony silence falls. I can't tell whether John's remark has insulted the captain because his eyes remained fixed on the letters in front of him.

"Patrizio and I have discussed this matter of the letters and Mrs. Constanzo's alleged absence," the captain says. My ears prick at the word 'alleged' and my stomach sinks. "Rest assured, we'll investigate today." He lifts his gaze, and it's as stiff as his smile. "I'd like to thank you for bringing it to our attention."

"But don't you want to hear all the details. I mean Celeste confided in me about her will and how her stepchildren could be planning to murder her and . . ." A gentle, yet firm touch of John's hand on my forearm halts my frantic appeal.

"At this stage, those details aren't required. Patrizio will firstly speak to the crew and visit Mrs. Constanzo in her cabin. There's no need to worry or concern yourself further until he's completed his interviews." Rising to his feet, the captain indicates the meeting's over, but I'm not finished.

"And what if Celeste isn't in her cabin?" I demand.

"Then we'll proceed with the next protocols." His voice sounds clipped and cold. "There's no need for alarm, Mrs. Daniels. We'll do everything we can to get to the bottom of this. I'm sure Mrs. Constanzo is fine. Have a pleasant day."

"As you can see, Captain, Mrs. Daniels is upset for her friend. As a matter of courtesy, you will advise us of how you get on?" There's a sharp, professional edge to John's voice. Not quite a command, but his message is clear.

Patrizio rises and towers over us, but because John stays seated, I do too.

"Of course. Patrizio will avail you of the good news that Mrs. Constanzo is safe and well. In the meantime, I suggest you enjoy the onshore excursion on Floreana Island today. It's very interesting." Gracious condescension tinges his voice.

"Well, if I'm right, the disappearance that happened on Floreana all those years ago has just happened on board your ship. And if I'm correct, Patrizio here will need all the help he can get." Infuriated, I stand and adjust my shirt. I've attended many board meetings with hard-headed, arrogant businessmen in my career, but Captain Rodriguez is in a league of his own. Small man's syndrome is what others would say. Barely as tall as me, he likes to wield his status as proof of his power. "Good day, Captain." I turn heel and march from the room. Behind me, I hear John perform a more courteous good-bye. My hands clench into fists as I tramp out of the bridge.

John hustles in beside me. "If that's your standard meet-and-greet manner, you sure could do with some improvement."

I spin on him ready to argue my case, only to find amusement glinting in his eyes. "Yes, well, what can I say? I don't think Captain Rodriguez is taking this seriously enough."

John opens the Staff Only access door and we step back into the passageway. Like passing through a wormhole from another dimension, normal shipboard life returns. "That's where you're wrong. He's taking this very seriously."

"What do you mean?"

"He's circling the wagons. I think the captain's worried. But he's not letting on. After all, we're just passengers. He needs Patrizio to conduct investigations. And if he finds that Celeste is missing, the captain has a serious problem on board his ship. That's when you'll see him take action."

"What are we supposed to do until then?" *I'm through being made to feel a fool and taking orders.*

"Go to Floreana. There's no point hanging around here. Come on. Grab your gear, and we'll have breakfast. There's still time."

"But—"

"But nothing." John clutches my hand and his mood swings to serious. "Up until this morning, I thought you may have been reading things wrong. But now, I don't think so. If Patrizio proves you're correct and something has happened to Celeste, everything will change on board the *Silver Galapagos*. We may as well make the best of it while we can. Grab your gear and let's get out of here."

★ ★ ★

"ARE YOU POSTING A LETTER in the post office box for the next visitors?" Derek's unmistakable voice whispers in my ear.

I send a stern sideways glance in his direction and press my finger to my lips. He ignores my silent admonition and winks.

I roll my eyes and shush him not to interrupt the guide's presentation. "Juan Carlos is talking . . ." I'm still stewing over the captain's dismissive manner at our meeting, and Derek's caught me in my lingering bad mood.

"But I'm more interested in how you are since last night." The warmth of his smile softens my disapproval, but this isn't the time or place for an update. My mind is elsewhere.

While a group of us mill around on the sandy beach of Floreana Island, the island where the mystery in *The Galapagos Affair* documentary took place, our guide points out the most notable structure on the beach—a make-shift post office box. With an old wooden keg barrel for its body, it's skewered on a corroded, metal pole about three feet above the beach. Like a giant cuckoo clock, minus the clock face, it's got a hinged door big enough to stick your hand through and is topped with a miniature Alpine ski-lodge-type roof.

The first inhabitants of Floreana, aka the Baroness, her two lovers, the Ritters and the Wittmers communicated with the outside world through this unsecured, letterbox. The sailors from passing ships dropped and collected mail from it, taking anywhere up to a year for the letters to reach their destination.

"Let's all take some letters and read them aloud," Juan Carlos says. He grabs a large handful of letters from within the box and hands them out. "These were left here by the last passengers from the *Silver Galapagos*. Perhaps there'll be one you'd like to keep and contact that passenger? You'd be surprised how many new friendships have started that way. When you're finished reading your letters, you can return them if you wish and post your own for the next passengers."

The excited chatter of the passengers as they unfold letters or flip over postcards is a normal response. After all, it's interesting to read about other travelers, where they've come from and where they're headed. But, of late, I've not had positive experiences with letters. As I stare at the four letters in my hands, my mouth dries, and my nerves send up tiny distress flares.

Derek edges closer. "Are you all right?"

"Yes. I'm fine." A lame smile proves I'm not.

"Here, let me take those." Obviously remembering the horrible letter we found in Celeste's mail slot last night, he removes the letters from my hand and slips them back into the post office box.

Meanwhile, my gaze scrutinizes the happy faces surrounding me. Was the person who left my letter last night one of them? I search the crowd, looking for John, but before I have the chance to join him, Derek returns. "Are you sure you're all right?"

"Yes. I'm fine. Just a little on edge."

"When I left last night, you didn't go and do anything that might be construed as TSTL, did you?"

"As you can see, I'm still here, so nothing too stupid to live."

"Good to hear—"

"Hello, Derek, it's so good to see you again . . ." A shrill, high-pitched voice grates our ears, and Derek winces. From behind him, a plump woman appears wearing a royal-blue one-piece bathing suit out of which her ample bosom bulges like giant marshmallows. Her face beams a beetroot red, probably from a touch of sun and a touch of infatuation with the handsome Scot.

"Ah, Mrs. Campbell, how delightful to see you again." He doesn't look delighted at all.

"Please call me Sarah. Remember, I'm divorced." When she bats her eyelashes, she looks like an aging Scarlett O'Hara from *Gone with the Wind.* Poor Derek.

"This is Diana Daniels." He steps aside.

"Nice to meet you." Before his silent appeal for help latches onto me, I excuse myself with a polite smile. "I'll see you later, Derek." The last thing I need is to witness the misguided advances of a desperate divorcee, and the gallant rebuttal of a gentleman. I stroll off alone, as the melodrama behind me plays out.

Cool sand slips between my toes, while around me birds chirp, dive and swoop into the thorny bushes lining the track that winds its way further inland. Before long, the sound of voices fade. I roll my shoulders and reach back to give my trapezius muscles a good rub. Having staked a permanent claim, the knot in my shoulder aches. I'll need some serious bodywork when I get back home.

On automatic pilot from the previous days' hiking, my legs continue forward, although I know I should turn back. But to be alone, without interruption, just me and Mother Nature stills my mind. I amble deeper into the backwoods of Floreana, lost in my thoughts. Under a tangled canopy of thickening, prickly scrub, the path narrows, and when I duck to miss its thorny grasp, there it is. The rock and lumber ruins of one of the original settlements on the island. At least, that's what it looks like from what I remember from the documentary.

I suspect the decrepit pile of building materials, curled fencing wire, and an assortment of rusted utensils and equipment probably belonged to either the Ritters or the Wittmers, as the Baroness's house had been further inland.

I pick my way through the overgrown shrubbery and debris toward the crumbling house. Nearly ninety years since it was built, it's now nothing more than scattered piles of rubble, except for the remnants of a drystone stacked wall which stands defiantly on the farthest corner. Careful not to twist an ankle, I tread gingerly between old garden implements, crates, broken furniture, and rusting bits of metal toward the last remaining wall. My fingers brush the craggy volcanic stone, trying to soak up the history of this mysterious place. I close my eyes and lean against the wall, its coolness chilling my back.

I recall the eager faces of the Ritters and the Wittmers when they first arrived here. And then Margaret Wittmer's odd expression when she said that a closed mouth admits no flies. She was right. No one opened their mouths here on Floreana all those years ago when the Baroness's lovers went missing. And the same is true now. No one's saying anything about Celeste. The ghosts of Floreana hover in my head, laughing at me for opening my mouth.

My eyes snap open at the sound of a branch breaking nearby. I slink behind the wall and freeze. Too stupid to live. *God, what am I doing?* Reality avalanches down on me. Alone. On Floreana Island. No one knows where I am.

"I did warn you that your longing for adventure would get you into trouble." Tom's voice echoes in my head. Little good it does me.

Another twig snaps.

I suck in air. Pain sears up my lower arms from digging my fingertips into the wall behind me. I scan the litter at my feet, hoping to find anything I can use as a weapon. Although it doesn't look like it can withstand more than one big whack, a garden shovel lies just out of reach.

Heavy footsteps resound on the ground not far away. Someone's followed me. This is it. I spring from my hiding place, snatch up the shovel and wield it above my head, ready to defend myself against my attacker.

"Hey, hey. It's me. Put down the shovel." Stopped in his tracks, John waves his hands in the air.

I blow out a pent-up breath and drop the shovel. "Sorry. I thought someone was after me." I double over as fear flees my body, leaving me shaking and unsteady.

"Seriously, Diana, you can't go wandering off by yourself." He helps me upright and meets my troubled gaze. "Come on. Let's get back."

Even though my heart's still racing, I force a nod and slow step beside him. I've no energy or inclination to argue. John's right. It was a stupid thing to do. I pause and look back. Derelict and ugly, the property and its inhabitants succumbed to some dark force here all those years ago. The atmosphere pulses with it. In an unconscious movement, I cross my arms and rub away the tingling sensation. "John, do you think people are born evil?"

"I don't know. Maybe they are. Or maybe they become evil because of what's happened to them. I don't know."

Facing him, I notice a deep weariness to his features. Perhaps it's a sign of having witnessed evil himself. "I think there was evil here on Floreana all those years ago. And I think there's evil on board now." My voice doesn't sound like mine. It sounds listless and distant. My skin's clammy.

He looks directly into my eyes and clasps my upper arms in a gentle squeeze. "I think you're right. That's why you can't go off on your own. Agreed?"

"Agreed." With a conclusive nod, I seal the deal. No more chasing rabbits down rabbit holes. No more trying to work out the mystery on board ship. The threatening letter left outside my cabin was right. None of this is my business. My business is to scatter Tom's ashes and get on with my life. Let the professionals handle the rest.

We walk back in silence to find a few other stragglers hanging around the post office box, waiting for the next zodiak to arrive. I bend down and collect my towel, giving it a good shake. Like one of Darwin's finches, a piece of paper flutters through the air and lands at my feet. The lump in my throat beats a frantic tempo while terror drenches me in a slime of sweat. My eyes focus on the paper John bends to collect.

Before reading it, he studies the faces of the remaining passengers, and I know. He's looking to see if any of them are wearing an expression of guilt or malice. Inside, I jitter like a frightened kitten. I want to curl into a ball and shut out the world. Instead, I listen to him read the note, "I told you to mind your business. You didn't. But you should have."

He refolds the paper and shoves it into his shirt pocket. He clenches my arm before my legs give way. With my weight suspended in his grip, we trudge down the beach toward the waiting zodiak that'll return us to the evil onboard the *Silver Galapagos.*

CHAPTER TWELVE

"W HAT'S GOING ON?" I ASK.

Not bothering with an explanation, Juan Carlos herds us into the Explorer Room to join what appears to be the entire passenger contingent. Facial expressions range from mild concern to disgruntled indignation, but like us, nobody seems to know what's happening.

"I told you." John guides me into the melee. "Guaranteed this is about Celeste. Let's grab those couple of seats in the front." We edge through the crowd and sit down. I search for Joey, Rose, and Tony, but with this many impatient people waiting for an explanation, it proves hard to get a fix on anyone.

"If I can have your attention, please." Patrizio's amplified voice fills the room. "If you could all take a seat, we'll try to get through this as quickly as possible."

Amid more grumbling and murmuring, everyone settles.

"What's all this about then?" Jim Pinkerton nudges me in the side. The episode at Floreana has jangled my nerves so much, I didn't notice him and Tippi beside me. I groan at the thought of listening to their commentary about the situation.

"Not sure, Jim." I shrug and return my gaze to Patrizio.

"Looks serious if the head of security wants to talk to us. What do you think it is?"

"As long as it's not a bomb threat, I'm happy."

"Everyone, your attention please." *Thank goodness for Patrizio.* "We apologize for this change to today's itinerary, but we ask for your patience for the next thirty minutes or so."

"What's going on?" an angry voice shouts from the back of the room.

"We need to conduct a quick search on board and while we do this, we need you all to remain here in the Explorer Room." A sense of panic elevates the murmurs. "There's no need for alarm. There's no threat to your safety, your person, or your belongings. There are refreshments here if you would like some while you wait" —he points at the two long tables either side of him set with hot and cold beverages, and snacks— "but please, don't try to leave the room until I say." I scan the two forward doors, which are closed, and suspect they have crew standing on the other side of them. Then like many others, I swivel toward the rear of the room where a handful of navy-uniformed crew gather in a group. Although they smile and nod, I've no doubt they won't let anyone pass.

"A search for what?" someone calls out.

"I'm not at liberty to say, however, there's no cause for alarm."

John and I exchange a look. My blood runs cold.

Jim huffs and folds his arms across his chest. "Looks like we're stuck here for a while."

"Seems like it. Why not grab a coffee or some pastries?" I nod to the tables laden with the ship's 'peace-offering.'

"Can I get you anything?" His brow lifts, and he angles a sideways glance at John.

"No, that's fine," I say. "We'll get something in a moment."

"Okay. Come on Tippi, let's see what's on offer." He grabs his wife's hand and heads to the front of the room.

Once they leave, John leans closer. "Looks like Celeste wasn't in her cabin when they went calling on her this morning."

"What are they doing now?"

"They'll search the ship top to bottom. Every cabin, every corner, everywhere."

"They're searching for her body, aren't they?"

"Maybe, maybe not. First, they'll assume she's shacked up in someone else's cabin. If they don't find her on this search, the next assumption will be she's the victim of foul play, and then, yes, they're looking for a body. I suspect they're doing both searches at the same time to speed up the investigation. That's why we're all sitting here. We'll be lucky if we get out of here within the hour. It's going to take a while to comb this ship from top to bottom."

"But what about Celeste's jewelry? I wonder if they even looked for it?"

"Good point. Come on." He fixes on Patrizio who's placating angry passengers, and we stride over. We wait until Sarah Campbell, Derek's admirer, finishes telling Patrizio she's going to write a long complaint to Silversea for this intrusion into her privacy. When she barks a final *harrumph*, we move in on Patrizio.

He pulls us to one side, so the other passenger can't overhear. "I conducted my initial investigation of cabin 430 this morning and didn't find Mrs. Constanzo. We scanned her lanyard. She's never left the ship since she came aboard. We'll know after this search, but it looks like your instincts were correct. Celeste is missing." He concludes with a series of humble nods.

I accept his olive branch. "Did you find Celeste's jewelry when you searched her cabin?"

"Our priority was to locate Mrs. Constanzo."

"You didn't check the safe?" A sense of urgency rises inside me.

"No." Patrizio frowns. "But we can do it now. Come with me." Even though other passengers clamber to speak with the head of security, he excuses himself, and with John and me in tow, he whisks past the crew on guard and up to the fourth floor.

On his belt rattles a ring of master keys and keycards, one of which he selects and uses to open Celeste's cabin. Once inside, John and I pause, our gazes skirting the room.

"This cabin's been serviced." John sounds disappointed.

"Unfortunately, yes. Jimmy came in this morning as per his roster."

"Damn it."

True to his training, Jimmy's left the room spotless and tucked in the bed tight. On the bedside table remains a small bottle of what I presume are Celeste's sleeping pills. I can see the lid's off. She said she was going to take one after I left on Sunday night. Maybe she took more?

Since the bed's made, there isn't any evidence of a struggle. And I doubt if Jimmy would have even noticed an upheaved bed. All unmade beds would be the same to him. Celeste's red Valentino gown is thrown over the sofa, which means she hadn't bothered hanging it up when she undressed. Even if she'd been deathly ill, it's strange that she'd leave such an expensive gown lying around for all this time. The rest of the cabin looks much the same as when I left, except it's been dutifully cleaned.

"What about the CCTV cameras I've noticed everywhere? Surely they must've recorded something?" John turns an expectant face to Patrizio, who returns with one of exasperation.

"There's no footage of Mrs. Constanzo since she took to her cabin," Patrizio says.

"What? She never stepped foot on her balcony?"

"The camera that covers the exterior of deck four through to the piano bar is out of order."

"You're kidding me, aren't you?" John's frustrated expression mirrors mine.

"I couldn't believe it either." Patrizio shakes his head. "It's the only section on the ship where the cameras are down."

"Down since when?" I ask.

"I spoke to the security detail in charge, and they advised that they expected a new camera to be delivered before we left on this expedition, but it never arrived."

I snort. "That's too much of a coincidence."

"What happened to the previous camera?" John asks.

"Faulty." Patrizio sounds annoyed.

"Since when?"

"The day before we docked and reloaded for this cruise."

"So, the new camera was ordered before you docked, you expected it to be delivered and waiting for you, but it wasn't," John says.

"Correct. And we set off without it." Patrizio's voice rumbles. I suspect heads rolled in the security detail for this non-compliance.

John shrugs. "It happens. Not your fault. The chain of command is only as strong as its weakest link."

"Still . . ." Discouraged, Patrizio marches to the closet, kneels, and sticks in his head. "There's nothing here, Mrs. Daniels."

"I saw her put the jewelry into the box and place it in the there." I bend over, looking into the empty black hole of the safe.

"Nothing here now." He straightens to his full height, his gaze on us both.

"But how did they open the safe?" I ask.

"Either they had a master key, or they knew the combination."

"Where can we talk in private, where we can't be seen or overheard?" John asks.

"We can use the medical center. The doctor doesn't have any patients currently. She's helping with the ship search. We can talk there."

We pace back along the passageway and down to deck two, while the ship, now anchored off Floreana Island, pitches and rolls in the deep-water currents. With a new bout of seasickness threatening to claim me, and the alarming episodes at Floreana, and now the confirmation that Celeste is missing, my world begins to spin out of control. I miss Tom more than ever. He was my rock. He'd have taken charge and . . .

"You can do this," John whispers, while Patrizio unlocks the medical center.

"I'm not so sure anymore."

"There's no turning back now. You need to tell Patrizio everything you know, everything you suspect. You're the only witness to most of this. Celeste's counting on you."

I breathe deep and square my shoulders. Whether Celeste is dead or alive, John's right. It's up to me. Not Tom.

Patrizio closes the door and due to the lack of chairs, we gather around the examination table. The second white clinical room I've been in today, except this one has walls lined with locked drug cabinets and the distinct smell of antiseptic. I stare at the table and shudder. In that instance, I visualize Celeste, lying there cold and dead. The image alarms me, and I hope my hunch is wrong.

Patrizio clears his throat. "Mrs. Daniels, in the captain's office this morning you said that if you were correct about Mrs. Constanzo, I'd need all the help I could get. Well, that's true. I do. I'm hoping you and Detective Nash will assist in my investigations and tell me everything you know."

Over the next hour, I recall every detail I can about Celeste, the bitter inheritance battle over Joe's will, her stepchildren's intense dislike for her, the conversations we had, and those I overheard. I explain my professional experience with human behavior and the Myer Briggs personality test, and the profile I believe each of the Constanzo's fit. I discuss my interactions with the Blum sisters, Jason Denham, the Pinkertons, Robert, and even meeting Derek. I leave out nothing.

"Then there's this." John takes my second letter from his vest. "We found this today in Diana's towel on Floreana after we returned from a walk."

Patrizio studies the letter, folds it, and slips it into his pocket. He runs his hand absent-mindedly through his thick black hair as if stalling for time. I get the impression he's out of his depth.

With a loud smack, John claps his hands together, shattering the inertia. "Maybe it's worth talking to Celeste's family first. Get a feel for them. Then interview Clare's lover, Robert . . .?"

Patrizio snaps back. "I think his last name is Sawyer."

"Good. Then, interview this Robert Sawyer about him seeing Joey leaving Celeste's cabin in the early hours of Monday morning." In a subtle, yet undeniable way, John takes charge, and I breathe a sigh of relief.

"I agree," Patrizio says. "The Constanzo's first. We can use the library. I'll block out the passageway windows for privacy. We'll do the interviews there. I'd like you both to sit in."

My heart leaps. At last, I can be of real assistance. Use my skills and instincts in a controlled situation. "Of course," I say before John has a chance to reply.

"We'd be happy to assist you in any way we can." Unlike my enthusiastic response, John accepts the invitation with professional deference.

"You're far more experienced in these matters than I am, Detective Nash."

"John," he corrects.

"I'm willing to follow your lead. The seriousness of this situation is above my pay grade."

"Then let's get to it. We need to see if your team turned up anything during their ship search. Then onto the interviews." He turns to leave, then stops. "Can you print off all the passengers and guides who went to Floreana this morning? One of them left that letter in Diana's towel. If we can narrow down who that was, it might give us a clue to the bigger picture."

"Of course." Patrizio jots a note in the book he's scribbled in since we started.

"Excuse me, Patrizio. If your team finds nothing during this search, what happens then? Are the excursions canceled?" I ask.

"The captain's decided that if Mrs. Constanzo is officially a missing person after this search, that the excursions will continue as per the itinerary, except with heightened security to ensure anyone who leaves the ship, returns. We'll allocate more guides to each group. More eyes on the passengers at all times."

"But what if there *is* a killer on board?" I'm certain there is.

"At this stage, there's no evidence of that."

My gaze sweeps to John who nods. "He's right. There's nothing to suggest that Celeste's been murdered. She may have committed suicide?" I shake my head and John continues. "Or she may have jumped ship and, with the help of an accomplice, purposely disappeared." He glances at Patrizio. "We need to talk to her daughter, Emily. Can you arrange a call?"

More scribbling. "Of course." Patrizio closes his notebook and wedges it under his arm. "I have to get back to the bridge to see if they've finished."

After sharing one more troubled glance, we leave the medical center to see what the full-scale ship search has turned up. I pray it isn't Celeste's dead body.

CHAPTER THIRTEEN

THE SEARCH TURNS UP NOTHING, and Celeste is officially declared missing. The passengers are released in a hubbub of petulant voices, and while lunch is served, Patrizio makes good on his promise to rig the ship's library with curtains, so no one can see our impending interviews. He's also stationed a permanent crew member outside the door. Wanting a clear head and steady stomach, I rush back to my cabin for another seasickness pill and on my way to the library, I'm hijacked.

"Diana." Derek bounds up the internal staircase just as I cross the foyer on deck four. "Is everything all right? Have you got news on Celeste?"

I maneuver him to one side so as not to be overheard. "Yes. She's officially missing."

"I knew you were onto something. You've got a real nose for a good mystery." He touches his finger to his nose, and I notice what I suspect is a glint of pride in his blue eyes. But I'm not feeling proud of myself. It's all too little, too late in my opinion.

"But I wish I'd been wrong. Celeste is nowhere on board. They've searched the entire ship."

"That's why they kept us in the Explorer Room . . . to search the ship?" I nod reluctantly. "Doesn't look good, I must say." He clasps my hands. "How are you holding up?"

"I'm okay, I guess." My shoulders sag.

He smiles. "As we say in the theatre, you're a trooper. You're professional, talented, and unstoppable. I know you'll solve this mystery."

For a moment, I lap up his encouragement, his vote of confidence lifting my spirits. "Thanks for that. Patrizio, John and I are about to conduct interviews in the library with people of interest to see if we can find out what happened."

"Well, you're in the thick of it now." Excitement rings in his voice. "Remember, intuition is like reading a word without having to spell it out. A child can't do it because it's had so little experience. A grown-up person knows the word because they've seen it often before."

I tilt my head. "What?"

"It's a line from *Murder at the Vicarage.*"

"You're kidding me?" I snort a short laugh. He's certainly the showman.

"But it's true. It's your intuition, your hunches, that sent up red flags all along about Celeste. And now, you've been proven right. When you go into the library, keep alert for what you've seen or heard before."

With a slow nod, I consider what he said. As odd as it sounded, the excerpt from one of Agatha Christie's novels crystallizes what I have to do. I shrug off the mantle of guilt that's settled on me and ready myself to find Celeste or her killer. If necessary, both.

"You're right . . ." I agree.

But before I have a chance to continue, he plants a quick kiss to my lips, then backs away. "Sorry. I shouldn't have done that."

My eyes widen. "That's okay," I reply because I don't know what else to say, though my lips tingle with prohibition and promise. "Anyway, I have to go. Thanks for the advice."

"You're welcome. Go get 'em."

Ignoring the swirl of emotion, I snap an about-face and head for the library.

★ ★ ★

WITH PATRIZIO SEATED IN THE middle, John closest to the door, and me nearest the starboard side windows, we line up solemnly at a long wood grain table. Its sheen befits an elite lawyer's office, and my mind wanders to Angelo—who I haven't seen since Monday's snorkeling on Punta Vicente Roca—and his warning to stay away from the Constanzo family. Yet here I am. Sitting across from Joey Constanzo, who is rigid and bristling with indignation. Patrizio's notebook lies open to a clean page in front of him. John's brought nothing but his sharp mind, and I position my laptop in front of me, ready to take notes or reference my Myer Briggs tests.

"What's this about?" Joey's tone telegraphs his contempt for the meeting as does his malevolent expression.

Patrizio launches in without pleasantries. "We're investigating the disappearance of your stepmother, Celeste Constanzo." Joey doesn't flinch. "After your altercation with Mrs. Constanzo at the Captain's cocktail party on Sunday night, witnessed by Detective Nash," he pauses for effect to let John's official title sink in, "and Mrs. Daniels." He nods to me. "Have you seen Mrs. Constanzo since then?"

A darkness veils Joey's eyes as his glare first falls on John and then lingers on me. "No, I haven't, and just because she's missing doesn't mean anything's wrong. She's probably jumped ship with some new lover. She was always a bitch, that one."

"There's no love lost between you and Mrs. Costanzo?" Patrizio's voice melts into a persuasive tone.

"Why would there be? She ruined our family and tricked my father into leaving her his fortune."

"Are you sure you didn't see Mrs. Constanzo after the cocktail party?" Patrizio asks.

In that fleeting moment, Joey blinks twice. Although a master of self-control, he couldn't stop the involuntary response. I catch his askance glance and smile. His glower proves I've seen something he hoped to hide.

"You do what you have to," he says, "but I had nothing to do with Celeste's disappearance."

"We have a witness who saw you coming out of her cabin early Monday morning around one A.M." John's voice sounds an octave lower than usual and reverberates in the small library like a deep-throated growl.

Joey locks eyes with him and sneers. Obviously, he considers Patrizio incompetent, but John, a worthy opponent. "Whoever told you that is lying?" He snarls and folds his arms across his chest. "From what I can see, there're too many people on board this ship punching above their weight. They should mind their own business." He nails me with a lethal glare.

"The witness is reliable." John recovers Joey's attention.

"The witness is a liar."

"You're denying it was you seen coming out of cabin 430 around that time?" Patrizio asks.

"How many times do I have to say it. It wasn't me."

Patrizio steers in a new direction. "Do you know the whereabouts of the jewelry Celeste wore at the cocktail party?"

"No. Why should I?"

"We have it on good authority that you informed the Misses Blum that Celeste was in the market to sell it."

"Maybe I did. What's it matter?"

"The jewelry seems to be missing as well," Patrizio says.

Joey barks a high-pitched, unctuous laugh. "That just proves what I said earlier. She's jumped ship and taken the jewelry with her. Mercenary bitch. Now if you don't mind, I've more important things to do than sit here and answer your questions about Celeste. If she's disappeared, I need to contact my lawyer and begin proceedings to claim our inheritance." His expression changes to one of triumph at the thought of being rid of his stepmother and claiming the fortune. He rises in one swift movement and straightens his navy-blue Armani jacket.

Patrizio reviews the excursion manifest in front of him. "Before you go Mr. Constanzo . . . I see you went ashore this morning, to Floreana?" He waves Joey back into his seat.

Joey huffs and drops. "Yes, with about a hundred other passengers. What of it?"

"In fact, there were only fifty-seven passengers that went ashore this morning," Patrizio says.

Joey shrugs. He's obviously bored with the proceedings.

"Did you notice Mrs. Daniels was also there?"

Joey's lip curl in my direction. "No, I didn't."

"You don't like Mrs. Daniels?"

"I don't like strangers sticking their nose into my family's business." Another belligerent glance in my direction.

"And you think that Mrs. Daniels did this?"

"Listen, what does my opinion of Mrs. Daniels" —he grinds his teeth on my name— "have to do with Celeste's disappearance?"

"Answer the question," John says. "Do you think Mrs. Daniels interfered in your family?"

"Yes. I think she put crazy ideas into Celeste's head."

"Ideas such as what?" Patrizio asks.

"I don't know. Maybe she arranged for Celeste to jump ship. To stay away until the will's sixty days survival clause expires. After that, Celeste will show up again and there's nothing we can do about our rightful inheritance."

My brow lifts in surprise. That Joey thinks I could conjure up such a slick plan means I've somehow threatened his well-ordered world from our first meeting. His agenda runs quick and deep. Much like his anger for anyone who he believes stands in his way.

"Did you know that someone left threatening letters for Celeste as well?" John asks.

A flash of a frown dips Joey's brow and is gone. "Really? What did they say?" He appears delighted that someone, seemingly not him, detested Celeste.

"That's confidential. So, you knew nothing about them?" John presses the point.

"No."

"For a smart guy, you don't seem to know much about anything." John's voice oozes sarcasm. He and Joey face off like a pair of boxers sizing each other up before a prizefight.

"Where were you round two-thirty this morning?" Patrizio breaks the stalemate.

"Asleep in bed."

"Someone left a threatening letter at Mrs. Daniels cabin around that time."

"Wasn't me."

"And then whoever it was left another letter in her towel on Floreana this morning."

Disinterest drags at Joey's face. "Not me."

I hear John push back his chair. He side-straddles the front corner of the table, threads his hands together, and leans forward into Joey's face. "You know, Joey, the wording of the letters left for Diana sounds a lot like your words."

Joey meets his challenge and leans forward as if daring him to take a swing. "How would I know? I don't know what the words are?"

John's patience pulls tight like a wire. Any minute, I expect him to smack the insolent expression from Joey's face. But being a true professional, he eases back. "Two letters threatening Mrs. Daniels to mind her own business have turned up within eight hours, and you know nothing about them?"

Joey shrugs again. "Nope." He's the typical cool-as-a-cucumber character with a deadly underbelly. My gut twists. Evil . . .

"Be advised, Mr. Constanzo, we'll get to the bottom of the letters, and Mrs. Constanzo's disappearance, and the missing jewelry. The statements you've made here today may be used against you." Patrizio twirls his pen in his fingers.

"No, they can't. I wasn't given the opportunity of a lawyer. Now, if you'll excuse me." Joey rises, his movement slow and deliberate this time. He buttons up his jacket and taunts us each with a sarcastic smirk. "Oh, by the way. Don't bother telling me not to leave the country, because come Saturday I'm out of this god-forsaken place. I never wanted to come on this cruise, to begin with." He pivots and marches out the door.

Still sitting on the table, John swings his leg in a lazy circle, unaffected by Joey's impudent bravado. "He's a piece of work that one. I bet he's left a trail of bodies no one can connect to him."

"He's definitely a man used to being in charge and getting his own way." I click on a profile on my laptop. "He's a classic ENTJ." John and Patrizio arch a brow at me, each wearing an expression of polite sufferance. "I'll keep it short," I say, though I'm unimpressed by their skepticism. "This personality type is assertive, will take charge and succeed. But if their energy isn't tempered, their assertiveness turns to aggression and then to recklessness. They become sadistic, abusive, tyrannical, and combative. They believe they're untouchable."

"Pretty much sums up Joey Constanzo." John tugs at his ear. "And since he's not been convicted of any crimes to date, he's every right to believe he's untouchable."

"Do you think he had anything to do with Mrs. Constanzo's disappearance?" Patrizio draws a line under his notes.

"Possibly. But he strikes me as someone who pays other people to do his dirty work," John says.

"More than likely. He's lying though, I'm sure of it," I say.

"I tend to agree with you. But about what?" John ambles back to his seat.

"With everything that happened, there are any number of things to choose from . . . Celeste, the jewelry, the letters."

John turns to Patrizio. "Let's get that Robert Sawyer in here. He's the one who supposedly saw Joey coming out of Celeste's cabin."

Speaking into a two-way radio, Patrizio instructs the crew member to bring in Robert Sawyer. He's been sequestered in another room to protect his identity. After initial questioning about his relationship with Clare, his suspicions about Joey killing Joe Constanzo, and his confrontation with Joey on the zodiak at yesterday's red mangroves excursion, John zeroes in. "Tell us what you saw on Monday early morning regarding Celeste's cabin."

"As I told Diana, I was on my way back to my cabin and noticed a man walking through the piano bar. I was sure it was Joey, so I followed him."

"But why were you sure it was Joey?" I ask.

"I know the way that guy walks. All full of himself, with a long loping stride. It was him alright." Robert scowls.

"What was he wearing?" John asks.

Robert's eyes cast upward. "A dark hoody and sweatpants."

"Can you be more specific?"

"I don't know, black, dark blue, maybe gray. The lighting was dim, so it was hard to see the color. And the hood was pulled up."

"Then how can you be sure it was Joey, and not someone else?" John asks.

"At first, I didn't see his face. When he stopped at cabin 430, I hid behind the wall in the foyer. He glanced back, probably to make sure no one was following him. That's when I saw his face. You can't miss that ugly Italian's hook nose and the black vacant holes that pass for his eyes."

Patrizio's hand rushes across the page trying to keep up. "Go on . . ."

"He jimmies the door open like an expert criminal, goes in, and comes out a couple of minutes later."

"Did he have anything with him?" John asks.

"Not that I saw. His hands were in his pockets. I dashed behind the reception counter and waited a few minutes to make sure he'd gone. Then I hightailed it back to my cabin."

"Robert." I draw his attention. "Are you absolutely sure that the man you saw was Joey Constanzo and wasn't anyone else?"

"Absolutely. I'm in love with his wife. I know what her bastard husband looks like because I see his face every night before I go to sleep. That's when I beat the crap out of him—in my dreams." Vengeance seeps from Robert's pores. I shiver and wonder if Clare hasn't fallen in love with a man much like the husband she fears.

"Do you know anything about the letters Celeste received?" I ask.

Robert cocks his head and frowns. "No."

"Have you seen her jewelry? The ruby and diamond necklace and matching earrings?"

"No. I hear it's amazing though. Clare told me about the day Joe gave it to Celeste. The whole family went ballistic. Spending all that money on her. That Joe was a mean bastard, playing his kids off against Celeste."

"Do you have any idea why he did that?"

Robert shakes his head slowly. "No idea. I think he just liked to piss everyone off."

I agree with Robert's assessment. From everything I'd discovered, Joe Constanzo gained sick pleasure from inflicting pain on others. While he was in the limelight, manipulating everyone else, he was a happy man.

"Is there anything else suspicious you've seen while on this cruise? Anything at all?" John asks.

Without thinking, Robert rushes in. "There's something going on with Tony. He and that young guy with the camera—"

"Jason," I say.

"I don't know what his name is, but he and Tony seem quite thick."

From what I saw yesterday afternoon on the zodiak, their body language signaled dislike rather than friendship. "Are you sure?"

"Yes. I've been keeping an eye out for Joey, so as not to run into him, and I noticed Tony and this Jason, the photographer guy hanging out together. Not with any of the family or anything. More by themselves. Come to think of it, they acted as if they didn't want to be seen." He glances upward.

"What is it?" I ask.

Robert shrugs and huffs out a breath. "I don't know . . . but if it comes to me, I'll let you know." He smiles at each of us and waits to be dismissed.

"Well, thank you for your time, Mr. Sawyer." Patrizio stands and offers his hand. "I suggest you continue to keep a low profile for the rest of the cruise."

Robert accepts the handshake. "I will." His mood suddenly darkens. "But if that asshole, Joey, so much as lays a finger on Clare, I'll—"

"Probably best not to say anymore." John rises next to Patrizio.

"Yeah. Right. Good luck finding Celeste. She seemed a nice enough woman." With a sharp nod, he leaves the library.

"What do you think?" Patrizio sits down and swivels a look at each of us.

"I believe him. I think he saw Joey going into Celeste's cabin." I reclined in my chair, my body aching for rest since I'd had so little sleep last night.

"Why do you believe him?" John cups his hands behind his head and leans back.

"Unlike Joey, Robert shoots straight from the hip. His eye contact is genuine. He doesn't try to stare you down, which is one of Joey's defense mechanisms. Aside from that, my gut says he's telling the truth."

Patrizio looks at John, who agrees. "Me, too. He witnessed Joey break into Celeste's cabin and come out a few minutes later. But how we're going to prove what Joey did in her cabin, is anyone's guess at this time."

"By the way, did you get onto Celeste's daughter, Emily?" I felt sorry for the poor girl. If she'd come on this trip for her birthday, perhaps none of this would've happened. Heartbreaking to think that Celeste's jewelry, which was supposed to be Emily's thirtieth birthday present, is gone.

Patrizio flips over to a page and consults his notes. "She hasn't heard from her mother since before the cocktail party on Sunday night. She kept calling her cell, but it just diverted to voice mail. We found Celeste's phone in her cabin and its call history verifies what Emily said."

"Did she try calling anyone else?" I ask.

"She said she tried ringing Rose and Tony but neither returned her calls. She says she was about to ring the cruise line's corporate office to see if they could help. Poor kid sounded frantic."

I launch to my feet and pace the small library from left to right. Though grateful for the extra space, I still unconsciously search for Tom as my sounding board. "So, she hasn't seen her mother?"

"No, and I believe her." Patrizio watches me like a tennis enthusiast follows the volley of the ball.

I agree with him. "Celeste didn't jump ship and take off somewhere, despite what Joey wants us to believe. If she stuck out a twenty-year marriage to her abusive husband, she had the guts to see an inheritance battle through to the end."

John stands, stretches, and tilts his head from side to side. "Agreed. No doubt in my mind, Celeste's fallen victim to foul play. The trouble is, without a body, we've got little to go on. We need to speak to the rest of the Constanzos. Let's take a break, grab some food, and be back in an hour."

"I'll arrange to have Rose and Tony ready by then." Patrizio closes his notebook.

"Can you also get Rose's husband, Angelo? I think he knows something, but again, I don't know what," I say.

"And you better have Joey's wife, Clare, join us as well," John adds.

"Sure. See you in an hour." Patrizio leaves the library, shutting the door behind him.

John faces me. "Do you want to grab something to eat?"

"Not really. I think I'll just type up some notes. Clear my head a bit. See you soon."

"Okay. But don't go walking around alone. We haven't caught whoever left you those letters. Make sure there're other people around if you go to get anything. Okay?"

"Okay. Don't worry. After the scare on Floreana this morning, I've learned my lesson."

"Good to hear. See you soon." When he opens the door, I notice him talk to the crew on guard, who glance at me and nod. John isn't taking any chances with my safety.

The door shuts with a soft *whoosh*, and I wander over to look out the window. A jewel-bright vista of blue on blue greets me, with no land in sight. Breathing deeply, I close my eyes. The gentle, rhythmic swell of the ocean rocks the ship like a mother cradling a small child. Instead of feeling seasick, I go with the flow of the waves, shifting my weight from foot to foot. As my center of gravity balances, my mind empties. I inhale a deep controlled breath and the knot above my shoulder begins to loosen. If ever I needed my sixth sense, it's now. I exhale, long and slow, and become one with this wild, forgotten place. What am I missing? Who wanted Celeste gone? Where was the jewelry? Why would someone write Celeste those letters? What was the secret she supposedly had? I cast my mind out to sea, willing it to find an answer. Like a patient fisherman, I wait. With Celeste's three letters as my bait, the solution circles . . .

What was it Celeste had to pay for? What had she done?

Snap! Of course. That's it. I grab my phone and scroll. There staring back at me is the answer. I need to check it out, just to make sure. And now is as good a time as any. With a sharp *smack*, I close the lid of my laptop and head for the door.

CHAPTER FOURTEEN

"I'M JUST OFF TO GET something to eat." On a mission, with little time to spare, I rush past the young crewman on duty before he has a chance to speak. Glancing at my watch, I realize I might be too late. The zodiaks have probably left for this afternoon's excursion—deep water snorkeling with sharks off Champion Islet. I cut through the Explorer Room and make a beeline to the port side door, where I step straight into the path of Joey Constanzo. He growls, and I recoil.

"Sorry," I say as an automatic, good-mannered response.

"You should be. You've caused nothing but trouble."

"I beg your pardon. I've done no such thing." Although righteous indignation peals in my voice, my eyes glance at the ship's side rail, no more than an arm's reach away. I know he won't throw me overboard, but the air crackles with his unconcealed hostility, and I involuntarily scope my surroundings. My blood pressure catapults like a slingshot ride and I decide on caution. "If you'll excuse me . . ."

Even though Joey's slight of stature and of average height, he's an experienced bully. He shoulders in on me, close enough so that his breath brushes my cheek on each exhale. "You should mind your own business," he says through gritted teeth.

I step back, lock eyes with him, and match his tone. "And you should stop leaving me threatening letters."

Without waiting for a response, I pivot and head back into the Explorer Room. Once inside, I slam my back against the wall and suck in a lungful of air. My heart thumps so hard,

I think it'll leap from my chest. I've no idea where my comment came from, and I'm not hanging around to gauge his response. After some combative business meetings over the years, I've joked that there was blood on the walls in the board rooms. But today, being confronted by Joey, I realize that in his world, blood on the walls isn't figurative.

I swallow the dry lump in my throat and rethink my plan. Best to return to the library. My hunch can wait. I rake my fingers through my hair, yank my polo shirt over my trousers, and head back the way I came. The chilly, air-conditioned air in the Explorer Room dries the beads of perspiration on my face, although it's got little effect on the knot above my shoulder which has resurfaced with vengeance.

When I walk into the library, the greeting from John is equally chilly. "What did you do?"

My cheeks warm. "I slipped out and accidentally ran into Joey."

"You what?" He shakes his head, disappointment tightening his face. "You'd have to be the most obstinate woman I've ever met. It's as if you *want* to get into trouble."

I dismiss his concern with a wave of my hand, which I notice trembles slightly. He catches it as well. "I'm fine." With the least amount of dramatics, I recount what happened.

"It makes sense though," he says, taking his seat.

"What?" I fold into my chair at the other end of the table and my knees breathe a sigh of relief.

"That Joey left you those letters to warn you off."

"I think so. But warn me off what? Looking for Celeste because he's murdered her? Or something else?"

"Too early to say. And we can't prove he left them. Not yet, anyway. We need a few more pieces of the puzzle to fall into place. But if he did write those letters, we'll get him." John reaches for the water jug, pours a glass, and offers one to me. I drink it all in one long pull.

When Patrizio arrives, I recap my Joey encounter and then proceed to explain the personality type of our next suspect. "Rose's personality type is an ISTJ . . . introverted, sensing, thinking, and judging. She's logical, methodical, and compliant to the rules and regulations of the world, as she perceives it. If we enforce the rules of this meeting in a systematic way, she'll probably follow them." Once we agreed on how to proceed, we get underway.

"Please send Mrs. Imperioli in," Patrizio says into his two-way radio.

Dressed in a utilitarian beige crepe skirt, bow-tie-neck blouse, and low-heeled pumps, Rose enters, resembling an old-fashioned school librarian. Her tentative movements match her wary expression. When she recognizes me, she falters a little before lowering into the chair, folding her hands and crossing her ankles.

"Thank you for coming in, Mrs. Imperioli." Patrizio does the introductions, during which Rose nods in forced politeness. "We're investigating the disappearance of your stepmother, Celeste Constanzo."

Rose's hands clench in her lap, turning a strained shade of pink. "I don't know anything about it." She sounds nervous.

"But you do know she's missing?"

"Yes, Joey told me."

"When was the last time you saw her?" Patrizio readies his pen.

"Before the Captain's cocktail party, on Sunday night. We were supposed to catch up for dinner afterward, but she rang down to say she wasn't coming."

"Doesn't it strike you as odd that you haven't seen her since?" John asks.

"I've enough going on in my own life, without worrying about her." Even though Rose defers to John's official status, she leaves her resentment toward Celeste unchecked.

Patrizio rolls his pen between his fingers. "And what *is* going on in your life, Mrs. Imperioli?"

She lifts her chin in a small act of defiance. "I'm not sure it's any of your business?"

"At this stage, anything that might have a bearing on Celeste's disappearance is our business." John sounds like a stern father, and I notice Rose's chin and eyes lower. He's set the rules, and she finds it difficult to refuse.

She spends the next five minutes talking about the family, her father's death, the inheritance, and the embittered relationship between Celeste and Joe's children which dates back over two decades. She explains the reason for this trip and how she and Joey didn't want to come, but since Celeste had bought the tickets, in the end, they relented. "As far as I was concerned, I didn't care if I didn't see Celeste the entire cruise."

"What is it you needed Tony's help with?" I ask.

Her eyebrows shoot up, and she blinks rapidly. "What do you mean?"

"I overheard you pleading with Tony to help you. Perhaps you intended to harm Celeste and you needed his help?"

Her fist clenching worsens. "No. No. That's not true. I admit I hated her, but I'd never—"

I press for an answer. "What was it you wanted Tony's help with?"

She slumps and releases her hands. "I've decided to leave Angelo. I can't stand his womanizing any longer. I'm sure he only married me to get his foot into father's business, but Dad loathed him. He told me I was a love-struck fool to think that a smart, attractive man like Angelo, who could have any woman he wanted, loved me. I didn't listen to him. But Dad was right. Angelo never loved me. Now that Dad is dead, and the fortune's been left to Celeste, Angelo's even worse. What you overheard" —she shot me an accusatory glare— "was me asking Tony to bankroll my escape to New York and start a new life. I'm sick of Angelo, sick of the betrayal, sick of it all." Fine, red lines rim her eyes as she battles for control. "That's why I didn't care about Celeste. She got everything when Dad died, and all I got was half-a-million dollars. That's not enough to divorce Angelo and start a new life." The reality of her desperate plight strikes her like a bolt of lightning and tears spill from her eyes. I whisk some tissues from the nearby box and hand them to her. "Thanks," she murmurs.

Clearly unmoved by Rose's tears, John forges on. "Can you tell us about the letters left for Celeste? Calling her a bitch and telling her she'll have to pay?"

"I don't know what you're talking about." She sniffles into the balled-up tissues.

John pushes harder. "But that is your favorite word for Celeste . . . bitch."

"So what?" Rose's head snaps up, her eyes flashing. "Joey calls her a bitch as well. Why single me out? I don't know anything about the letters or what happened to Celeste." She dissolves into sobs.

"And what about her jewelry? That's gone missing too." Patrizio regards her closely.

"What! That beautiful necklace and earrings that Dad bought her? Oh, no. He'd be devastated." Obviously, Rose cares more for the jewelry than she does Celeste.

"You don't have any idea where it is?" I'm hopeful she might divulge something.

"Of course not. Why would I?" She reaches over, tears a couple more tissues from the box, and composes herself. "I hated Celeste and yes, I'm not sorry she's missing. Whether she's dead or alive is of little consequence to me, except if she's dead I won't need any financial help from Tony to leave Angelo."

"And what about your brother, Joey?" John asks.

Rose's demeanor toughens. "I've no idea what Joey does. He reports to no one."

"Are you sure there's nothing you would like to add?" John tries again, but Rose remains stoic.

John, Patrizio, and I exchange looks. "Thank you for your time, Mrs. Imperioli. If you remember anything that might help us in our investigations, please tell us." Patrizio hands her his card.

She sniffs with disdain. "I doubt I'll recall anything about Celeste, the letters, or her jewelry." She hands the card back to Patrizio. "I had nothing to do with any of it, and neither did Joey." And as an afterthought, she adds, "Or Tony for that matter." With a toss of her head, she turns to leave.

"Perhaps it's time to stop covering for the men in your life," I say. She stops. Her frosty gaze narrows on me. "Your father, Joey, Angelo, even Tony . . . The worm can't turn if it keeps heading in the same direction." I cock a brow, hoping to remind her of her previous promise to herself.

She pivots toward me, her face contorted in malice. "You think you're so much better than me, don't you? You're just like Celeste. You and your superior attitude. Pretending to be concerned for people when all you're doing is snooping and raking up the muck in people's lives. You should mind your own business." She spits the last words with such ferocity, it stuns me.

John jumps in. "Perhaps you can tell us about the letters left for Diana saying as much?'

"I've no idea what you're talking about. I wouldn't waste my time." After giving me a final death stare, she storms from the library, and I lower into my chair, shaken from her outburst.

John flips a wave. "Don't let her bother you."

But she did. I empathized with Rose. I understood how hard it must've been when her father remarried. How displaced she must've felt. I'd experienced those feelings too when I was younger. Despite my genuine efforts to help Rose, she viewed me with as much contempt as she did Celeste. On an intellectual level, I know she's hurting, lashing out. But on an emotional level, her comments cut. What the hell am I doing sitting in this room, thinking I can help with a serious criminal investigation? This isn't what I'm trained for.

"Let's see what her younger brother has to say." Patrizio instructs Tony to be brought in. With no time to further doubt myself, I open another file in my PC and title it, Tony.

"What personality type is Tony?" John asks.

"Not sure yet, but when Celeste introduced us, he seemed caring, calm, personable, and he tried to get along with her and his siblings. If I had to guess, I think he's an ESTJ—extraverted, sensing, thinking, and judging."

"Meaning?" Patrizio looks confused.

"He focuses on fact, details, logic, reason, and he systemizes his life in a way that brings structure to his world. For him, the proof is the past."

"Okay, bring him in," John says.

The questioning follows the same line as Joey and Rose, except Tony is friendly and forthcoming, as I suspected. He seems genuinely concerned that Celeste is missing. "You don't know what's happened to her at all?"

"Not as of yet," John says.

"God, it's like a curse, isn't it?"

"What do you mean?" I rest my elbows on the table, intrigued by his use of words.

"I can't remember a time when there wasn't some sort of drama going on in our family."

"Go on," I say.

I notice Tony's face slacken as his memories surface. "Even when I was little, Dad had awful fights with Mom. It was terrifying. She'd be cowering in a corner. Sometimes, it was just me and Mom home. I tried to protect her, but I couldn't." He hesitates and closes his eyes. "Then he sent her away. We all hated him for that. He was a cruel, wicked man." A dark emotional cloud passes across his handsome features.

"And Celeste? Was she to blame?" I keep my voice low so as not to break his reverie.

He opens his eyes and shifts his gaze to the bookcase behind me as if tapping into his past. "Not really. If it hadn't been her, it would've been some other woman. I liked Celeste. She tried hard to keep him off our backs, but he abused her too. I remember Mom's funeral . . . Celeste looked lost. As if she wasn't sure how to act. Dad avoided everyone, including Mom's brother who'd come all the way from Sicily. Then as the years went on, it just got worse. Dad's criminal activities"

—Tony glances at John who merely nods— "and his unreasonable demands on all of us. I was glad when he died. Maybe now we can be free of the curse."

"But you don't really believe in curses, do you?" I press him for a more reasonable explanation.

He sighs. "I guess not. But being cursed seems a whole lot better than just being a fucked-up, dysfunctional family."

A soft snort escapes Patrizio's mouth, and he pinches his lips from smiling. "Tell us what you and Rose were planning on Tuesday, just after lunch?"

Tony considers for a moment. "She's going to leave Angelo. About time too. He's a prick. She asked me for money, so she could get away. She wanted me to go to New York with her, but I told her I couldn't. But I'll give her some money. My sister has some mental health issues. She takes medication like Mom used to. The least I can do is help her out until she gets back on her feet."

"Do you think Joey might have killed Celeste to get the inheritance?" John's question lands with a thud.

Tony remains unfazed. "I don't want to think what my brother is capable of, but I suspect he's capable of anything that serves him."

"For instance?"

"I'm not in Joey's confidence. He knows I disapproved of Father's illegal dealings. So . . ." He skewers each of us with a meaningful stare. "In his own strange way, I guess he protects me by not telling me what he does."

"Is there anything else you want to tell us?" I ask.

"Not at the moment, but if I think of anything, I'll let you know." He flashes an expensive, white-toothed smile to demonstrate his cooperation.

"Even if it means divulging information that might incriminate your brother or sister?" John's voice holds a hint of suspicion.

"Ah, Detective, that I won't confirm or deny. Cursed or not, we are all Constanzos." Tony stands and surveys us one last time. Like a young heir apparent, he possesses a strength of character and will underneath his good-hearted, unruffled exterior.

"Before you go." Patrizio motions him to sit, but Tony declines.

"Yes?"

"You went to Floreana this morning on the post office excursion."

"Yes, that's correct."

"Did you leave anything behind?"

"Like what?"

Patrizio nods in my direction. "A letter addressed to Mrs. Daniels?"

"You mean in the letterbox? No. Of course not. Why would I? I read the letters left by the previous passengers. I've even taken one to follow up when I get back home." With his boyish, good looks, he answers the question with ease and confidence.

"Very well, Mr. Constanzo. You're free to go," Patrizio says.

Tony strides from the library more like a movie star than a person of interest. I smile. He's a high achiever and an expert at building rapport. The perfect combination for a successful stockbroker.

When he leaves, Patrizio purses his lips. "He's a bit too sure of himself for my liking."

"Why do you say that?" I ask.

"He's . . . what do they say? Ivy League. Too well-educated, too self-assured, too successful." The scowl on Patrizio's face carries a hint of jealousy, I think.

"But even if he is Ivy League, how does that make him a viable suspect?"

He huffs. "All that rubbish about being cursed. It's a cover-up."

"It's a cover-up for the corruption and crimes the Constanzo family is known for," John says. "But is it a cover-up for Celeste's disappearance?"

"I don't think so," I say. "Because of his father, Tony's pretended all his life to be someone he's not. He admitted to Rose in that conversation I overheard that he's gay. That's what he's covering up."

Patrizio grunts. "I knew there was something about him I didn't like."

John and I exchange a worried glance. That the ship's head of security possesses a homophobic attitude while conducting a serious investigation means we'll need to pay attention to Patrizio's judgment call when it comes to Tony. Or any other gay persons-of-interest for that matter.

John claps his hands together. "Let's move on. Is Clare Constanzo ready?"

Patrizio glances at this watch. "I think we're on a shift changeover. I'll get Mrs. Constanzo myself and bring her in."

As soon as he's gone, I pour more water for all of us. "I notice you didn't say anything to Tony about Jason?"

John nods a thanks for the top-up. "Neither did you? Why not?"

"I figure it can keep . . . at least for a little while."

"Well played. I agree. The opportunity will arise when we'll need to put Tony on the spot about Jason." He sips from his glass.

"Or vice versa."

The door opens and Patrizio ushers Clare inside. While she fidgets in the chair, I notice her inflamed cuticles, the result of increasing stress. She's like a beautiful, bewildered doll, frightened of being broken. Patrizio explains the circumstances of Celeste's disappearance, the letters, and the missing jewelry, while Clare sits wide-eyed, listening.

"Did you know your husband was seen coming from Celeste's cabin in the early hours of Monday morning?" John asks.

She blinks. "Who saw him?"

"We can't say who the witness was," he says. "But was Joey with you at this time?"

"I don't know. I was asleep." She picks at the cuticle on her index finger.

"You don't recall waking up and noticing he was gone?" From experience, if Tom got up, I woke up. It took only the slightest movement to stir me from sleep.

"My husband keeps strange hours at the best of times, so I've become accustomed to sleeping through." Her fingers work overtime trying to tear off the stubborn strip of skin.

"Clare, it's okay. We're just trying to piece together this puzzle," I say, trying to soothe her anxiety.

She slumps, her hands limp. "I'm sorry I can't help you. As I told you on Monday night in the toilets, I wanted to talk to Celeste but hadn't seen her. And I've not seen her since. I don't know what's happened to her. As for my husband, I try not to upset him. He's been on edge more than ever. I don't know what's wrong." Tears swim in her eyes, but she holds firm.

"What about Robert?" I ask.

"Robert and I haven't been anywhere near each other since that awful episode at the red mangroves yesterday afternoon." Her breath hitches. "I just want to get off this ship." Her shoulders tremble as she reaches for the tissue box on the table. A woman trapped in a debilitating marriage with a husband who terrorizes her, and a lover who possesses a smoldering fuse. My heart went out to her. Being beautiful, graceful, and accomplished has brought her nothing but misery.

John hands her a glass of water which she sips slowly, using the time to collect herself. When she's calmer, he asks, "Has your husband said anything to you about being interviewed?"

"No. He stormed into our cabin a while ago, ranting about people sticking their noses into our business and that there are spies everywhere. I said nothing and kept out of his way. He rushed out not long afterward. I don't know where he's gone."

"Do you want us to put a guard on you, Mrs. Constanzo?" Patrizio asks.

"Heavens, no. That'll only make him worse. So long as I do what he tells me, I'll be fine. We've only got another couple of days before we disembark. I'm sure I can keep the peace with Joey until then."

"But what are you going to do after that?" I'm concerned about her long-term sanity and safety.

"I'm not sure. If I try to leave him, he'll take the children. I . . ." Her breath rushes in and out.

"Take this, Mrs. Constanzo." John hands over his business card. "When you return to L.A., feel free to call me. Maybe there's a way we can get you and your children out of the situation, safely."

For the first time, I glimpse hope in her eyes.

"Thank you, Detective Nash. Thank you.

"Make sure you put that card where Joey can't find it," I say.

She nods.

"Thank you for coming in, Mrs. Constanzo. If there's anything else you remember or if you want our help, please call me on my direct shipboard number." Patrizio proffers his card. "You're free to go."

Clare pushes up from the chair. Her designer clothes hang limply on her body, and I notice that she's shrunk in the few days she's been on board. She looks like a strong wind could blow her down. Her health will continue to suffer unless she finds a way to positively reframe her situation. Instead of seeing herself as a victim, she needs to see herself as championing her life. Easier said than done, but if she doesn't take assertive action soon, she might be the next missing person on the ship.

After she leaves, I slump in my chair, rubbing my forehead. "I could use a coffee."

"Good idea. Let's take a break and meet back here in fifteen minutes." Patrizio collects his notebook and pen. "I need to give the captain a quick update."

John strolls over to the window and stares out to sea. "This whole affair strikes me as strange. There're too many motives . . ."

I edge beside him. "What do you mean?"

"For starters, there's greed with the stolen jewelry and the inheritance. Then there's the psychosis and mental issues that both Joey and Rose suffer from. I suspect there's also Joey's obsession with power and status. He's got an underlying belief that he not only deserves his father's money but his position in the crime world."

"Still, I still don't think Celeste's murder is a crime of passion where someone loses their temper and snaps in a fit of rage," I say.

John tugs at his ear. "Then there's the secret that was mentioned in each of Celeste's letters. What's that all about?"

I swipe my hand across my mouth. I don't want to tell him my theory on that just yet. Not until I've researched it a bit more. "And don't overlook the greatest motives of all. Love, sex, and jealousy. There's plenty of the latter when it comes to how people perceived Celeste. She attracted green-eyed monsters."

"We need to clear our heads for a while. Take a walk around the deck."

"I'm with you." Fresh air is exactly what I need.

"You bet you are. I'm not letting you out of my sight this time." He cups my elbow and guides me to the door.

CHAPTER FIFTEEN

ASIDE FROM ONE CREW AT the reception counter, there isn't a soul to be seen on deck three. "Seems everyone's gone swimming with the sharks," John says, as we head toward the internal staircase.

"I'm not sure I would've gone. A little risky for me."

"Funny. You don't strike me as someone who's risk-averse." He barks a laugh. Its happy sound deflates the pressure from the last couple of hours of questioning.

I mirror him with my own mocking tone. "Very funny, but until now I was probably the most risk-averse person I knew. Given the choice in any situation, I'd err on the side of caution and play it safe." We reach the top of the staircase and wander to the piano bar, which also looks deserted.

"And what about your husband?" It's the first time John asks about my personal life, and it's the first time I don't emotionally flinch at the mention of Tom.

"Tom was the risk-taker. He loved doing different things, particularly when we traveled. I tagged along really."

"But how would he have coped if you took the lead, set the pace, and chose the adventure?"

While we wait at the bar to order our coffee, I cast John an askance glance. He's deliberately, yet subtly questioning me, steering me in the direction he wants.

"Oh, you are good." I give him a sly smile.

He shrugs. "That's my job. But seriously, how would have Tom reacted if you'd expressed your true spirit? The one I've witnessed."

That's the question I don't want to answer. One that I buried long ago when I decided to let Tom take charge in our personal life. Sure, I established a successful career and business in my own right, but personally, I deferred to Tom's judgment on many things. Friends, family, cars, holidays . . . even my clothes were more Tom's taste than mine. Keeping the peace was something I learned to do when my father remarried all those years ago. After losing Mum, the last thing I wanted was to lose Dad, so compliance had been my coping mechanism. Back then, being the peacekeeper minimized the risk of loss. If I didn't rock the boat, my life would be safe and predictable.

Rock the boat.

The phrase flashes on and off like a marquee neon sign in my head. My brain synapses work overtime connecting an array of seemingly random dots. Could my seasickness really be telling me it's time to rock the boat in my life? To go where the currents take me, without reservation? To live the life I want, rather than the life Tom wanted? A familiar flutter in my stomach says yes.

"Here's your coffee." John eases the cup toward me. "I didn't want to interrupt, so I ordered you a cappuccino."

I stare down. The coffee's perfect head of foam disguises the delicious, warm beverage lurking below, waiting to be upturned and enjoyed. Tom had been my foam, and our life together had disguised my deep longing for adventure lying underneath. His death had upturned my world. And now it's time for me to enjoy my new life. *Could it be that simple?*

"Thanks. Perfect choice." Instead of spooning out the froth like usual, I bring the cup to my mouth. Dipping my lips into the fluffy foam, I tilt it until the rich, roasted coffee flavor awakens my taste buds. An act of communion. A holy communion with me and my new life.

"Good?" he asks a twinkle in his impossibly green eyes.

"More than you'll ever know." I tingle with anticipation, while we drink our coffees at the bar. After a few minutes, it's my turn to broach personal matters. "Have you spoken to

Sharon?" By the incline of his head and upturned mouth, he appears cooperative.

"I have. I took your advice and told her not to worry about our future. That we'll talk about it when I get home." He drains the last of his long black coffee.

"And . . .?"

"I've decided to tell her how I feel and to take a second chance."

"Excellent. Expressing your feelings is a good start. I've always thought that communication leads to compromise. And compromise is when each person thinks that their slice of cake is no bigger or smaller than their partner's."

He smiles. "Sounds tricky, but I'll keep that in mind."

"And are you going to take your own advice? Are you going to let Sharon take the lead in some things? Set the pace? Choose the adventure?" I purposely use the key phrases that he spoke only minutes before.

"I've got to give it to you. You don't miss a thing." He reaches over and clenches my shoulders in a big, playful hug. For a moment, I'm worried he's going to ruffle my hair. Lucky for him he doesn't.

The sound of zodiak outboard motors and shouting drifts up and into the piano bar.

"Looks like the snorkeling excursion is back," he says.

But when we walk out onto the aft deck, our curiosity turns to alarm. Panicked voices, strident shouts, and revving engines mingle into a chaotic cacophony of sound. Holding onto the railing, we lean over and spy Patrizio directing crew on deck three below. I notice a couple of zodiaks circling erratically off the ship's stern. That isn't where they're supposed to be after an excursion.

John hollers above the commotion. "Patrizio, what is it?"

"We found something. At Champion Islet . . ." Patrizio's voice fades.

I grip John's arm and point. "There. In the farthest zodiak. Without any passengers. On the floor."

"Damn it." The muscles in his arm clench.

"Under the blanket . . . it's a body, isn't it?" My heart goes cold.

"It looks like it. I'm sorry, Diana."

"I bet it's Celeste."

"Possibly."

I swivel my head to face him. "We have a body now." I hate to hear the words, but at last, we have proof.

"We'll find whoever did this. I promise."

"Thanks, but *I* promised Celeste to help her. And I'm keeping that promise, whether she's alive or dead."

★ ★ ★

THE THREE OF US LINE up in a row as the crew carefully carries the body on board. Like watching a car crash, I want to avert my eyes, but I can't. I have to see. Have to bear witness for Celeste's sake, if, in fact, it is her.

Patrizio leans closer. "One of the guides found the body caught in some rocks when he was snorkeling with his group. He called it in and offloaded his guests to another zodiak."

"We'll need to talk to him." John appears unfazed by the spectacle before him. All in a day's work for him, I guess.

As for me, I watch in disbelief while four men struggle to haul the blanketed body onto the medical gurney. I nudge John and point. "The sharks have been at it." From under the body, tattered pieces of silky apricot fabric hang where their teeth ripped it, obviously curious to see if it was worth eating. The fabric reminds me of an expensive nightgown, something worn by a Hollywood starlet in the old movies. It calls me closer.

"Don't." John's hand brushes my arm but fails to stop me.

I bend over and carefully lift the cotton blanket. I have to know. Underneath lies a slender forearm turned a hideous blue from the cold and the exposure to the water.

John moves in beside me. "Wait until we get to the medical center."

I turn to him, a desperate plea swimming in my eyes. He avoids my stare.

When I lift the blanket a little higher, my gaze travels down to the long slender wrist, then along the fingers, to the long acrylic nails tipped with red polish. The same color red that Celeste wore at the Captain's cocktail party. Heaving a breath, I slowly lower the blanket and nod to Patrizio, who instructs the crew on their duty.

"I think it's Celeste." My voice is a raspy whisper.

John straightens beside me. "We'll need to notify the next of kin for an official identification of the body."

"We're not going to let Joey or Rose identify her? They hated her. Surely, we can't do that." I imagine the spiteful delight they'll take in seeing their dead stepmother laid out cold on a table in front of them.

"We'll get them all in. Including Tony. It's going to make no difference to Celeste, but their reactions might give us some clues if they had anything to do with it. Death is never pleasant, but murder is a crime. And this certainly looks like murder."

"You don't think she committed suicide?" Patrizio asks.

I shake my head. "No way. She needed to stay alive for at least sixty days to inherit. Even if Celeste wanted to kill herself, which she didn't, she'd never have done it because of Emily, her daughter. She wanted to secure her future with the inheritance."

"I agree," John says, his stony expression matching mine. "I doubt Celeste threw herself overboard. I think it's foul play."

Patrizio nods to the crew, and like mourners at a funeral, we march behind the gurney as it winds its way through the staff access passageways to the medical center. "Unfortunately, word has spread through the passengers that a body's been found during the snorkeling excursion. At this stage, we don't think anyone knows who it is. But it won't be long before the identity will be common knowledge."

"Then we're in trouble," John says. "Once everyone knows that it's one of the ship's passengers, they'll realize there are three options. Accident, suicide, or murder. When the third option is confirmed, they'll panic that a murderer is on board the *Silver Galapagos*, perhaps looking for their next victim."

"God damn it." Patrizio tries to rub the escalating dilemma from his forehead.

I shudder. The thought of controlling one hundred panicked passengers is daunting enough, without having to find a murderer in the mix.

After snaking through a warren of passageways, we file into the medical center's examination room and wait until the crew depart. "Can you give us a moment please, doctor?" Patrizio eyeballs Doctor Garcia, who hovers in the corner ready to conduct a preliminary examination. With her saucer-round eyes and plump, taut skin, she looks like she's just graduated from medical school. Probably took this job thinking the most she'd deal with was seasickness. She nods respectfully, shoves her hands in her lab coat pockets, and scuttles out in a hurry.

John takes control. "We need to move as quickly as we can now. Before we get the Constanzo family in here to identify the body, we need to interview Angelo. Then I'd like to talk to Jason. What about the butler crew responsible for deck four passengers?"

"That's Bruno, the butler manager, and Jimmy, deck four's personal butler. But I've already taken statements from them," Patrizio says.

"Maybe so, but I'd still like to talk to them. In the meantime, get the doctor in here to see if she can shed any light on the cause of death. Let's not tell the Constanzos anything yet. We need as much time as we can get." John's cool, professional stare settles on me. "You good to go?"

My eyes sweep the covered body on the gurney and I nod.

"You sure?"

"Yes." I steel myself.

Careful not to dislodge any evidence which may exist on the body, he gingerly raises the blanket and peels it back on one side of the head. Pasted to the high cheek-boned face are lashings of chestnut hair, above which one opaque eye stares sightlessly at me. Below the classic nose, her generous lips press together, bloated, and tinged an ugly shade of purple. My heart pounds in my ears. Celeste Constanzo. In the prime of her life no more.

"It's her," I whisper, and John carefully replaces the blanket.

"Right." He claps his hands together. "Let's get on with it."

★ ★ ★

ANGELO STRIDES INTO THE LIBRARY and drops into the assigned chair. "What's going on? Is the body they pulled from Champion Islet, Celeste?" My ears prick at the undercurrent of anxiety I notice in his voice. Although his outward demeanor is exaggeratedly masculine, inwardly I sense fear lurks just under his façade. "I was there, you know? Snorkeling. Tell me the truth."

Patrizio ignores Angelo's demands. "I understand you're a defense attorney, Mr. Imperioli?"

"Yes, but I fail to see what that has to do with a body being hauled from the water." He tweaks the collar of his pale blue Ralph Lauren polo shirt, crosses his legs, and pinches the crease.

"Perhaps Celeste discovered something unsavory about you?" A wheedling tone laces John's voice. "Maybe even about your business dealings?"

"I've no idea what you mean." Angelo's indignation appears genuine, but a pink blush tinges the lower part of his neck at the V-collar of his shirt.

"Maybe Celeste threatened to expose you in some way, and you decided to kill her?"

177

"Are you mad?" He leaps to his feet, hands clenched by his side. "I liked Celeste. She's about the only sane one in the entire family."

Patrizio motions his hand up and down. "Please, sit down, Mr. Imperioli."

With a huff, Angelo resumes his seat and proceeds with the same posturing as before with his shirt collar and trousers crease.

"What do you mean, about the only sane one in the family?" I keep my voice even and friendly.

"Well, you've met them. They're nuts." He rolls his eyes. "Joey's a loose cannon. Rose is—"

"Your wife, Mr. Imperioli." Patrizio slants him a glance.

"I know, but she's always whining about why her father married Celeste. For God's sake, that was over twenty years ago. Rose suffers from major depression, she complains about her headaches, about her health, about everything. Honest to God, the woman drives me crazy."

"So why do you stay married?" John asks.

"Because of the money, man. Isn't it obvious?" Try as we might, I'm sure the three of us visibly balked at Angelo's forthright, mercenary answer. Undeterred, he continues, "Then the old man goes and leaves it all to Celeste, just to spite his children. Joe was a mean bastard. Anyway, now that Celeste is dead—"

"We've neither confirmed nor denied that the body is that of Celeste Constanzo," John says.

"Oh, come on. Of course, it is. I'm a lawyer remember." He shoots a smug smirk at each of us in turn. "Anyway, now that Celeste is dead" —he pauses for effect— "Joey will be itching to get his hands on the old man's money. Rose will get her share, and by association, I will too."

Not if she divorces you first.

"Assuming the body is Celeste's, who do you think killed her?" John asks.

"My first thought would be Joey. But something about it seems odd. Why would he take the risk here? Much easier to get one of his cronies to do her in back home. It doesn't make sense. Aside from him, I couldn't tell you. Either way though, he'll get what he deserves."

Patrizio taps the pen in his hand. "You mean the money?" Angelo presses his lips together and stares out the window. "Mr. Imperioli, what do you mean?"

Angelo returns his gaze, his eyes hard and watchful. "Under the circumstance, I think it's best if I tell you."

"Tell us what?" John angles forward and folds his hands on the table.

A loud knock precedes the door flying open. The distressed face of the young crewman relays his plight as the Pinkertons barrel into the library.

"I beg your pardon," says a shocked and disgruntled Patrizio, springing to his feet.

Likewise, surprised, John and I stand, as the Pinkertons steamroller our meeting. With his hand outstretched, Jim's effusive welcome leads the way, while Tippi titters a whinnying greeting behind him. Suddenly, the six of us resemble too many sardines in a can. The Pinkertons' overpowering presence fills the small room, disturbing the previous professional atmosphere.

"I'm sorry, sir, but . . ." says the young crew member, trying his best to herd them back outside.

"That's fine. You can go." John waves him away and turns his attention to the two intruders. "Do you mind telling us what all this is about?"

The moment the door closes, they stop the kerfuffle. Like theatre performers removing their costumes and makeup, the Pinkertons figuratively defrock in front of us. Standing side by side, they no longer resemble the brash Texan tourists. They transform into seemingly taller, slimmer, and fitter versions of themselves. Gone is their air of arrogant ego, instead replaced by professional decorum, one of intelligence and authority. "Due to the current circumstances, I think it's time to introduce ourselves. Agent Rick Sullivan and Agent Trisha Mackenzie, FBI."

I gasp, wondering if I've heard correctly. *FBI agents? The Pinkertons? No way.*

"What?" Patrizio lands with a thud in his chair.

"ID," John says, without missing a beat. Once he scrutinizes their badges, his face splits in a lopsided grin, and he strikes out his hand. "Detective John Nash, Monterey County Sheriff's department." He flashes his badge as proof. Like players from the same football team, they form an instant bond.

"Sorry for the subterfuge, everyone, but we're on a case." Agent Sullivan looks directly at me. "Particularly to you, Mrs. Daniels. I know we pestered you a few times, but we were only doing our jobs."

Still collecting my thoughts, I accept his apology with a hesitant nod. For a moment, I think I'm on a movie set. Murder, FBI agents, missing jewelry . . .

I glimpse Patrizio beside me who obviously feels the same, but his expression fluctuates between disbelief and annoyance. "Please explain what you're doing on board this vessel without first alerting me to your presence."

Agent Sullivan scans the room. "You got another couple of chairs?" His voice is efficient and polite. Nothing like the bellowing tones of his shipboard alter-ego, Jim Pinkerton.

While Patrizio begrudgingly calls for two more chairs, Agent Sullivan bends over to Angelo. "What have you told them?"

"Nothing."

"Good."

I notice the amused glint in John's eye, but I've no idea what's going on. When the extra chairs arrive, the agents sit either side of Angelo, shoulder to shoulder. Squeezed between them, he no longer exudes his usual machismo but appears contrite and wary. His self-confidence is replaced by an air of acquiescence.

"Let me explain," Agent Sullivan says. "The FBI's been investigating a number of cases of money laundering and fraud, primarily through reputable law firms." He cuts a stern glance at Angelo. "In the process, we came across Mr. Imperioli here." Angelo avoids everyone's gaze.

Agent Mackenzie takes up the story. "When we discovered what he's been doing, Mr. Imperioli offered up a bigger fish to save his own skin." She pauses. "Joey Constanzo."

The air sucks from the room. Patrizio and I exchange startled expressions, while John, at the other end of the table, folds his arms and smirks.

Agent Sullivan continues, "In return for all charges to be dropped against him, Angelo agreed to be a CI, criminal informant, against Joey."

"Is that why you warned me to stay away from Joey when we came back from the red mangroves?" I say.

Angelo nods. Agents Sullivan and Mackenzie swivel their heads toward him and frown.

"Sorry," he says to them, "but I was worried about Mrs. Daniels getting into trouble with Joey. What with all the questions about Celeste's absence, I tried warning her away, but it didn't make any difference."

"Tell me about it," John says, under his breath.

I bristle. "Thank you, gentlemen, for your concern. But if it wasn't for my persistence and refusal to be warned away, no one would've even realized anything was wrong until Celeste's body was found. And if it hadn't been found, then what?" Every man in the library receives one of my best condescending stares and thankfully, chooses to remain silent. Agent Mackenzie's lips twitch a furtive smile, her eyes twinkling in my direction. I suspect she too reckons with the indignation of mansplaining. When I first met her, she appeared to be a stereotypical, middle-class Texan housewife, and now, here she is, a competent, law enforcement agent. That's what I saw on Monday night. When I glanced back after having dinner with them, I thought they'd changed into different people. They had. They'd changed into their real selves.

I give her a nod of solidarity, and she continues, "Anyway, Joey's been under investigation for money laundering, fraud, and other criminal activity for quite some time now. All cash, nothing on the books. We haven't been able to get anything on him until Angelo turned informant. Now, we've got just about everything we'll need to make a case stick. It looks like Joey will serve real prison time."

"So why are you on my vessel?" Patrizio's still upset.

"Precautionary, really," Agent Sullivan says. "Just keeping an eye on Joey and Angelo. Making sure neither of them skips out instead of returning to the States. By the time we get back, the case should be solid enough to make an arrest. Sorry about not telling you, but the captain knows."

"What?" Patrizio's face reddens.

"Yes." Agent Sullivan scratches the back on his neck. "I thought he'd have told you. Anyway, I'll leave that for the two of you to work out."

Patrizio growls and lowers his head. I glimpse his pen working overtime on his notebook.

"And what do we do about Angelo being a suspect in Celeste's murder?" John asks.

The FBI agents scrutinize Angelo.

The color fades from his face. "What? Do you think I had cause, motive, or opportunity with you guys watching my every move? I'm turning state's evidence to stay out of jail, remember?"

After exchanging a smug smile with his partner, Agent Sullivan says, "Since knowing Mr. Imperioli and his pathological dislike of going to jail, in our professional opinion, I can't see any reason as to why he'd be a serious suspect in Mrs. Constanzo's murder."

Angelo slumps on an audible exhale. He offers the agents a grateful, sheepish grin. If only Rose knew the truth about her philandering, ambitious husband, she'd have no hesitation in serving divorce papers, with or without the funds she needed to move to New York.

"Agents, would you mind if Angelo waited outside for a moment, and we speak in private?" John asks.

"Not at all." After Angelo leaves, Agent Sullivan asks, "What is it?"

"As you may or may not be aware, there's an awful lot going on with the Constanzo family. Point of order being Clare, Joey's wife, is having an affair with Robert Sawyer, who came on board this cruise to confront Joey and demand he divorce Clare."

Both agents snort. "Is the guy for real?" Agent Mackenzie asks. "I suspect Joey would soon as kill them both than divorce Clare."

"That's what I told them when they confided in me," I say.

Agent Mackenzie raises her brow in my direction. With the daylight flooding through the window, her short, corn silk hair reminds me once more of an angel's halo. "You're a secret keeper, aren't you?" There's a hint of wonder in her voice.

"Excuse me?"

"That's what my grandmother used to call them, secret keepers. They're people that others, even strangers, confide in, knowing their secrets will be safe. I felt it when we were having dinner. I wanted to tell you who we were, but of course, I didn't. Secret keepers draw people to them. That's what you do, Mrs. Daniels."

I acknowledge her with a modest smile. "In my line of business, it's called hyper-empathy. I think that's why Celeste confided in me. She sensed I understood and that I could be trusted. I was someone she'd not had in her life for some time. Being hyper-empathetic has its advantages and disadvantages. In this instance, information was given to me that hopefully will help solve the case."

John squints at me. "I'll be damned. No wonder you were so insistent."

I shrug. "That's what they pay me for."

He turns back to the agents. "Anyway, Robert told us he's had a PI tailing Joey for a while. Seems this guy has evidence that Joey was somehow complicit in his father's death. Robert reckons the police know and that an arrest is imminent when they return to the mainland. Have you heard anything about this?"

Agent Sullivan frowned. "No. We're working the fraud case."

"But if Joey's dirty little prints are on Joe's death, we want to know," Agent Mackenzie says.

"Thanks for telling us," Agent Sullivan says. "If it's doesn't interfere with your investigation, do you mind if we speak with Mr. Sawyer and see if we can find out more?"

"I'm sure he'll be more than happy to tell you everything he knows," John says. "If there's nothing else, we'll leave you to debrief Angelo. Use the library if you want. I know you'll impress on him the need for confidentiality."

"Of course." The agents rise. A spontaneous smile flits across my lips as I imagine them assuming the Pinkerton persona once more.

"Okay then, you know how to find us," John says. After he and the agents shake hands, the three of us leave. Once outside, he glances at his watch and then at Patrizio. "Can you arrange to have Joey, Rose, and Tony at the medical center in an hour's time?"

"Sure." Patrizio checks his watch. "See you then." Glowering, he pivots and hurries off.

"Off to see the captain, no doubt," I say, as we watch him take the stairs two at a time.

"Not a happy man. But that's what happens when you're on a lower rung in the chain of command. Listen, I need to clear my head before we ID the body."

"Me too. I wouldn't mind freshening up a bit."

"How about we meet in fifteen minutes up on deck five? Grab something to eat."

"Great. See you then." I turn to take the same route up the stairs to deck four as Patrizio, but there's no way my legs can take the stairs two at a time. They're as heavy as my heart.

CHAPTER SIXTEEN

AFTER A SCALDING SHOWER AND a fierce body scrub, my mood brightens, matching the ruddy glow of my skin. Standing in front of the narrow closet, I thumb through my limited choice of clothes, my mind elsewhere. *Too many loose ends.* First, Celeste's letters. Who sent them? I've got an idea, but I need to check out my theory. Perhaps it's over-reach. Still?

My focus returns to the job at hand. Hanging in front of me is an uninspiring trio of slacks. Dark olive green, dark navy blue, or dark chocolate brown. When did I become so dull? I throw the drab, olive green pair across the cabin, missing the bed. While I ponder them lying on the floor, my mind wanders to the two letters left for me—one at my cabin door and the other in my towel. My gut squirms. If my suspicions about Celeste's letters turn out to be true, was it the same person or someone else?

Back to the clothes. Cream blouse with long sleeve, cream blouse with short sleeve, cream blouse, sleeveless. *My God, I'm boring.* Closing my eyes, I shuffle the clothes and recite, "Eenie, meenie, miney, mo," and grab whichever my hand falls on. "Fine, sleeveless, it is."

Making a mental note to throw out my entire wardrobe when I get home, I tuck my lackluster blouse into my dreary slacks. A sharp knock at the door startles me so much, my feet fumble, and I nearly topple onto the bed. My nerves are more jangled than I realize. Slipping on my watch, I notice I've five minutes before I have to meet John. Otherwise, he'll send out a search party for me, no doubt.

I crack open the door, without unlatching the chain.

Familiar cornflower blue eyes blink at me. "Can I see you for a moment?"

"Of course. Come in." When I open the door, Clare wastes no time stepping inside. "Please sit down." I indicate to the sofa, where she tucks the plastic shopping bag she's brought, beside her. "What can I do for you?"

"I'm not sure I should be here." While her hands twist in her lap, I notice her cuticles have been bleeding.

"It's okay. You're safe. What can I do for you?" She reaches down and hands me the plastic bag. "What's this?" I ask.

"I'm not sure if it's anything to do with Celeste's disappearance."

I open the bag and peer inside. Dark clothes? Not that I need any more of them. Frowning, I pull an item from the bag and hold it in front of me. Sweatpants. I rummage for the second item and a hollow feeling punches my gut. A hoody. I stare hard at her. "Where did you get these?"

"They're Joey's."

"Why would you bring them to me?"

"After speaking with you in the library, I went straight back to our cabin. When I walked in, he was fumbling around with this plastic bag. I obviously surprised him, because he stuffed it in the garbage bin. I asked him what he was doing, and he said he just was throwing out some rubbish. He asked me what I said in my interview, which I told him. Then he said he'd be back later."

"And?"

"I stood for a long time, wondering if I should look at what he stuffed in the bin. Eventually, I pulled out the bag and came straight here." Her eyes implore me for help.

On my lap lies what I suspect are the clothes worn by the person who left the letter at my cabin door last night. They look identical to what I remember. However, there's no real way to tell. "Thank you. I'm not sure if these clothes have any bearing on what's happened, but I'd like to keep them just the same. Show them to Detective Nash and Patrizio."

"That's fine. As far as Joey's concerned, he threw them out. So, he won't know any different. I just thought I should bring them to you . . . just in case." She appears visibly relieved. "I better get going." Rising to her feet, she manages a stiff smile.

I stand beside her. "Are you sure you're okay?"

"I'm sure." Her gaze hardens. "If Joey's involved in this business with Celeste, I want him caught and punished. When I married him, somewhere deep inside I knew who he was, and what he was capable of, but I ignored it. Now I'm paying for it. The only way for me to get out is to help put Joey away. Maybe those clothes will do the trick."

"Thank you for bringing them to me. But promise you won't tell a soul about this." I clasp her hands with a gentle squeeze.

She squeezes back. "I promise."

"If there's anything else, you know where I am." I escort her to the door, and we exchange gazes, hers troubled, mine compassionate. She walks away, her head held a fraction higher than before.

After she leaves, I go inside and lay the pants and hoody on the bed, studying them closely. Every bone in my body tells me these are the clothes. The slight flutter of recognition in my gut confirms it was Joey who tried to scare me off with the letters, which means he ranks as our number one suspect in Celeste's murder.

★ ★ ★

ASIDE FROM THREE TABLES OF passengers playing cards in the undercover section of deck five, John's got the open deck all to himself. Clutching the *Select Poems of Tennyson*, I slide into the chair beside him. After the hours we spent in the library, the warmth of the afternoon sun on my arms feels good. I'm pleased I ended up wearing my sleeveless blouse.

He eyes the little red book. "What have you got there?"

"It's Tennyson. Tom bought it for me years ago. I take it everywhere. Whenever I need to clear my head of something, I sit and read poetry."

Nose wrinkling and mouth twisting, he looks like he's sucked on a lemon. "Really? Poetry?"

"Really." I match his sarcastic tone. "Hear, let's see if there's a poem for our current situation." I ignore his barely audible tongue-clucking and open the tattered little book to a random place. "Well, I'll be." I tap a triumphant finger on the page.

He groans. "Let me see."

I spin the book around toward him, still tapping the page. "How's that?"

He leans over and reads aloud. "The Revenge. A Ballad of the Fleet. 1880."

"See, I told you." While John chuckles softly, I peruse the poem. "Can you believe it's a poem about a battle at sea? And the title? Revenge."

"What? You think it's some sort of omen for Celeste's murder?" He chuckles louder this time in unconcealed disbelief.

I pout and shut the book. "Well, you have to admit, it's odd. Here we are investigating a murder at sea and the poem that bursts forth on the page is called Revenge. Maybe that's the motive for the murder?"

"Coincidence." He sounds a lot like Ebenezer Scrooge.

"Coincidence, my butt. There's no such thing." I shake the book at him like a zealous preacher with the holy bible.

He angles me a look. "Are you trying to say that life is pre-destined?"

"Not exactly. But I know that nothing happens by chance. Everything is cause and effect."

Even though he groans, his lips twitch a smile. "Okay. Here's what I know. My stomach's grumbling, that's the cause" —he pauses, his eyes dancing with humor— "and the effect is to call a waiter and order food."

I tut loudly while he waves over one of the staff. After ordering a club sandwich each, I cease our esoteric conversation and explain Clare's recent visit to my cabin with her gift of Joey's clothes.

"Sounds like we've got what we need to persuade Joey to come clean about leaving you those letters?"

"I'm certain they're the clothes, but is it enough? I saw the person running down the passageway dressed in the same sweatpants and a hoody, but I never saw the person's face. I can't positively say it was Joey."

"But *he* doesn't know that. Clare caught him trying to get rid of the clothes, so he thinks they *can* identify him. It also adds weight to what Robert said about seeing Joey coming out of Celeste's cabin on Monday night. He said he didn't see Joey's face until he looked back. Why?"

"Because he was wearing a hoody." I gesture my finger in true Sherlock Holmes style.

"Correct. Joey probably wore the same sweatpants and hoody on both nights. That's why he's getting rid of them. But now that we have the clothes, we can use them as evidence, if not, at least a damn good bluff, to get inside his head a bit more."

"Okay, but we have to protect Clare. Joey must never know how we came into possession of them."

"Understood. We'll tee it up with Patrizio about one of the staff finding them when they sorted the garbage below ship. Brought them up to Patrizio, etcetera."

"Good."

Two plates loaded with hot chips and double-decker sandwiches of crispy bacon, mayo chicken and salad layered between thick slices of toast slide in front of us. Without another word, we each wrangle a half of our monstrous club sandwich and stuff our mouths until our cheeks stretch like chipmunks. Exchanging childish grins, we devour our meals amid appreciative moans and small talk.

★ ★ ★

BY THE TIME JASON DENHAM stalks into the library, my dark olive pants strain at the waist, and my stomach groans. I not only ate the entire club sandwich, but also every chip on my plate, followed by a double glass of sparkling mineral water.

"Why am I here?" Jason pushes his glasses up his nose toward his bad-tempered frown. Despite his good looks, he's obviously convinced that life has dealt him a 'bad hand.' No doubt being summoned to the library only adds to his pity party.

"Can you tell us what brought you on this expedition cruise?" Patrizio's manner has softened since he left us, which I infer means his conversation with the captain ended amicably.

"As I told Mrs. Daniels . . ." He slants me an impudent glance, as if all this is my doing.

"Diana," I say again, despite the pang in my stomach.

He sneers. "I'm a photojournalist. I came on this cruise to take photographs and write articles to sell to travel magazines."

"What sort of photos do you take?" John looks relaxed. Obviously, not feeling bloated like me.

"Who are you and why should I answer any of your questions?"

"I'm Detective John Nash, Monterey County Sheriff's department."

Jason's eyes dart around the room, while he shoves his glasses up with a jab.

"Please answer the detective's question," Patrizio says, pen at the ready.

He pouts. "I take photos of animals, birdlife, landscapes, anything that's unique to the Galapagos." His frown deepens. "Do you mind telling me what this is about?"

John ignores his request. "What sort of articles have you written since you've been on the ship?"

While the young man answers John's questions, Derek's words float back to me, "Keep alert for what you've seen or heard before." Something else interests me more than Jason's articles. With one eye and ear on the conversation, I scroll through my phone. When I find what I'm looking for, my gaze fluctuates between it and Jason. *Could it be true?* I linger a little longer before another spasm interrupts my concentration, and I switch off my phone.

"I still don't know why I'm here?" Jason says, impatience growing in his voice.

Patrizio reaches into his folder, slides the papers toward me, and I clear my throat. "I asked you this morning about these, but you refused to answer—"

"So that's it, is it?" Jason snaps.

I hold up the images of Celeste. "Actually, it's about a whole lot more than these."

"I'm a photojournalist. I take photos for a living."

"But you just got through telling me about the type of images you take and at no time did you mention photos of people." John folds his arms on the table in a show of one-up-man-ship.

Jason's gaze sweeps us, while we study him like cats with a cornered mouse. "Listen, I took photos of her because . . ."

"Because?" I ask.

"Because I wondered if she was some sort of celebrity. One I didn't know. I thought if I got a candid shot of her, I could sell it when I got back to the mainland and make some real money."

"Paparazzi?" Patrizio's voice drips with disdain.

John's brows lift. "And that's the story you're sticking with?"

Jason faces him. "Yes."

"I think you're lying. No, wait. I know you're lying." My face hardens as he tosses me a glare.

"What do you mean?"

"Because when we were both on deck six early Monday evening, I asked if you knew Celeste, which you denied point-blank." I wait a beat to see if he knows where I'm headed. He doesn't. "And you replied . . .?"

He shrugs, while I covertly rub my belly under the table.

"Your exact words were, 'and this Constanzo woman you refer to . . . I wouldn't know her if I ran into her.'" I stare hard at him, but his vacant expression indicates he still hasn't understood. I slow my pace. "If you didn't know Celeste, how did you know her surname was Constanzo?"

A jarring silence plummets in the library like a frigate bird diving headlong into the sea. Realization flushes Jason's face. Patrizio, John, and I recline in our chairs, our gazes fused on him.

"I can't remember saying that." He pushes his glasses further up his nose. "Anyway, what does it matter?"

"Because Mrs. Constanzo is missing." John's voice is flat.

"What do you mean, missing?" As Jason straightens in his chair, I notice concern pass over his face.

"She's not been seen for days," I say.

"But . . ."

"But what?" My stomach grumbles louder.

Again, his eyes dart around the room.

John's voice deepens. "It's odd really because before she disappeared, she received three letters threatening her that she'd have to pay for what she'd done. Do you know anything about those letters?"

"No, why should I?" But the quaver in Jason's voice indicates he might.

"Maybe you know more about Mrs. Constanzo than you're admitting? Maybe you were blackmailing her? Threatening her? And when she didn't pay up, you made her disappear?" John lunges across the table.

Jason recoils. "No, I didn't. Why would I do that? I didn't know her?"

"Are you sure you didn't know her?" I ask.

He juts his chin upward. "I didn't know her."

"But did you *want* to know her?"

His lips twist. "No, I didn't want to know her." He sounds unsure.

"And what about today?" Patrizio asks. My breath hitches, and John and I trade confused glances. What's Patrizio doing? We just backed Jason into a corner. John huffs out a terse breath and shakes his head, but it's too late. The conversation has been redirected. "Did you go to Floreana this morning?"

Jason seems visibly relieved. "Yes. I got some great shots of the old post office box."

"And did you post any letters?" Patrizio is oblivious to his blunder.

"No."

"You didn't leave any letters for Mrs. Daniels, perhaps?"

"No. Why should I?"

"And what about Tony Constan—?"

Before Patrizio has a chance to stumble into that bramble briar, John jumps in. "Jason, I don't think you understand the seriousness of what's going on here. There's no doubt you're lying, but about how much is the issue. Celeste Constanzo has disappeared from the ship." He pauses for added effect. I know he doesn't want to divulge she's been found murdered until a formal ID has taken place. "I suggest you go away and think long and hard about what you've told us. Very soon, it'll be too late to recant your story. If we find that foul play has befallen Mrs. Constanzo, I can assure you, you'll be front and center on our suspect list." He drives the last point home by tapping his index finger three times on the wood grain tabletop.

"But why me?" A thin tone squeaks in Jason's voice.

"Because you're lying," I repeat. "And it's in your best interest to tell us the truth. All of it. No matter how confronting or upsetting it may be."

For the first time since entering the library, Jason's indignant, churlish persona tempers. Behind his glasses, his brown eyes soften. I wondered if the heavy, horn-rimmed glasses are prescriptive or merely cosmetic to protect his real self from being seen. He and I exchange a look of quiet understanding. I lean forward, ready to hear the truth, but the compression on my stomach makes me wince. In that split second, Jason's mood changes. The shutters to his true story snap closed, leaving me with nothing except escalating stomach cramps.

"As I said, I don't know anything about Celeste Constanzo or these letters you say someone sent her. I took pictures of her hoping she was a celebrity, so I could sell them. If you'll excuse me, I have an article to write." Without waiting for permission to leave, he walks to the door.

"Before you go . . ." Though John halts his hasty retreat, Jason remains with his back to us, his hand ready to turn the handle. "Make sure our discussion here remains confidential."

Jason glares over his shoulder. "Who on earth would I tell? I'm here alone."

It's my last chance. "Perhaps *that's* why you're fascinated with Celeste?"

He quarter-turns, confusion on his face. "What do you mean?"

"She was alone as well." I wait a beat. "Surrounded by a family she didn't belong to. Perhaps you had that in common?"

He opens the door and leaves, but not before I notice the color drain from his face.

Patrizio and John stare at me. "I'm not sure what you're on about, but whatever it is, you hit a soft spot with Jason, that's for sure."

"Let's say I've got a hunch that there's more going on here than we first thought."

"Well, out with it."

"Not yet. I need to confirm a couple of details."

"Okay, but if you're right, those hunches of yours will turn me into a believer, yet," John says, with a good-natured chuckle.

A piercing jab lifts me to my feet. "If you'll excuse me, I need to take a break." While my hand clutches my stomach, my skin beads with a clammy film of perspiration.

"Are you okay?" He strides over and grasps my hand. "You've gone as white as a sheet."

I gather myself as best I can. "I just need to visit my cabin. I'll be back shortly." I force a weak smile before making an unsteady beeline for the door. Once outside, I clamber up the stairs, along the passageway to my cabin, race into the bathroom, and make it just in time before I soil my pants.

My stomach cramps are so severe, I'm going to turn inside-out. I rock back and forth clutching my groaning belly, while my head spins at breakneck speed. Then, without warning, my lunch demands a dramatic reappearance. Before I projectile-vomit everywhere, I swivel around and lunge head-first into the toilet bowl. My senses reel while my body purges itself, over and over. Exhausted, I collapse into the narrow space between the vanity and the doorway.

I lie prostrate on the cold, marble floor, and within moments, the shivering sets in. Unable to move, I struggle to focus on the overhead light fitting as the room pitches and rolls.

But it isn't the movement of the sea or the ship making me sick. This I know for sure before I lose consciousness.

CHAPTER SEVENTEEN

"Diana, are you all right?" John's voice drifts in from my right side, his concerned face hovering in mid-air.

I blink a few times, trying to focus. "Where am I?" My voice sounds groggy. Had I overslept? I wonder where Tom is, and then I remember.

"You're on the bed. In your cabin. We found you on the floor in the bathroom."

The memory of every orifice of my body purging itself crashes into my consciousness, as does the mortifying thought of the state of my bathroom. *How embarrassing.* Fully clothed under the heavy double blanket on top of me, I'm toasty warm, no longer shivering. My eyes scan the ceiling and then slowly, side to side.

On my left stands Doctor Garcia. "How're you feeling now?" She reaches over, and takes my pulse, her fingers cold.

"I'm not sure. Better I think." Except the ugly smell of puke and excrement lingers in my nose.

"Your vitals are stable. That's a good sign." She releases my wrist and folds her stethoscope into her pocket. "Take these anti-nausea pills. They'll settle your stomach."

"Thanks." I accept the two tablets and wash them down with a mouthful of water from a small disposable cup. "How did you get in?" I ask John.

"When you didn't return after fifteen minutes, we came looking for you. There was no answer when we knocked, so Patrizio used his master key to open the door." He indicates to Patrizio standing at the far end of the sofa. With a hangdog expression, he resembles Berty whenever I was confined to my bed. A mixture of guilt, concern, and failure grace his face because he can't make things better.

"You were unconscious," Patrizio says, without moving closer.

"Do you remember what happened?" John asks.

"I got these terrible stomach cramps during the interview with Jason. Then, diarrhea and vomiting. I felt like I was going to die."

"Sounds like food poisoning." The doctor's bedside manner is as dry as toast.

"Maybe . . . I've had food poisoning before, but never like this." I avoid her gaze and instead find John's.

"When do you think she'll be able to resume our interviews?" he asks Doctor Garcia.

"Hard to say. It's up to her. Whenever she feels well enough."

"Thank you, Doctor." I want everyone to leave so I can talk to John. "I'm sure I'll be up and about in no time. If you don't mind, I'd like to take a shower, freshen up a bit."

"Of course." She gives an official nod.

"Are you finished in there, Jimmy?" Patrizio calls.

"Jimmy?" I push up in bed, while John restacks the pillows behind me.

Jimmy strides out from my en suite, ripping off a pair of plastic gloves. "All done, sir."

I groan. "Oh, you didn't have to clean . . ." No one's cleaned up after me since before my mother died. Aside from the humiliation, I detest my present state of helplessness.

"No trouble at all, Mrs. Daniels." He bends and collects his bucket, mop, and cleaning products before making a humble exit.

"We'll leave you to it." Patrizio guides the doctor in front of him.

"Hang on a moment." While John follows them outside, I shuffle higher in bed and stare outside between the open curtains. Gray clouds brush the sky in feathery strokes, while in the distance arches a faint rainbow with its legendary pot of gold at its end. *If only.*

When the sound of the zodiak boats' two-stroke engines drifts up through the open balcony doors, I glance at my bedside clock. Four-ten. The excursion to Punta Cormorant just left. Although disappointed to have missed the opportunity to see the flamingoes of Floreana, I'm grateful to be conscious and recovering. My cabin door opens and in walks John. "So, how are you feeling, really?"

"Once I have a shower, I'll feel much better. Can I have some water please?"

"Sure." He brings a bottle over from the mini bar, opens and hands it to me. "What do you think made you so sick?"

"Well, if it was food poisoning, it sure came on quickly and was awfully acute." I gulp down a few mouthfuls, feeling stronger with each swallow. "I've had food poisoning before but nothing like that. Maybe someone slipped something into my food?"

"You think?" He props on the arm of the sofa.

"I remember when I was at Uni at one of those end-of-term parties. I never drank too much because I liked to keep my wits about me. But suddenly, I dropped to my knees, slurring my words. I'd only had a couple of glasses of wine, but I couldn't stand. Luckily, my friends bundled me into their car and took me to their place. I stayed all night, trying to recover. I swear someone slipped something in my drink. What I just went through was like that. Not food poisoning in the traditional sense. Think about it. This is a six-star vessel. I suspect their food quality is of the highest possible standard. Not only that, but we also had the same thing for lunch. The club sandwich. You're not sick, are you?" I swallow another mouthful of water.

"No. Not a bit. But if you're right about someone contaminating the food, only the staff had access to your meal."

"Not necessarily. Have you noticed how they manage the lunch service? The meals come out and are left on the counter for the waiters to collect. Anyone could have tampered with them?"

"If you'll excuse my language, but they'd have to have some balls to do it."

"Agreed. But we've met one notable suspect so far with that sort of arrogance." I drink more water.

John nods. "Joey Constanzo."

"Yes. But I don't recall seeing him when we were on deck five. Do you?"

"No. But we were facing out to sea. We'd have had no idea what was going on behind us."

"True." I finish off the bottle, but still, my thirst isn't quenched.

"You know, if someone did mess with the food, it mightn't have been meant for you." John slants me a grave look.

"My god, you're right. Maybe it was meant for you?"

"Or maybe it didn't matter? Either one of us was good enough for a warning."

I stare outside once more. The clouds have gathered in billowing layers of gunmetal gray, swallowing the rainbow and mirroring the dense, darkening events on board. Knowing that a murderer was on the ship is one thing, but being their target brings a new perspective to what I initially thought was an adventure. I shift my gaze to the bedside drawer, wishing for Tom. "What do we do now?" A question both for him and John.

"Leave it with me. I'll talk to Patrizio. I'm sure he can arrange for our food to be prepared and served by staff he can trust." John's confidence reassures me a little.

"I don't think I could go through another bout of that." I incline my head in the direction of the en suite.

"I understand. Don't worry about it. Now, I've got the guide who found the body at Champion Islet waiting. You don't need to come."

"But . . ."

"I'm sure it'll be straight forward. Murderers seldom draw attention to themselves by discovering their own dead victims. It'll be a standard interview. I'll fill you in on the details later."

"Okay," I say, reluctantly.

"Grab a shower. See how you feel. We're interviewing Jimmy and Bruno in about thirty minutes. If you're up to it, join us then."

"Okay. Say, five?"

"Five it is." He flashes me a warm smile then strides from the cabin. *A man on a mission.* Which reminds me. I slide over to the side of the bed and pull Tom's ashes from the drawer, cradling the box in my hands. "I'm sorry Tom. I know this trip was supposed to be for you. But I've got to finish what I've started." After a fond caress, I slip the box back into the drawer and march to the en suite.

★ ★ ★

AFTER A THOROUGH SHOWER AND dressed in a pair of navy slacks and a long-sleeve cream blouse, I'm back in my usual chair beside Patrizio in the library. Thankfully, my stomach resembles a tranquil lake, most of my mental acuity has returned, and the liberal lashings of my Chanel No. 5 fumigate my nostrils. When John flicks over a page on a small notepad, I can't help but smirk. Although he's a champion at retaining information and details, I wondered how long it'd take before he needed to keep some sort of chronology of the past few days. While I watch him and Patrizio prepare for our next person of interest, a flutter of pride at what a fine investigative trio we make lifts my spirits—me with my laptop, Patrizio with his notebook and bulging folder of notes, and now John with his simple notepad. A veritable vault of confidential information about Celeste and our list of suspects.

"Now, Jimmy, you're responsible for the passengers on deck four. Correct?"

"Yes, Detective Nash, that's correct." Sitting ramrod straight, Jimmy maintains his professional manner, although the quickened rise and fall of his chest indicates he's more nervous than his outward demeanor suggests.

"Do you remember our conversations about Mrs. Constanzo?" I ask.

"Yes, Mrs. Daniels." His mouth lifts in a faint smile, reminding me of a conscientious student, eager to please.

I match his tentative grin. "Can you tell us what you remember?"

"I believe it was Monday morning when you first asked me had I seen Mrs. Constanzo." His brown, puppy-dog eyes blink at me.

"Go on."

"You said you'd planned to go on an excursion with her, but she wasn't answering when you knocked on her cabin door. I said I hadn't seen her, and you instructed me to tell her you'd been looking for her."

With a nod at Patrizio and John, I confirm Jimmy's recollection of events. "And when else did we talk about Mrs. Constanzo?"

"The next time was early Monday evening. Mrs. Constanzo had placed a do-not-disturb sign on her door. You were knocking and calling for her when I interrupted you."

"And?"

"I informed you that Mrs. Constanzo was ill and didn't want to be disturbed."

"But when did she tell you this?" John asks.

"She didn't. Mr. Bellassai told me. He'd looked in on Mrs. Constanzo earlier that day."

"And did you see Mrs. Constanzo any time after this?" Patrizio refers to the statement he'd already taken from Jimmy.

Jimmy's eyes drift upward. "No, I didn't."

"Didn't you service her room or deliver room service?" I ask.

"I took dinner to her cabin in the evenings. I left the tray outside her door and knocked. Then came back to collect it later. In regards to servicing her room, Mr. Bellassai serviced it on Monday and yesterday. I serviced it this morning."

"What time?" John asks.

"About thirty minutes before the zodiaks left on their first excursion. I was finished by nine."

John looks up from his note-taking. "When you serviced the room this morning, did you notice anything out of place or strange?"

"Not that I can think of. Our job is not to disturb any of the passengers' personal belongings. Just to tidy up, make the bed, change the linen, and clean wherever necessary."

John taps his pen on the pad. "Why didn't you service Mrs. Constanzo's room on Monday and yesterday?"

"It's company policy that if a passenger is sick, the Butler Manager liaises directly with the passenger, and services the cabin. By having only one staff near the sick passenger reduces the risk of infection or contagion."

"Did you meet or know Mrs. Constanzo before now?" I ask.

"No, Mrs. Daniels."

"Do you know if any of the staff or crew knew her before?"

"No one mentioned knowing her."

My gut squirms. This time with a persistent tickle of intrigue. I stare at the shelves of books behind Jimmy's head as if they hold the answer to my hunch. While John and Patrizio exchange a few whispered words, I can't shake the feeling that Jimmy knows something, but he doesn't know he knows it. "Do you know anything about Mrs. Constanzo's jewelry?"

His expression brightens. "You mean the jewelry she wore to the Captain's cocktail party?"

"Yes. Did you see it?" John pounces on the topic.

"No. I wasn't there, but all the staff and crew talked about it. They said it was amazing. Big diamonds and cluster of rubies." The thrill in Jimmy's voice fetches a fierce sideways glance from Patrizio. "I'm sorry." His reserve returns. "We don't often have passengers bring valuable items like that on board the ship. When it happens, everyone gets excited."

"Have you heard any of the passengers talking about the jewelry?" I'm determined to unearth the information I suspect he knows.

"Not that I recall. I do most of my work when the passengers are off the ship. I don't hear a lot of what they talk about. The other staff hear more than I do."

I shoot him a cranky frown. "So, you haven't overheard any conversations that might help us with Mrs. Constanzo's disappearance or about her jewelry." To think that he hasn't heard or seen anything suspicious seems unlikely. I tap my foot under the table.

"I'm sorry, Mrs. Daniels, I can't think of anything."

Either he's so well-trained not to eaves-drop or so well-trained not to admit to it, I can't tell. I huff out a breath and type.

"If you do hear anything, anything at all about the jewelry or Mrs. Constanzo, make sure you tell Patrizio," John says. "Thank you. You can go."

Jimmy rises and gives his vest a sharp tug over his trousers' waistband. "Thank you, Detective, Patrizio, Mrs. Daniels." He nods at each of us and exits in a slow shamble.

My gaze locks on John and Patrizio. "I've a hunch that Jimmy knows something. I don't think he's lying, but he's seen or heard something and not thought it was important. There's something."

"Yeah, he strikes me as the fall guy," John says. "The poor sap who's in the wrong place, at the wrong time, but doesn't know it."

I snort a soft laugh. "I agree. I don't think he's the sharpest knife in the drawer as we say back home. He's too trusting."

Patrizio joins in. "I've seen some of the staff take advantage of him."

"In my opinion, he's a good-humored underachiever, not capable of any crime." I save his file as such in my laptop while they agree.

"Wait a minute," John says. "What about the waiter from the restaurant yesterday? The one you asked about seeing Celeste at lunchtime? Did you get his name?"

I sigh. "I was too seasick to notice. Sorry."

"That's okay," Patrizio says. "We'll get the staff who were on shift in a line-up. Do you think you could remember him?"

"I think so. If not, he'll sure remember me since I nearly made him lose all his plates."

"Good. Leave it to me." Patrizio jots down another task in his notebook.

"Okay." John rubs his hands together. "We've lost time, and we still need to ID the body. Let's get Bruno in here."

Bruno Bellassai appears incongruous to the escalating events taking place on board. Unflappable by nature, diminutive in stature, fastidious in manner, and humble to the point of subservience, he waits inside the doorway to be invited into the library.

Patrizio motions to the chair. "Please, be seated."

A persnickety man, Bruno positions himself with precision, feet flat on the floor, back upright and hands laced in his lap. Despite his appearance, I suspect he's a tough taskmaster. In front of the guests, he complies and obliges. With his staff, he demands, expecting them to be as industrious as him.

After Patrizio performs the formal introductions, he says, "I know I've taken your statement, but Detective Nash and Mrs. Daniels would like to hear your version of the past few days regarding Mrs. Constanzo."

"How may I be of assistance?" Bruno's even, unemotional voice matches his composed manner.

John begins. "Can you tell us about your interactions with Mrs. Constanzo?"

"Well, Mrs. Constanzo became ill after the Captain's cocktail party."

"How do you know that?"

"She phoned me and asked if I had any seasickness pills."

"What time did she call you?" I ask.

"It was before midnight as I recall. I took her a couple of pills and left."

I'd left Celeste around eleven-thirty, and Robert had seen Joey, allegedly, breaking into her cabin at one o'clock. Bruno delivering pills before midnight, fitted the timeline.

John glances up from his notes. "And when did you see her after that?"

"I checked in on Mrs. Constanzo the next morning."

"Monday morning," I say.

"Yes. I wanted to see how she was feeling. But Mrs. Constanzo was still sickly."

"When was the next time you saw her?" John asks.

"I checked in on her Monday evening, and by Tuesday morning when I visited her again, she was feeling better. If you recall, Mrs. Daniels, that's when I informed you that Mrs. Constanzo had removed the do-not-disturb sign from her door." His heavy-lidded eyes open a little wider in my direction. "After you returned from the morning excursion to Caleta Tagus?"

"Yes, I remember. I went to her cabin and the sign was gone, but I couldn't find her anywhere. By the time I got back to her cabin, the do-not-disturb sign was on the door again." I scratch the nape of my neck. A wild goose chase then, and the same now.

"Did you see Mrs. Constanzo after that?" John scribbles on his pad.

"No. Since she'd recovered, I relieved myself of her duty-of-care and informed Jimmy he could continue with his duties. Which he did the next day, Wednesday, when he serviced her cabin in the morning."

I shuffle time-coded colored cells around on the gant chart in my laptop, plotting the chronology of events and people. Like a chess game, every time a player makes a move, an opponent scuttles the play with another move. Glancing upwards, I thank Tom for teaching me the strategy behind chess many years ago. It comes in handy. I narrow my gaze on Bruno. "Did you know Mrs. Constanzo previously?"

"No."

John twirls his pen in his fingers. "What did you think of the jewelry she wore to the Captain's cocktail party?"

"I can't say I remember."

A sly smile widens John's face. "Come on. You were there as a member of the senior management team. You must've noticed it."

"I did notice it, but it'd be unprofessional of me to discuss any guest's personal items." He raises his chin as if declaring an end to the topic.

I decide on a new direction. "How long have you been working for Silversea?"

"I worked on their Mediterranean luxury cruises before being transferred to the *Silver Galapagos Expedition* cruise two years ago."

"Why the Galapagos?" John asks.

"I always wanted to see this part of the world."

"I thought all crew on board the ship had to be nationals. You're not Ecuadorian. You're Italian, aren't you?" I ask.

"Head office approved my transfer request based on my previous employment performance with the company."

"Do you have family back in Italy or did they come with you?"

"I haven't any family."

"So, nothing or no one to keep you in Italy then?"

"No." His eyes lower.

"One more question," John says. "When you were caring for Mrs. Constanzo, did she mention that she'd received nasty letters here on the cruise?"

"No, she never mentioned it."

John checks with Patrizio and me before concluding. "Thank you. You may go."

Rising to his feet, Bruno buttons his jacket and pulls his shirt cuffs down. He swivels a turn and steps lively out the door.

John consults his notepad. "He's an odd character."

"Bruno's hard-working and efficient to the point of brusqueness," Patrizio says. "He's very good at his job and extremely loyal to the company. Head office views him as an asset. That's why they approved his transfer. I've his personnel file here if you want to look at it."

"Thanks." I reach over and peruse it quickly. "Can I hang onto this for a day or two?"

"Sure. Do you want Jimmy's as well?"

"Thanks." I accept his file and tuck them both beside my laptop. "Do you know Bruno personally?"

Patrizio shakes his head. "No one really knows Bruno. He keeps to himself. Doesn't talk about his personal life."

"Mmm." I open my Myers Brigg file and scroll through the tabs. "I think he's an ISFJ."

"Okay, let's hear it." John's voice holds a familiar weary tone to it, which I ignore.

"Introverted, sensing, feeling, and judging. In a nutshell, the big characteristics of this personality type are a deep devotion to family, loyalty to traditions, and the embodiment of service above self."

"That's Bruno," Patrizio says.

"Certainly seems to fit," John agrees.

"But don't you think it's strange he said he's got no family? I mean everyone has some family, even if they're twice removed. And as an ISFJ, he'd be committed to finding them, so he could feel whole."

"Maybe he did, and he didn't like what he found." John snorts. "I think he's got some seriously high expectations."

"I wouldn't like to be his family," Patrizio says. "If they're anything like him, they wouldn't be much fun."

While they chuckle over Bruno's shortcomings in the enjoyment stakes, I consider how desperately sad it must be to have no one at all.

CHAPTER EIGHTEEN

IN THE SHIP'S SMALL MEDICAL center, the four of us, including Doctor Garcia gather around the examination table. In front of us lies Celeste's naked body covered for modesty. The tight pull back of her hair and its cascade over the head block, emphasizes the symmetry of her face. Her closed eyelids give the impression of a sleeping beauty, and she is a physical beauty—slim, tall, and well-proportioned. Or more correctly she'd *been* a beauty. Seeing Celeste's cold, lifeless body brings back the terrible sense of loss and wasted life of Tom's death twelve months earlier. I deflate at the memory and at the tragic sight in front of me.

"Tell us, Doctor, what do you think was the cause of death?"

"It's difficult to say, Detective. I've no idea of the time of death or how long the body may have been in the water."

John hovers closer. "I've seen bodies pulled from the water before, and it's hard to know how long they've been there, just by looking at them. They can stay underwater for a week or more before they float to the top. Go on, Doctor."

"As you can appreciate, I'm not qualified to give an expert opinion, but from my initial examination, there doesn't appear to be any wounds that indicate death by an object or brute force. There are marks here on her right shin, which look like shark teeth marks." We all lean over for a look. "But there doesn't appear to be any obvious physical signs as to cause of death. A toxicology report may find foreign substances or poisons which she ingested. But that sort of report will take weeks. I don't know whether the body's submersion in saltwater will impact that or not. In short, I can only tell you what I think didn't happen. Not what did happen." A tinge of failure blushes her face.

"You've done a sterling job, considering the circumstances," I say.

"Thank you, Mrs. Daniels." Her shoulders sag. "I'm sorry I couldn't be of more help."

"That's fine," Patrizio says. "This is an extraordinary circumstance and not one in your job description, I expect."

"That's for sure." She exchanges a relieved smile with us.

"Where are the clothes she was wearing?" Patrizio asks.

"I've bagged them." She indicates to the large black plastic bag on the counter behind her.

"Anything of interest there?" John asks.

"No. She wore a long, apricot silk nightgown. Expensive by the look of it. No underwear or footwear. No jewelry or hair adornments."

"Thank you, Doctor Garcia." He nods for her to cover the body, then inclines his head toward the door. "If you'd give us a moment and wait outside. We'll need you when we get the next of kin in to identify the body."

I stare down into Celeste's once-beautiful face. "Who hated you so much that they'd go to all this effort, my dear?" I wait as if expecting an answer. Straightening, I eyeball my two colleagues. "If she wasn't physically marked, I think she was probably drugged or poisoned. Possibly in her sleeping pills. Once she was dead, the murderer tossed her overboard. It wouldn't be that hard to do. She doesn't weigh much by the look of her. The murderer probably hoped the sharks would make short work of her or that she'd stay down long enough for the ship to depart these waters."

John folds his arms and angles me a quizzical look. "And what do you base your assumption on about the sleeping pill substitution?"

"What just happened to me. I didn't have food poisoning. I'm sure someone slipped something into our lunch, meant for either of us. If we find that person, we find who murdered Celeste. I bet they substituted sedatives or poison for her sleeping pills. She took a couple and didn't wake up. No struggle involved."

"Plausible, I guess." John tilts his head. "But your assumption implies that this was premeditated, by someone who knew Celeste would be on the ship for this particular cruise."

"As I said earlier, Celeste's murder doesn't feel like an impulsive crime of passion. I think someone planned this from the start."

"You're convinced she didn't accidentally fall or jump overboard?" Patrizio's voice is tinged with hope. I suspect that an accident or a suicide would be much less trouble for head office than a murder.

"The best approach is to treat Celeste's death as suspicious," John says. "We don't have much time to solve this. When the ship docks in a few days, our window of opportunity shuts."

"You better get the bottle of sleeping pills from Celeste's bedside table in her cabin. It could be evidence," I say to Patrizio, who writes a note in his book and circles it.

He sighs a heavy breath. "Okay, but what about the jewelry?"

"Maybe that was part of the motive. Celeste was murdered for her jewelry." But somehow that doesn't feel right either.

"Or maybe when they stole the jewelry, Celeste caught them, and they killed her." Patrizio clutches for a simple solution.

"No." John's answer is definitive. "If that was the case, they'd be some indication of a struggle. I tend to agree with Diana. This was planned. Probably down to the last detail. Celeste was a dead woman before she walked on board the ship."

To think that while Celeste and I sat talking, someone watched, waiting for their moment to kill her. Now, that same person could well be planning my demise. Fright marches over my skin in stiletto-heeled shoes.

"Right." John claps his hands again, in what I presume is one of his trademark leadership moves as a detective. "We have a body, which based on where it was found, obviously went in the water sometime late last night or the early hours of this morning. We're assuming Celeste didn't fall in by accident or commit suicide. Let's get Joey, Rose, and Tony in here and gauge their reactions. Patrizio, please send Doctor Garcia in to prepare the body for the viewing before you bring them in."

"How did you go with the guide who found her?" I ask John, while the doctor covers Celeste's face with the sheet.

"As I suspected, standard stuff. He's pretty shaken. Found her tangled in some deep-water seaweed. By the sound of it, she might've stayed there for ages unless he found her."

I sneer. "Unlucky break for the murderer."

Patrizio pokes his head in the door. "They're here."

"Right. Bring them in."

Joey, Rose, and Tony single file into the medical center, their gazes fixed on the covered body on the table.

"Oh, God." Rose reaches out for her younger brother.

"It's okay." Tony wraps a comforting arm around her shoulders as the doctor ushers them to the opposite side of the table. He steadies Rose beside him, while Joey stands silent and stony-faced at the head of the table.

Patrizio clears his throat. "As you know, we conducted a search earlier today for your stepmother and found she wasn't on board ship."

"You don't mean, that's her?" Tony hugs Rose tighter. Their expressions convey shock and disbelief, while Joey's remains unmoved, almost frozen.

"We believe so."

Rose buckles at the knees and groans. "Oh, no. This can't be happening. This can't be happening."

Tony scoops her up, taking her weight.

"For God's sake, Rose, pull yourself together." The icy fire in Joey's glare knocks her upright. She composes herself, mumbles a barely audible apology, and accepts a couple of tissues from the doctor.

John takes charge. "A body was found at Champion Islet during this afternoon's shark snorkeling excursion . . ." — Rose moans softly— ". . . and we believe it's Celeste. You've been called here as next of kin to formally identify the body."

Taking a deep breath, Tony steels himself and clutches Rose tighter. Joey's indifferent, as if a dead body, particularly Celeste's, is of little consequence to him. "Go ahead."

While the doctor folds back the sheet from Celeste's head, I study each of their expressions. Tony's eyes glisten with tears before he looks away. He appears genuinely upset at the sight of his dead stepmother. Rose buries her mouth and nose in the tissues, but she can't hide the incredulity on her face.

"Yes. That's her. Celeste Constanzo. Can we go now?" Joey's reaction is exactly as I expected, heartless.

John nods to the doctor to replace the sheet and leave the room. "We've reason to believe that your stepmother was murdered."

"What?" Tony shoots Joey a quick sideways glance.

"You mean this wasn't an accident?" Rose teeters on the edge of hysteria.

"At this stage, we're treating her death as suspicious," Patrizio says.

Joey casts a stern eye at his siblings. "Well, don't think one of us did her in. We mightn't have liked her, but we didn't kill her."

"But you all had the most to gain by her death because of your father's inheritance." John skewers a look at each of them before locking on Joey. "You even threatened Celeste at the Captain's cocktail party that if she wasn't dead within sixty days, the three of you would contest the will."

Tony stares at his brother. "You didn't tell me that."

Joey's top lip curls. "Not now."

A brooding silence stretches while Tony obeys his brother.

"Despite what you did or didn't know, Joey made his threats in front of witnesses." John swivels on Joey. "You had the most to gain from Celeste's death. Money is one helluva motive as is long-festering hatred. You were also seen coming out of her cabin in the early hours of Monday morning." Rose gasps. "That's an opportunity. And you had the means to kill her."

"I told you it wasn't me. It's all conjecture on your part. Now, we've identified the body. Can we go?"

"Who's going to tell Emily?" Rose whispers in a frantic voice.

"We will," I say. "We'll contact her shortly."

"Thank you." Tony sounds relieved. He shakes his head while staring at Celeste's white-sheeted body. "Cursed . . ." I know he refers to the description he'd given of his family earlier, although it's obvious neither Rose nor Joey understand. Out of the three of them, he seems saddened by Celeste's death, whereas Rose spirals into worsening confusion and mania. Her breathing's quickened, and she's gulping back little sobs behind the tissues over her mouth. She looks as if she'll hyperventilate if she stays much longer.

"We'd appreciate it if you'd keep this to yourselves for the time being. Joey and Rose, you can tell Clare and Angelo, if you like. But we don't want this becoming public knowledge just yet. Can I have your promise on that?" John sounds sympathetic yet authoritative.

Tony and Rose nod, leaving only Joey. "Well?" I meet his defiant gaze.

"Okay." He sneers. "But when can I contact my lawyers about the will?"

Rose sucks in air, her eyes round and wide.

"You mercenary asshole." Tony growls the words through tight lips.

Joey bares his teeth, his stare, scathing.

I step in before the friction escalates. "I doubt there's much your lawyers can do until you get an official death certificate."

"They can freeze the estate." Another threatening glare from Joey. This time at me.

"Under the circumstances, I think it's Emily's responsibility as the direct next-of-kin to contact her mother's lawyers who'll then take the correct legal action." Outwardly, I maintain a calm manner, while inside, I'm seething. Tony's right—Joey's an asshole.

Joey murmurs in reluctant agreement, but I have a hunch he'll be on the phone to his lawyers the moment he gets back to his cabin.

"Thank you for your time. Our sympathies for your loss." As Patrizio escorts them from the medical center, Rose clings to Tony while Joey pushes past in a rush to call his lawyers, no doubt.

"What do you think?" I ask John.

"Joey's definitely hiding something, but I'm not sure it's murder."

I pause, piecing together random thoughts, before facing Patrizio. "You know how you said that the camera for deck four never arrived before we embarked on this cruise?"

"Yes . . ."

I turn to John. "What if the camera *did* arrive, and it was misplaced on purpose? All planned by the murderer or an accomplice." My sixth sense dances in happy circles.

"That's a bit of a leap, even for you." John closes his notepad. "More than likely, the murderer got a lucky break."

I crinkle my nose in disgust. "If Celeste was dead-woman-walking and this was pre-meditated, surely the camera was part of the plan?"

John rubs his chin. "If that's the case, we need to broaden our list of suspects or accomplices to the entire crew."

Patrizio groans and looks around as if searching for a chair to collapse onto. "There's no way we can interview the entire crew before debarkation. There's not enough time."

"Okay. Let's not get ahead of ourselves," John says. "We need a break." Patrizio and I agree. "It's nearly six o'clock. Let's have dinner and regroup back in the library at nine. That gives us time to clear our heads, go over our notes, and decide on the next course of action. What do you say?"

"Perfect." Relief washes over me. I need quiet time.

"Suits me," Patrizio says.

"What about Emily? We need to contact her." I'm concerned she might find out about her mother through her stepsiblings before we speak with her.

"I'll make the call." Patrizio's pained expression relays how he really feels about being the bearer of such sad news.

"I'm happy to help if you like," I say.

"No, that's fine, Mrs. Daniels. This is official company business. I'll update the captain on our investigation. He may choose to make the call instead."

"Well, if I can be of assistance, you know where to find me."

"Thanks." Patrizio tucks his notebook and folder under his arm.

With another clap of his hands, John concludes the meeting. "See you in the library at nine." And we go our separate ways.

★ ★ ★

SITTING ON MY BALCONY, SIPPING a glass of delightfully cold sauvignon blanc, I breathe in the unpolluted air of the Galapagos. Beside me on the table rests the box of Tom's ashes and my little red book of Tennyson's poems. "Oh, Tom, what an adventure I've got myself into," I say aloud, with a hint of excitement in my voice. "I know you'd disapprove of my involvement, but to be honest, I'm enjoying the mental exercise of it all and having a chance to unravel my hunches in real-time. It's more important, and much more fun than recruiting staff."

In my mind, I hear Tom tutting me with a good-natured laugh. It brings me a sense of peace to imagine him so close. I swallow a hit of wine and recline in my chair, rolling my head from side to side. The knot in my shoulder has called it quits for the day which adds to my relaxed mood. In a swath of deep purple, dusk surrenders to the velvety veil of night. My cue for dinner.

When I stand, my gaze travels from the ocean to the silver box in my hand and back again. I waver, waiting for a sign. Nothing. "Not yet, my darling." But soon, I'll have to let him go. Soon. Just as I'm about to slide my balcony door shut behind me, a knock taps at my cabin door.

"Just a minute," I call before slipping the box in my bedside drawer and returning my glass to the counter.

Rushing past the full-length closet mirror, I check myself and fluff my hair. Why I've no idea. Despite, or maybe because of Celeste's tragedy, I'm feeling useful again. Like I've rediscovered my purpose in life.

Cracking open the door without sliding the chain, I giggle at the person peering in at me. "What brings you here?"

"I figured after everything that's been going on today, you'll need a kindred spirit to buy you dinner."

"But dinner's included in our tariff," I say, in a cheeky tone.

"That it is, but still a superlative amateur sleuth like yourself can't possibly dine alone."

I open the door with a grateful smile. "It's good to see you, Derek. Come in."

Like a man used to making an entrance, he strides into my cabin looking as grand as an English Duke, in navy-blue jacket and trousers with an open-necked pale blue and white striped shirt.

"I was just getting ready to leave for dinner, but would you like a white wine?"

"Of course. A pre-dinner drink sounds perfect. Thanks." While I pour two wines, he asks, "How did it all go today?"

"It was harrowing, challenging, and I loved every bit of it." *Well, not the vomiting and diarrhea.*

"'Atta girl." He accepts the glass. "I knew you had it in you. Cheers." He clinks his glass to mine, and we sip. "I hear they found a body at Champion Islet today during the shark snorkeling expedition." His face drops. "Was it Celeste?"

I decide to confide in him, hopeful that I'm as good a judge of character as I believe myself to be, and that Derek isn't a viable suspect. "Yes, it was, but we're not making it public yet."

"I'm sorry. I know you'd become quite fond of her."

I sigh. "Yes, I had. We're treating her death as suspicious."

Derek's brows lift on his forehead. "Murder?" I nod. "Suspects?"

"Increasing as we speak." I sip some more.

He salutes me and drinks. "Well, with you and your gut instinct on the case, I'm sure you'll find the fiendish fellow or woman who murdered her."

From outside, we hear splashing water. "What on earth is that?" I move toward the balcony with Derek behind me. Standing side by side, we lean over the railing, and I gasp. "Oh, my God."

"It's sharks." Stretching along the eighty-eight-meter starboard side of the ship, in a band at least three meters wide and even more meters deep, thrash schools of sharks. "Good lord, there are thousands of them."

In a mighty commotion, the sharks try to catch the nocturnal seagulls as they skim across the water's surface after fish. This night-time ritual is obviously part of the expedition, as the ship's massive floodlights tilt downward onto the water, so the passengers can witness the sight. Excited voices carry on the still night, cheering the seagulls' perilous escape from the sinister smiles of their foe beneath.

"Unbelievable." I watch the feeding frenzy, unable to tell who's winning—the seagulls, the sharks, or the fish. The noise of churning water, smacking shark tails, snapping jaws and squawking seagulls surges louder. A lethal game of do or die. My skin turns clammy and cold. "That's why the murderer threw Celeste overboard in these waters. So, she'd be mauled by the sharks." As much as I try not to, I imagine Celeste's pretty, apricot nightgown and delicate body being torn to pieces by the sharks. Horrible.

Derek squeezes my hand. "But she wasn't torn to pieces by the sharks. Because of you, she was found. You thwarted the murderer's plan."

"A lot of good that's done her." I finish my wine in one hard swallow, hoping it'll wash away my guilt. It doesn't. My gaze lingers on the turmoil below.

"Maybe you didn't save her, but I've got faith in your powers of deduction."

"Why?" I face him, unable to hide the frustration in my voice. "You don't even know me."

"I can't rightly say why, and yes, I don't really know you, but there's the hint of the Grand Dame about you."

"I don't understand."

"Christie was a master inventor of crimes on the page. Why? Because she was an astute observer of the human condition. And you are, too. You see things that most people don't. And it's because of that, people gravitate toward you. I've no doubt you'll find your murderer, and you'll get to the bottom of whatever else is going on board ship connected to Celeste Constanzo."

I blow out a breath. "I'm not so sure. But thanks, for your vote of confidence."

"Come on. Let's go to dinner. Talk about other things than murder and mystery."

"I'd like that." But before I follow him back into my cabin, I glance over the side of the ship once more. Whoever murdered Celeste hated her with a passion so deep and enduring, that they wanted her to be mutilated by sharks. The Tennyson poem must be an omen—Revenge.

CHAPTER NINETEEN

Just before nine o'clock and after a delightful dinner, Derek and I stroll up the internal stairs to deck three. "Thanks for taking my mind off everything."

"My pleasure." A seductive gleam twinkles in his eyes. "Perhaps after your meeting, you'd like to come to my cabin for a night-cap?"

I pat his arm. "Not this time."

He inclines his head and pouts. "But I've a lovely suite on deck five you know."

I giggle. "I'm sure it's wonderful."

"And there's only me and a couple of old ducks up there from what I've seen."

"What do you mean? Old ducks?"

"Elderly gray-haired ladies dripping in diamonds." He chuckles. "Funny old dears."

"They're the Blum sisters. Jewelers from L.A." I shuffle us to one side for more privacy from passing passengers. "Tell me more."

"I haven't spoken to them except to say hello, but they're an odd pair. I hear them chattering away when they're coming and going from their cabins."

"What've you heard?"

"They keep prattling on about some jewelry they acquired. How marvelous it is and what a shrewd deal they've done."

My heart beats faster. "Did you hear them say what it was? Or when they did this deal? Or with whom?"

"Not that I can remember. But if you want me to, I can schmooze them, and see if I can find out details."

"That'd be wonderful." In a moment of uncharacteristic fervor, I wrap my arms around his neck and kiss his cheek.

He laughs a soft, throaty sound. "If I'd known it was this easy to get a kiss from you, I would've offered to chat up old dears before now."

"Don't be silly." I slap his arm, playfully. "I've got to go. Keep your eyes and ears on the Blum sisters."

"Aye, aye, my captain." He gives me a sharp salute. "I'll report back when I've further news."

"Thanks."

"You're welcome." He plants a gentlemanly kiss on the back of my hand, smiles, and heads to the higher decks.

I enter the library re-energized and find John and Patrizio reclining in two plush leather armchairs, their notebook, notepad, and folder closed on the coffee table between them.

"Sorry, guys." I slip into my usual chair at the end of the table and set up my laptop.

"That's okay, we only just arrived. Feeling better?" With his long legs stretched out and crossed casually at the ankles, John brackets his hands behind his head and grins.

"Yes. Those few hours worked wonders. How did you get on with Emily?" I ask Patrizio, who, by his relaxed posture, also enjoyed the time off.

"The captain made the call. Emily's going to arrange to meet the ship at Baltra on Saturday and fly home with the body."

"Won't it have to stay in Ecuador until an autopsy has been conducted?" John asks.

"Yes, but she's determined to meet the ship and sort it out from there. She's bringing her lawyer."

"She sounds a tough young woman."

"Like her mother, I've no doubt." Though the memory of Celeste makes me sad, it seems she taught her daughter well. "Did Emily say anything else?"

"No. It was a short conversation. I suspect she'll want to know everything once she arrives with her legal advisor."

John jerks upright and claps his hands. "Okay. As nice as it'd be to sit here and do nothing, we better get started and make sure we've got notes on everything." He eyeballs me. "You seem to be the most efficient out of the three of us in note-taking. Would you mind?"

"No problem." I flick open my laptop and review my notes to date. "Today we've interviewed Joey, Robert Sawyer, Rose, Tony, Clare, Angelo, Jason, Jimmy, and Bruno."

"And we discovered the true identity of the Pinkertons aka FBI Agents Sullivan and Mackenzie." Amusement flickers in his green eyes.

"But are we any closer to finding out who killed Celeste, stole the jewelry, or wrote the letters to you or Celeste?" Patrizio's eyes dim with worry.

"Why not do the easy one first?" I say.

Patrizio brightens. "What do you mean? 'Easy one'?"

"The letters. I think Joey's behind the ones left for me. He told me to mind my business and keep my nose of out his family's business, and those were the same words repeated nearly verbatim in the letters."

John rises to his feet. "Yes, I think you're right."

"Then there's Celeste's letters. When she showed me the first letter after the cocktail party, my impression was that it looked like it'd been written by a person using their less dominant hand. Trying to hide their handwriting. Why don't we get everyone we've interviewed so far to do handwriting tests? Use the text from both sets of letters, and get them to write it with their dominant and less dominant hands?"

John props against one of the bookshelves. "It can't hurt. It won't be conclusive though."

"I know, but it might steer us in the right direction. At least with the letters." I gaze past him to the books on the far wall.

"I've come to know that glassy-eyed look of yours. What's going on? Another hunch?"

I return my focus. "I think we should get them to fold the letters as well."

"Why's that?" Patrizio asks.

"Because the letters left for Celeste were folded in half while the letters for me were folded in thirds."

"Now, that's attention to detail." John nods impressed.

I smile coyly. "Thanks. But I noticed it straight away with my letters. Folded three times with neat creases whereas Celeste's were folded in half, and not always exact. Even if the senders of the letters try to mask their writing during the tests, I think they'll fold them unconsciously."

"Good thinking. It might work as an added clue."

"Do you think the letters were written by different people?" Patrizio asks.

"I'm not sure," John says, his gaze settling on me. "But judging by the expression on your face, you have a hunch as to who wrote the letters to Celeste. Correct?"

"Yes." I press my lips tight.

"But you're not going to share just yet."

"No. Not yet. I want to be sure."

He chuckles. "All right. You follow your hunches with the letters, but when you're sure, I want to know. Okay?"

"Thanks."

He cuts me a cautionary look. "Just don't go getting in Joey's way."

"I won't."

Once we agree it'd be better if Patrizio conducts the tests in his official capacity, I explain what I need and how to go about it.

"Got it." Patrizio glances at his watch. "It's not too late. I might see if anyone is around and begin doing the tests one at a time, tonight and tomorrow."

"Terrific," I say. "By the way, did you get the sleeping pills from Celeste's cabin?"

"Yes. I have the bottle and the remaining pills. Doctor Garcia bagged and tagged them. They'll go to the authorities with everything else."

"It's a shame we won't know if there's any trace of a foreign substance until well after we dock," I say.

"What's the captain's official stance on all this?" John selects a book from the shelf and thumbs through it, as if distracted.

"His powers are far-reaching in these types of cases. He's got the power to stop disembarkation from the ship and to prevent the planes leaving Baltra with any of the passengers from this expedition."

"At least that's something. But we can't hang around for weeks while forensics do their job." My previous sense of hope fades.

"Stranger things can happen." John returns the book to its place. "You never know. The murderer might confess."

"Very funny," I say, with a derisive grin.

"It's true." John becomes serious. "The end game comes down to who's left standing. Sometimes, murderers simply want revenge and recognition. They want to be credited with doing what they think was justified, and they want the world to know."

"A savior syndrome," I say. "They believe by getting rid of the person, they're saving the world, so to speak."

"Yes. And if this is pre-meditated murder, as we suspect, and if revenge is at the root of it, the murderer may want to shout his or her success from the proverbial rooftops."

"We can only hope." Patrizio sounds disheartened. "If we don't get some serious leads soon, this is going to turn very ugly for the cruise line, and for the passengers who'll get caught in the formal protocol."

"Hang in there, Patrizio. We've only just started, and we've still got over two days before we reach Baltra." John's voice is upbeat, as he strolls to another bookshelf and rifles through the books.

"You're the detective. I hope you're right." Patrizio bundles up his notebook and folder, bids goodbye, and leaves to begin his handwriting tests.

"You know, Diana, despite anything I've said up to now, everything you've suspected, seen or heard has been critical to this case. Without you, I doubt we'd be this far in finding out what happened to Celeste and her jewelry."

"Thanks, but I agree with Patrizio. I don't think we're close at all. There are a lot of loose ends."

"When I was a rookie cop, I worked with a senior detective in homicide. Back then, I felt like you, as if we weren't getting anywhere, that there were too many loose ends. And you know what he used to say?" I shake my head. "Pull one loose thread and the rest will unravel, leaving you with an undistorted image."

"Won't that just leave you with nothing?"

"And nothing is the clear undistorted image of the obvious." He selects a book and opens it, giving me time to digest his words of police wisdom. He raises his head, pinning me in his gaze. "You have an eye for the obvious. Whatever your gut tells you, pull the thread." He circles back to the armchair and gets comfortable with his book. "You may find reading poetry clears your mind, but I like reading books on mechanics and engines. Helps me fit the pieces of a case together." He holds up the book on marine engineering he found on the shelf.

"I'll leave you to it." Closing the lid on my laptop, I consider whether to share my hunches with him. After all, he is a detective and far more experienced in crime investigation than me. But I want to solve this. I want to prove that I still have value and a purpose now that Tom's dead. "This wasn't how this trip was supposed to turn out," I say out loud, more for myself than him. "I was supposed to come away, throw Tom's ashes to the wind, and prepare for my new life."

His eyes lift slowly. "And you're doing just that." He shares an intimate smile with me before returning to his book.

Without another word, I tuck my laptop under my arm and leave him to his solitude.

★ ★ ★

THE CLANGING OF THE ANCHOR chain wakes me from a surprisingly good night's sleep. Overnight, we've traveled from Floreana to the eastern side of Santa Cruz island, leaving behind the sharks and the place where Celeste's body was found. I scramble out of bed and check the day's itinerary. This morning's excursion promises a long hike at Cerro Dragon, named after the masses of land iguanas which populate the area. "At least they're not smelly." My nose twitches at the memory of the marine iguanas from a few days before.

Shrugging on my fluffy robe, I wander to the sliding doors and draw open the curtains. The day sparkles jewel-bright with a cloudless sky, and because the ship's anchored close to land, the waters are calm and glassy. *Good, no seasickness pills required.* For a moment, I wonder what John's got planned for the morning and how Patrizio got on with his handwriting tests. But why think about them? Why not follow my own leads?

"Good morning and welcome to Santa Cruz, everyone. The excursion to Cerro Dragon departs shortly. Please muster in the Explorer Room in one hour if you want to experience some of the island's unique wildlife."

Israel's morning call is my cue. Inspired, I strip off and leaving a trail of clothes behind me, march to the en suite.

★ ★ ★

BY THE LOOK OF IT, every one of the hundred passengers musters in the Explorer Room ready for the excursion. Except of course, for one—Celeste.

Amid the milieu, I can't see any of the Constanzos, but I spy Agents Sullivan and Mackenzie in a couple of seats at the back, guffawing in their brash Pinkerton fashion. I suppress a smile. Damn fine undercover agents. I follow their sightline to Angelo sitting mutely beside Rose. With the expression of a thundercloud, she looks ready to rain down on anyone who gets too close. The poor woman has no idea what's going on with her traitorous husband and the FBI. She's caught in a trap she doesn't know exists. The same as Joey, but I've no sympathy for him.

My gaze moves to a circular table in a corner booth, where Tony seems intent on the person beside him, though they act circumspectly. This is my chance. I glide across the room and in less than a minute, stand in front of them, smiling my sweetest, motherly smile.

"Good morning, Tony, Jason. How are you this fine day?" A little theatrical, but I think I carry it off well.

Jason visibly recoils while Tony flinches only slightly. "Hello, Diana. We're fine, thanks."

My ears prick to Tony's polite reply in the plural. "Do you mind if I join you?" Before either object, I squeeze in next to Jason, trapping him in the middle. "I assume you're both doing the Cerro Dragon excursion?" Obvious question.

"Ah, yes, we are." Tony fidgets.

Now or never. I reach across and pat Tony's forearm. "I'm so sorry about your stepmother." He mumbles a thanks. "She was a lovely woman. It's all very tragic." I know I've said too much and overstepped my position in the investigation, but I need to follow my hunch.

Jason's head swivels to Tony and back to me. "What do you mean?"

"Oh, didn't Tony tell you?" My voice is low and sympathetic. "The body found yesterday at Champion Islet was that of his stepmother, Celeste Constanzo."

Jason's face drops. He slumps back into the booth and a big breath escapes him. "But when you interviewed me, you said she was missing."

"She was. Unfortunately, she was then found, dead." I emphasize the last word to give it finality.

"Oh, that's terrible." The words tumble from Jason's mouth.

Tony and I watch the color drain from his face. "Are you okay?" Tony asks, but Jason remains mute. "Jason, are you okay?"

"That's so sad. I'm sorry for your loss." He chokes on the words and grabs Tony in a hug.

Obviously uncomfortable with the public display, Tony unravels Jason's arms while checking the room to see if anyone saw it. "Thanks. Celeste's death was a terrible shock. Despite what my brother or sister say about her, she tried her best to be a good mom."

"Really?" Jason pushes his glasses up the bridge of his nose.

"Yes. She was always there for me. Out of everyone she understood."

I tilt my head and regard Tony closely.

He pauses, mirroring my expression while Jason sits between us, a confused expression growing on his face.

Not breaking eye contact with Tony, I say, "It's not a curse, you know. Don't you think the time's come?"

Jason's frown deepens. "Time's come for what?"

"It's been *my* curse. My terrible secret. Why now? Why here?" By the sound of his voice, Tony wavers on an emotional brink. He's spent all his life hiding the truth about himself and the thought of exposure terrifies him.

"Because I overheard you tell Rose, that it was time to be who you really are. Right now, is as good a time as any."

He huffs out a breath and narrows his gaze on Jason. I sense he's running scenarios in his mind, trying to pick the best approach. In the end, he opts for honesty. "I'm gay, Jason. I'm sorry I didn't say anything sooner, but since meeting you, I've enjoyed your company a lot. I didn't want to ruin a new friendship by you thinking I was hitting on you, so I just didn't say anything."

Jason's face opens into a wide, relieved grin. The first genuine smile I've seen on his face since meeting him. "Is that why you were so stand-offish on the zodiak cruise to the red mangroves on Tuesday afternoon?"

"Yes. We got on so well at lunch, that I thought I'd come on too strong. I just clammed up. Sorry. But being 'out there' is not something I'm good at."

"Don't worry about it." Jason nudges him in the ribs. "It took me a while to get the hang of it too." The expression on his face illuminates our table.

"Really?" Tony straightens, matching Jason's glow.

"Really."

Having faded into the background, I watch the two young men chat about their awkward experiences about finding themselves and each other. An enriching experience, but not the ultimate reason I joined them. "May I suggest something?"

"Of course. You seem to be full of good ideas." Tony winks at Jason.

"Why don't you tell Jason a little more about Celeste? I think he has a sympathetic ear and would like to hear about the woman who helped you overcome, what you call, your curse."

Tony smiles, obviously liking the idea, while Jason's eyes glint with fear. I acknowledge his dread with a soft touch to his forearm. "As I said when we first met, Jason, you remind me of my stepbrother. You're a young man who feels deeply because you've been disenfranchised."

He pulls a face. "You also warned me not to lose my way."

"A warning you chose not to heed." It's more a question than a fact. He replies with a slow, deliberate nod. "Perhaps this time, you'll take my advice."

"Thank you, Mrs. Daniels—"

"Diana," I remind him. "Now listen to Tony's stories. I think they'll help."

Slipping out from their table, I know I've solved one crime. Only three to go.

CHAPTER TWENTY

A FAMILIAR HAND CUPS MY elbow and steers me across the Explorer Room to the port side door. "Good morning, I see you're hard at it." Derek's warm breath tickles my ear.

I exchange his smile with one of my own. "Good morning."

"How did your meeting go last night?" He ushers me outside onto the narrow external passageway of the ship.

"Very well, thank you. And your nightcap?" Standing beside him, I fix my gaze on the horizon.

He edges in closer in a conspiratorial manner. "I didn't return to my cabin. I went in search of the Blum sisters."

I face him, surprised and delighted. "Really?"

"I found the dears in the piano bar, playing cards. I offered to get them a round of drinks and they dealt me into their poker game."

"You cunning wolf. And?"

"I lost, of course. Those two are card sharks. Took my last five dollars."

I laugh. "That doesn't surprise me one bit. Go on."

"Well, they told me all about their jewelry business in L.A., and how they've supplied some spectacular pieces to celebrities and stars."

"Did they mention Celeste?"

"Nothing about her personally, but they puffed up like miniature bullfrogs over the jewelry Celeste wore at the Captain's cocktail party and gloated how they'd sold it to her husband, Joe. I then informed them that I was in the market for a piece like that, and their eyes lit up like fire rubies. I swear those two are the devil's spawn."

"Don't be silly. Go on."

"They intimated they could arrange to sell that exact necklace and earrings to me for the right price."

"Really?"

"They conditioned the sale by saying it couldn't be finalized for a few more days. I gave them my card and told them to call me once they were ready." His face breaks into a proud grin. "Does that help?"

"It does." My mind works overtime, fitting another piece into the puzzle. "If you'll excuse me, I need to check up on a couple of things in my cabin. Thanks for the info. See you later." I cast him a grateful smile before leaving him neglected and alone on the deck.

When I open my laptop, the email I've been waiting for from Harrison pings in my inbox. I read its contents and cross-check it with my notes and files. *Excellent!* My son's connections have paid dividends. Crouched over my notebook, I jot down the sequence of events until I've mapped out what I think is a reasonable conclusion. But it needs to be conclusive, not just reasonable. A sharp *rat-tat-tat* at my cabin door interrupts my train of thought.

John and Patrizio hover in the passageway, both wearing serious expressions.

"Agents Sullivan and MacKenzie have asked to see us in the library," John says.

"Right. I'll grab my things." I rush back inside and collect my laptop, notebook, and files. The three of us march down the passageway side by side in silence, like patrolling troops. When we come to Celeste's cabin, we instinctively slow down to pay our respects before striding off to complete our mission.

"Thanks for coming so quickly," Agent Sullivan says. After brief hellos, we take our seats, and he continues, "Since our meeting yesterday, we spoke to Robert Sawyer about his suspicions that Joey had something to do with his father's death."

"And?" A chill scampers up my spine.

"It doesn't fit as neatly as Mr. Sawyer implied," Agent MacKenzie says.

"Go on," John says.

"We spoke to the private investigator that Mr. Sawyer hired to keep an eye on Joey. His name's O'Rourke. He says he's got some solid evidence that Joey *is* culpable in a man's death, but it wasn't Joe's. It was another man who owed Joey money."

"But why would Robert say he thought Joey was involved in Joe's death?" Patrizio asks.

"Grandstanding in the hope of getting Joey arrested." Agent Sullivan snorts and crimps his lips. "After speaking to O'Rourke, we questioned Mr. Sawyer who then admitted to overstating Joey's involvement in the old man's death. But as far as he was concerned, Joey was guilty of someone's death, and Joe's was as good as any."

"The classic battle of the male of the species—the interloper does whatever it takes to topple the dominant male, so he can claim the female. In this circumstance Robert embroiders his story, hoping to convince Clare of his suitability to be her new mate," I say.

"Got it in one. Boys will be boys." Agent MacKenzie's comment is met by a couple of raised male eyebrows, which she ignores. "It seems the local police have O'Rourke's statement and photographs. Robert told the truth when he said the police were working on O'Rourke's evidence. They're in the process of building a case against Joey for the man's death."

"Will they arrest Joey when he returns to the States?" I ask.

"Not likely at this stage," Agent Sullivan says. "That was wishful thinking on Mr. Sawyer's behalf. He'd hoped to get Joey out of the picture as soon as possible to safeguard Clare. In some ways, his motives were in the right place, but his methods weren't. We've put his mind at rest about Joey returning home with Clare though."

"How so?" John asks.

"By the look of things, our case will be strong enough to arrest Joey the moment he steps back on U.S. soil. He can cool his heels with us for a while, which will give the local boys a chance to build their murder case."

I repeat what Angelo said. "Joey will get what he deserves."

"It looks like it." Agent Sullivan seems rightfully pleased with himself.

"But where does that leave us with Mrs. Constanzo's death?" Patrizio asks.

Agent Sullivan shrugs. "Sorry, we can't help you with that."

"Based on what you've found out, do you think Robert's an unreliable witness?" John eyeballs the agents in turn.

"No, I don't think so. Why?" Agent MacKenzie asks.

"Because he told us he saw Joey coming out of Celeste's cabin at around one o'clock Monday morning."

Agent Sullivan's eyes cast upward. "You got any corroborating evidence it was him?"

"Only Joey's clothes which Robert said he saw him wearing. Those clothes match what the person wore who left me a threatening letter at my cabin," I say.

"That sort of reckless behavior sounds like something Joey would do. He flies off the handle now and again like that; sends incriminating emails, has unguarded conversations, or verbally threatens people. It fits Joey's M.O.," Agent MacKenzie says.

Agent Sullivan agrees and shares some examples from their investigation into Joey's case.

"Right." John claps his hands as if satisfied. "Unless you've got anything else, I think that covers it."

"Thanks for your time. We'll get back to keeping an eye on Angelo and Joey and leave you to it." After more handshaking, the agents depart, and Patrizio sinks in his chair.

"What happened with the restaurant staff?" John asks him.

"When I called them for a meeting to arrange a line-up, Edwardo, the waiter you spoke to . . ." —he glances at me— ". . . admitted he hadn't seen Celeste at lunchtime."

"What? Why would he say he did?" I ask.

Patrizio shakes his head. "He's trained to say yes to guest's requests. He got scared about dropping his tray and making a scene. So, he just said yes in the hope you'd let go of his arm." Patrizio shrugs and looks defeated.

John chuckles and shoots me a glance. "You certainly have an effect on people."

"Be quiet," I scold.

Sounding like a football coach rallying his players, John redirects to Patrizio. "How did you go with the handwriting tests, then?"

Patrizio pulls on a pair of plastic gloves and fumbles out pieces of paper from an envelope. "Here are the original letters left for Mrs. Constanzo and Mrs. Daniels." He lines up the letters across the top edge of the table. "I was able to only get four handwriting and folding tests so far. Each written with the person's dominant and less dominant hands." While he recites the names, he places the sample letters in front of us under the corresponding original. "Clare Constanzo."

John and I study the samples. "Nothing matches there at all," he says. I agree.

"Rose Constanzo." Patrizio lays out her samples, which we reject. "Tony Constanzo." Nothing. "Joey Constanzo."

When Patrizio opens the folded pieces of paper and places them beneath the original letters, John and I grin.

"Well, look at that," John says. "There seems to be a match of sorts." He points to a couple of loops and swirls in the sample made by Joey's less dominant hand. "It's harder to disguise how your less dominant hand writes compared to your dominant."

"And Joey's the only one who folded his samples neatly in three crease lines." I indicate the obvious difference between the letter samples. "I knew it was him. He all but admitted it yesterday, still threatening me to stay out of his business. Arrogant . . ." Two sets of eyes train on me.

"Arrogant what?" John teases.

"Arrogant prick. I'll sort him out."

"I'm sure you will." He chuckles. "I bet Agents Sullivan and MacKenzie, and the local police working the murder case would appreciate this information. Another strike against Joey Constanzo."

"Perhaps Clare will get her wish to be free of him, sooner than she expected." For her sake and her children's, I hope this will be the case.

"But we still don't have any matches to Celeste's letters yet," Patrizio says.

"You'll find them." John claps the head of security on his shoulder. "We're one step closer."

But I already knew.

"If it's all right with you, I'd like to pop back to my cabin and finish what I was working on." I gather my things.

John inclines his head. "What is it?"

"Nothing really. I'm mapping out the sequence of events and who fits where." I try for a nonchalant tone, but I think my inner excitement betrays me.

John's hand moves up and down. "Sit down and spill it."

I huff but obey. "I think I've worked out how this fits together, except there's one piece missing."

"Go on."

"I think Jimmy is the key." They frown. "Jimmy knows something, I'm sure of it. But I need to lead him to what he knows."

"And you think whatever that is, will solve Celeste's death and the missing jewelry."

I nod. "It's the final piece."

"*Final* piece," John says, surprised.

"I think so." I purse my lips unwilling to say more.

"Do you have more than your hunches to back you up?"

"I do. But a lot of it's circumstantial." I wince, hoping it'll be enough.

John waves a dismissive hand. "What are you waiting for? Go find Jimmy."

★ ★ ★

BY THE TIME JIMMY ARRIVES, another two hours have passed. But it's given me time to crystallize my thoughts. He stands at attention in my cabin, a panicked expression on his face.

"There's nothing to be afraid of, Jimmy. I just want to ask you a couple more questions. Please sit down."

Reluctantly, he perches next to me on the sofa. "But I've already told you everything I remember about Mrs. Constanzo."

"But I think there's something you witnessed that you don't realize is connected with Celeste." I speak in a gentle, reassuring voice, about his job, his responsibilities and duties, his rostered hours, and other professional topics which aren't emotionally charged. After a few minutes of easy conversation, he relaxes. "Tell me about any unusual guest requests you've had on this trip?"

"I can't divulge their names, but there's a couple on deck four who have late-night requests for whipped cream, fruit yogurt, or ice-cream." He hints at the sexual inference with a naughty smirk.

"Oh, I see." I raise my eyebrows. "And how often have they made these requests?"

"Not every night, but—" Suddenly, his mouth slackens, and his eyes widen. Recognition floods across his face, and he lapses into silence.

"Go on. What is it?" I whisper.

He swivels to me, a vacant expression on his face. "Oh, Mrs. Daniels . . ."

"It's all right, you can tell me."

And he does.

★ ★ ★

THE LUNCHTIME RUSH ON DECK five is in full swing by the time I get there. I study the staff, trying to understand the systems they employ to deliver their quality service. The wait staff drift in and out behind the counter while serving and kitchen staff remain behind it. A hand-held bell is rung whenever meals are placed on the 'pass,' a small section of counter space next to the coffee machine, waiting for collection. The perfect time someone could go unnoticed and tamper with the meals. The coffee machine acts as a cover, of sorts, giving someone just enough time to slip something into a meal resting on the 'pass.' I analyze the system for another ten minutes or so, until the service lulls. Paulette, the maître D, is on duty so I stroll over.

"Second last day before we disembark." I smile. "Looks like everyone is up here taking advantage of the beautiful weather and food."

"Yes, it's busy today." She watches the staff go about their duties while talking to me.

"Are the staff the same today as yesterday?"

"Yes, they work the lunchtime roster here for the entire expedition. Then change over on the next cruise." She casts me a sideways glance tinged with curiosity.

"Do any of the crew ever come up here during lunch?"

"They're not allowed in the guest areas, particularly during service. Is there something wrong?" She faces me, concerned.

"No, no. Of course not. But when I came up yesterday afternoon after the lunch rush, I don't remember seeing you here."

"I finish at three o'clock so if it was after that, no, you wouldn't have seen me. We keep a skeleton staff on for late-lunches after three."

"Who was the skeleton staff working yesterday?" Although visibly unsettled by my questioning, she points out Louis, the chef, and two waiters, Ricardo and Manuel. "Ah, yes. Manuel served us. He's very good." I know complimenting her staff might alleviate some of her worry.

"Thank you. He and Ricardo do a fine job. If you'll excuse me." She manages a polite smile before dashing to another passenger whose cranky expression needs soothing.

I check my watch. Two o'clock and my rumbling tummy reminds me I didn't eat breakfast. May as well have lunch and wait until I can speak to the skeleton staff. I scan the deck for a seat. None. Nevertheless, I take my chances and help myself to the salad buffet, which never fails in freshness. With a plate piled high of colorful vegetables, I hover, waiting for someone to leave. On cue, I spot the Blum sisters readying themselves to vacate their table. Not only do I want the table, but I also want to quiz them about what they'd said to Derek. I weave between the other tables and chairs, hoping they won't leave before I get there. With a giggle, I remember what Derek said about them being the devil's spawn and true to his assessment, they swivel on my approach as if they've got eyes in the back of their heads.

"Oh, how lovely to see you," they say, their jewelry shimmering in the sunlight.

I place my plate on the table. "You too." I lean forward giving them both an air kiss to their proffered cheeks. "Would you like to stay for a few minutes?" I motion to the chairs, which they promptly reclaim. "If you'll excuse me, I haven't eaten yet."

"Oh, don't mind us, dear, you go ahead." Judy waves at the cutlery.

"Have you enjoyed your cruise?" I ask, before tucking into my lunch.

While I eat, they regale me with their stories of adventure to which I respond through mouthfuls of food. When I deposit my cutlery and signal the waiter to clear my plate, they lapse into silence.

After he leaves, Judy moves closer. "What's happened?"

"What do you mean?" *Here it comes.*

"All that searching of the ship yesterday. And then there's gossip about a body being found at Champion Islet. Do you know anything about it?" As much as they're gossip merchants of the highest order, I sense that Judy's curiosity is heightened by anxiety—or is it guilt?

"I don't rightly know." I speak with a not-so-subtle inference that I do know but I'm not at liberty to say.

Judy presses harder. "Go on, dear. You can tell us."

"I understand you've some jewelry to sell." I drop the question like a ten-ton weight. They recoil from the table, like startled fish caught on an outgoing tide, only to be drawn back in again by the current. My gaze nails each of them in demand of an answer.

"We don't know what you mean." Defiance rings in Nancy's voice, as she sits ruler-straight in the chair, her hands clenched in her lap.

I cock a brow at Judy, who hasn't recovered her poise as fast as her sister. "Go on, dear. You can tell me." I mimic what she just said to me with a cheeky twist of my lips.

She avoids my eyes.

In a gentler voice, I try to win them back. "I know all about your offer to the handsome Scotsman." They gape at me and try as they might, the thought of Derek brings a soft memory to their faces. Despite everything, they're lonely spinsters, who probably long for love, and Derek has pricked their hearts. *Understandable.* "Listen, ladies. I'm not going to ask you now, but there'll come a time very soon when you'll be required to tell the truth. All of it. Do you understand?"

"But we haven't done anything wrong?" Nancy sounds alarmed.

"I can't be the judge of that. But if you tell the truth, I'm sure everything will get sorted out. Can I count on you?"

They exchange worried looks. "Yes. We'll tell the truth," Judy says, while Nancy agrees with numerous nods.

"Good. Now promise me you won't speak to anyone about this conversation."

"We promise," they say.

"Enjoy the rest of today and wait for me to contact you. Okay?"

"Yes. Of course."

After saying our good-byes, I go through my mental checklist. The only thing left for me now is to talk to the staff. Hopefully, they'll fill in the last piece of the puzzle.

CHAPTER TWENTY-ONE

WITH LATE AFTERNOON CREEPING IN through the window, the light washes the library in an eerie glow before it diffuses through the spectrum to purple. We've spent hours in this room listening to people tell the truth, massage it for their own ends, and outright lie to protect their despicable actions. This room has been a safe haven for the innocent, while for the guilty, their undoing. And I'm certain, I've discovered who's who. Now, having spent an hour explaining my conclusions to John, we stare down at the wood grain table littered with my notes, papers, and charts.

"So that's it, John. What do you think?"

When he looks at me, I'm once more struck by what a handsome, gentle, good man he is. Sharon's a lucky woman. I hope they make it.

"I must say. I think you've nailed it." His face splits into his lopsided grin, and I exhale a breath of relief. He points to a couple of clues on the table. "That's clever work."

"Thanks." I think I blush.

"When do you want to do this?"

"What?"

"Get everyone together and expose them?"

"Me? I thought you'd take it from here since you're the detective."

He laughs. "Remember, I've no jurisdiction on a ship. And there's no way our dear friend Patrizio can get his head around this. You solved it. It's your 'collar.'"

"Really?" Inside me, a whirling dervish spins in ecstasy.

"I think it's only fair." He hesitates. "You're not scared, are you?"

"Hell, no. If I can deal with difficult CEOs, I can deal with a murderer, or two, if the need arises." I sound smug, but I don't care. I want my moment in the spotlight.

"Right." He claps his hands together. "Let's get Patrizio to gather everyone on your list—"

"Plus one." I hold up a finger.

"Okay, plus one, to meet in the Explorer Room tonight after dinner. Nine good for you?"

"Perfect."

* * *

A DIFFERENT ENERGY RESONATES IN the Explorer Room at night to when the passengers muster for the daily excursions. Like the atmosphere of a cinema before the movie feature starts, it's full of suspense and anticipation. Patrizio has done a terrific job setting the room to my wishes, arranging sixteen chairs around a group of three tables. Nathaniel has printed place cards with the attendees' names on them, which I've set with jugs of water and glasses.

I step back to view the finished product before everyone arrives and my stomach flutters like a trapped butterfly. In my mind, doubt rears its ugly head, but my gut tells me I'm right. The time for second-guessing is over. The knot in my shoulder twists, trying to get my attention, but I ignore it. The seasickness pill I took earlier, just to be safe, has kicked in. Primed in front of me is an adventure, at once surreal and deadly serious, waiting to unfold. A shiver of nervous excitement races over my body, and I glance at my watch. It's time. John walks in, looking crisp and smart dressed in his tan trousers, white shirt, and dark brown blazer.

He also wears a reassuring smile. "Ready?"

"Yes." My voice quavers slightly.

"Patrizio's got them waiting outside, and in the library as per your instructions. Including your plus one."

"Good. Send him in first, please."

John goes to the door and returns with Derek.

"John, this is Derek Stewart. Derek this is Detective John Nash from the Monterey County Sheriff's department." They follow my lead of formal introductions and shake hands.

Derek's eyes twinkle. "You figured it out then?"

"Yes, she did." John nods his head in my direction. "Her investigative work's been impressive." I lower my eyes in embarrassment, while Derek congratulates me.

"It was a team effort." I smile at Derek. "And since you were instrumental in helping me, I thought you might like to sit in."

"Yes, please. You know me and a good mystery." He winks, and I lead him to his chair furthest from the front, on one side of the table. "You won't be able to make any comments though." I angle him a look.

He mimes zipping his lips shut. "Not a word." He slides into his chair and waits like an obedient schoolboy.

I heave a breath and glance over my shoulder. My two surprise guests give me a 'thumbs-up' from their hiding spots. Then I call to John. "Okay, let's do this."

The first is Captain Rodriguez, in full dress naval uniform, who sits in the middle at the far end of the table, befitting his authority. Patrizio and John sit either side of me at the other head of the table. Amid murmurs and whispers, the others wander in. They mill around the table, reading the place cards and on finding their name, take their assigned chair. Once everyone settles, I breathe in, square my shoulders, and begin.

"Thank you for coming this evening—"

"We didn't get a choice." To John's right, Joey interjects in his trademark, ill-tempered tone.

Though my heart rate rockets, I'm not going to let him commandeer my meeting. "Let's get one thing clear from the start, that kind of behavior won't be tolerated, so either shut up or Patrizio will throw you in the brig." I nail him in a scathing stare, which he returns, but with his mouth shut.

"Good. Let's keep it that way . . . everyone." My stern gaze circumnavigates the startled faces around the table, sweeping finally past John, who suppresses a smile.

I adjust the lapels of my black blazer and resume. "As some of you may or may not know, Celeste Constanzo was officially deemed missing yesterday."

To my left, Nancy and Judy Blum gasp and clutch each other's hands. "Oh, dear," Nancy says.

"Shortly after, her body was discovered during the snorkeling-with-the-sharks excursion at Champion Islet."

"Oh, no." Judy claps her hand to her heart. She faces her sister and both women comfort each other with gentle cooing noises. Even from where I am, I notice their hands trembling. Nancy's backward glance over her shoulder tells of their horror at the news. *Good, I want them shaken.*

"Take your time. We'll wait," I say.

Joey rumbles a low growl, his eyes glued on the Blum sisters. In a flash, John reaches over, and tugs on his sleeve, like an owner pulling on the leash of a wayward dog to make it behave. It shifts Joey's attention and he obeys, teeth bared.

After the Blum sisters recover, I continue, "We've reason to believe that Celeste's death was not accidental. That in fact, it was murder, and that one of you seated here is the murderer."

Pandemonium breaks loose. Voices of shock, denial, and suspicion ride on the sideways glances aimed around the table. Only the captain, Patrizio, Derek, John and I remain silent, watching and waiting.

I clear my throat. "Before I expose the murderer." I pause for effect and heads swivel from side to side. "There are a couple of other details which need finalizing. I'll begin with the easiest and most obvious." I snap on a pair of plastic gloves and extract from the folder beside me, my two letters and Joey's handwriting tests. Laying them out carefully on the table, I explain, "Around two o'clock on Wednesday morning, I was woken by a sound. When I opened my cabin door, I found this letter" —I lift it up— "and saw someone running away down the passageway. It reads, 'This doesn't concern you. Mind your own business.'" I glimpse a muscle flinch in Joey's jaw. "Then, when I went on the Post-Office-Box excursion on Floreana Wednesday morning, I found another letter" —I raise the second one— "tucked inside my towel. It reads, 'I told you to mind your own business. You didn't. But you should have.'"

Clare, sitting directly across the table from her husband, stares daggers at him, which he deflects. I continue, "Patrizio has conducted handwriting and folding tests with each of you. From these, we've matched the author of these letters to Joey Constanzo."

While every pair of eyes glower at him, Joey launches from his seat. "What a load of crap. What the hell is going on in this tin-pot operation?"

John jumps up and shoves him back into his chair. "Sit down and shut up."

"Further to this, the person who left my first letter wore these clothes." Like a magician, I pull Joey's sweatpants and hoody from the plastic bag hidden at my feet.

"You bitch, what've you done?" Hurling expletives, Joey launches toward Clare, who pushes back onto her feet. John grapples him back into his chair while from the other end of the table, Robert springs up and runs to Clare's side.

But she shoves him away. With her gaze burning like the fires of hell, and hands clenched at her sides, she screams at her husband. "I'm through with you. You don't scare me anymore. You good-for-nothing piece of shit. Once I get a divorce, I'm testifying against you. I'm taking the children, and you're going to jail for the rest of your life." Her body trembles with rage, her face contorted and blazing red. When Robert reaches out to soothe her, she slaps his hand away. She whirls on him with a similar vengeance, and he skulks back to his seat. Clare's fury acts like a bombshell, distracting everyone from the entrance of my two surprise guests. By the time, they're positioned either side of the captain, a distinct chill fills the room.

"Thank you, Mrs. Constanzo. We'll definitely follow you up on that." Agent Sullivan's resonant voice rings with authority.

"But Mr. Constanzo will be arrested as soon as he returns to the States." Agent MacKenzie sounds as imposing as her partner. No longer dressed for their Pinkerton charade, they wear well-cut, dark suits, and look the epitome of FBI agents.

"Who the hell are you?" Joey asks, before John clips his shoulder.

"FBI Agents Sullivan and Mackenzie. We've been working undercover for some time building a criminal case against you, Mr. Constanzo."

Joey sneers amid more gasps and murmurs and raising of brows.

"You've got nothing on me." Venom infuses his words.

"Yes. They. Do." Angelo jumps to his feet and takes to the floor like the accomplished attorney he is. He orates his involvement in the case, and how delighted he is to bring down his corrupt brother-in-law.

Rose glares across the table at her husband, livid with his betrayal. She likewise screams her intention to divorce him, but Angelo dismisses her outburst as nothing more than another one of her crazy fits. Bemused, I watch the antics for a while, giving them leeway to vent before raising my voice and hands in protest. "Enough. You can sort out your family issues later. We've more important matters at hand."

With their gazes on Joey, the agents slip into their chairs either side of the captain. I suspect they want him to step out of line, so they can, at last, cuff him.

"Let's continue. Next, is the matter of the letters left for Celeste. Three letters, on three separate occasions." I finger them from my folder. "I was with Celeste on Sunday night after the Captain's cocktail party when we discovered this one in her mail slot. 'Bitch. You think you could keep this a secret. Well, you can't. And now you're going to pay.'" The Blum sisters shake their heads. "The second letter was left for Celeste on Monday evening. It reads, 'Time to own up to the secret, bitch. I'm here and you're going to pay." More head shaking, this time Clare and Robert join in. "And the third letter which appeared on Tuesday night, reads, 'Time's running out. I'll find you and make you pay for what you did. Bitch.'"

"Oh, that's horrible." Nancy tuts. "Who would write such terrible things about such a lovely lady?"

"Her son." My answer hits the table like a felled tree.

"What?" Tony asks.

"Her *real* son."

A prickly silence hangs in the air, but I want to give him the chance to reveal himself.

"I'm sorry. I shouldn't have done it. But . . ." Jason's apology drifts from the far end of the table. He slumps beside Derek, his head hung, avoiding everyone's gazes. Especially Tony's.

In a gentle voice, I ask him, "Do you want to tell the story, or should I?"

"You go ahead."

"Very well. When Celeste and I went back to her cabin after the Captain's cocktail party she explained to me how this trip was to celebrate her daughter's birthday, but that Emily couldn't make it. Celeste was disappointed because she'd planned to give Emily the exquisite necklace and earrings Joe had bought for her, from Blum's Jewelry in L.A." I glance at the sisters, who wait for my cue. *Not yet.* "Celeste was convinced her stepchildren were planning to kill her." I raise a brow at each of them, my opinion, clear. "She made me promise that if anything did happen to her, I was to give the jewelry, worth over five-million-dollars, to Emily on her behalf."

Jimmy whistles. "That's a lot of money."

"The piece is worth every cent, young man." Judy cold-shoulders him.

"Celeste air-dropped images of Emily to my phone with her contact details, just in case. At the time, I thought nothing more about it, but I did ask what the secret was that the letter alluded to. She said something about her past and making a mistake, but she didn't go further."

"But how did you connect Jason to Mrs. Constanzo as her son?" the captain asks.

"That came later. When I first met Jason, he denied knowing Celeste, even though he knew her last name. His vehement insistence on the matter reminded me of my young stepbrother. In my line of business, I've found that if a person reminds you of someone from your past, there's a message there. An insight into that person. I had my suspicions that Jason was stalking Celeste and leaving her the letters, but I didn't know why. Until the family resemblance hit me. Emily looks just like her mum, and so does Jason." I stare at him. "Glasses."

He removes his glasses, and a few others gasp. Staring back at us is Celeste's heart-shaped face framed by dark, chestnut hair, her wide-set, dark eyes, classic nose, and an expression of endearing naivety. So sad.

"When I confronted him about his obsession with Celeste, he denied it. Even when I caught him with photos of her he'd printed on the ship, he tried to fob us off by saying he thought she was a celebrity, and he was going to sell the photos to a gossip magazine or such. But I knew that wasn't it. Jason is Emily's twin brother and the son Celeste adopted out when she chose to only keep her daughter."

Pity escapes on a collective exhale and whispered laments.

"I'm sorry, I left those nasty letters," Jason says. "But I wanted her to know what she did to me, by giving me away. I grew up thinking my adoptive parents were my real parents. When I was fourteen, my father died in a car accident, leaving me to fend with a bitch, alcoholic mother. By the time I turned eighteen, I'd had enough. During one of our fights, she screamed that I wasn't even her son. That some slut by the name of Kovak was my real mother, and that she'd had twins, but only kept the girl and gave me away. I packed my bags and left. I never went back. From that day, I searched until I found Celeste Kovak, who'd become Celeste Constanzo."

"But how did you know she'd be on this cruise?" Tony asks, his expression clouded with confusion and disappointment.

"I used an app to keep tabs on every time the name Celeste Constanzo appeared online. It alerted with a news article in some magazine about her taking her daughter away for her thirtieth birthday on this cruise. I bought my passage, planning to confront her. I never meant to hurt her with the letters. I just wanted to get my own back. I'm so sorry. I wanted to meet my real mother, but I screwed it all up and now she's . . ." Jason dissolves into silence, his head in his hands.

"So, what? Who cares? I hope you don't think you can barge your way into our family?" Rose's voice is filled with spite. "You're not entitled to any money, you know."

"Rose, stop it." Tony turns on her. "Enough with the money."

"I doubt Jason was motivated by money," I say, softly. "More likely, it was a longing to be part of a family, with his biological mother and sister."

He nods but doesn't lift his face.

"Unfortunately, you've missed your chance with your mother. That's why I wanted you to listen to the stories about Celeste that Tony told you this morning. To hear she was a good woman, who tried her best. Perhaps over time, you'll learn to forgive her . . . and yourself."

I reach for my glass and drink a mouthful of water. While most of the others do the same, I make a mental note. Two down, two to go. "Now, we come to Celeste's jewelry. When she and I returned to her cabin after the cocktail party, she locked it away in her safe. We planned to take it to the captain the next morning for him to secure in the ship's safe. However, by the time we discovered Celeste was missing, the jewelry was gone. I knew that the Blum sisters had tried to buy it back from Celeste on this cruise, but she'd refused. So, who stole it? Was it taken by the murderer? Was it the motive for the crime?" Rigid expressions meet my inquiring gaze.

"We didn't steal it." Judy's voice echoes with distress.

"But you have it, don't you?" I ask.

A short pause fills the room. "Yes, we do. We bought it fair and square," Nancy says.

"But who did the exchange?"

The Blum sisters point across the table. "He did."

Before Joey has a chance to object, John stands, as do Agents Sullivan and MacKenzie. Defeated, Joey huffs and says nothing.

"Go on." I open the floor to the Blum sisters.

"He came to us Monday morning with the jewelry," Nancy explains.

"He said Celeste changed her mind and that she was willing to sell it back to us,' Judy says.

"He said she only wanted four million dollars for it."

"We jumped at the chance." Judy nods at her sister, who agrees.

"When we arranged for the transfer of money, Joey told us not to say anything to Celeste if we saw her as she was upset at having to sell her jewelry, but she needed the money. We agreed not to speak to her about it. We didn't want to upset her, her being a widow and all."

I glimpse Derek mouth "six-six-six" and suppress a smile. "Just for the record, how did you get the jewelry, Joey?"

"Exactly as they said." He cocks his head in the sisters' direction across the table.

"You're saying that after everything Celeste told me about gifting the jewelry to Emily, that she decided to have you play the intermediary and sell it back to the Blum sisters for one million dollars less than its market value?"

Sniggers rise like sparks from a fire.

"That's a lie," Robert shouts across the table from the other end. "I saw you break into Celeste's cabin at about one o'clock Monday morning and come out not long afterward. Don't try to deny it. I saw your face. And those clothes" —he points to the sweatpants and hoody— "were the clothes you wore. I'd swear it in a court of law." He folds his arms and snarls. "You're going down, Constanzo."

"Are you seriously going to believe the addled imaginings of two dementia sufferers, and the lies of the man obviously screwing my wife." Joey barks a strident laugh. Gone is his ranting and raving, replaced instead by a talkative, elated mood. I double-check the signs. He's jumpy and on edge, his self-confidence even more elevated, and he's abnormally upbeat, considering the severity of the circumstances. A manic episode. I suspect his lawyer will plead mental incapacity when he finally gets his day in court.

I continue, "At this stage, it appears that the Blum sisters are telling the truth. Patrizio will recover the jewelry from them tonight and lock it in the ship's safe. I'm sure the FBI will trace the account into which they deposited the four million dollars and find it's yours, and not Celeste's. You misled the Blum sisters into coming on this cruise with the promise of buying back Celeste's jewelry, when all along you intended to steal it, sell it to them and abscond with the money."

"Pay-back." He snorts. "For taking my rightful inheritance."

"But what about our money?" Misery bleaches Nancy's face.

"Don't worry, Ms. Blum," Agent MacKenzie says. "We'll make sure your money is returned to you, once we get the evidence to prove Joey sold it to you under false pretenses."

The Blum sisters sigh with relief, while Joey sulks in silence.

"By the way, Joey, didn't Celeste wake up when you went into her cabin?" Like a black widow spider, I lure him into my trap.

"No. She was aslee—" *Bingo!* He clamps his mouth shut and rolls his eyes at his own stupidity.

"You're almost right. She didn't wake up because she'd been drugged with a heavy sleeping sedative substituted for her sleeping pills." Though we couldn't prove this yet, John agreed I should present it as if it's true.

"I didn't do it."

"We know that. You did a lot of other terrible things, but surprisingly enough, you didn't kill Celeste, although you threatened to do so."

"I stood up for you, Joey. I knew you didn't do it." Rose sounds like an infatuated cheerleader.

"Shut up, Rose."

She recoils like a timid child. *So much abuse.*

I indicate to my right. "The Butler Manager" —I then indicate to my left— "and the deck four butler, have provided us with first-hand accounts of Celeste's whereabouts during those first days on board. Bruno advised that Celeste called him on Sunday night around midnight for some seasickness pills. This would've been about an hour before you" —I nod at Joey— "broke into her cabin. Then Bruno said he tended to Celeste for the next couple of days while she was unwell. Is that correct, Bruno?"

"Yes, Mrs. Daniels. That's correct."

"But there's one thing I don't understand. Why did Celeste ask for seasickness pills?" I arch a brow at him, and all eyes turn to Bruno.

"Because she said she was feeling seasick."

"But how can that be? When I first met Celeste, she informed me how much she and Emily enjoyed cruising and that they often took shipboard holidays together. I ask you again, are you sure Celeste called you for seasickness pills."

"Yes." Like the aperture of a lens, Bruno's eyes widen and then retract.

"I put it to you that Celeste didn't call you at all. That while the cocktail party was underway, you left unnoticed and slipped into Celeste's cabin and substituted powerful sedatives for her sleeping pills. After I left her cabin, you gave her enough time to prepare for bed, take a pill, and fall into a deep, drugged sleep. At around midnight, you entered her cabin and made sure she didn't wake. If she wasn't already dead, you probably smothered her. An easy thing to do to someone who is heavily sedated." Sharp inhales and shocked murmurs swirl around the table. "Your timing couldn't have been better, because you were gone before Joey turned up to steal the jewelry."

"Some guys have all the luck," Joey murmurs.

"This is preposterous," Bruno says. "Why on earth would I want to harm Mrs. Constanzo?"

I ignore his question. "Celeste lay dead in her bed while you hung the do-not-disturb sign on her cabin door, where it stayed all day Monday. But when I questioned you directly on Tuesday morning, by lunchtime you'd removed it. You advised me Celeste was feeling better and was taking lunch. You had me running around on a wild goose chase trying to find her until I returned to her cabin to find the sign back on the door. You continued to engineer this charade of Celeste's illness until the ship cruised into shark-infested waters. Then in the early hours of Wednesday morning, somewhere between Isabela and Floreana Islands, and between one o'clock and two o'clock, you hauled Celeste's body from her bed and threw her overboard, hoping the sharks would make short work of her, and that her disappearance would be deemed as an accident or suicide."

"Mrs. Daniels, I must respectfully say this is nonsense." Bruno's professional demeanor doesn't budge, but I forge on.

"We have a witness who places you coming out of Celeste's cabin during those hours Wednesday morning." *There it is.* The first hint of disturbance with a twitch to his left eye. That's what I need. "Jimmy had been summoned by some guests on deck four and he remembers seeing you coming out of Celeste's cabin. He thought nothing of it, but on further consideration, he remembered you were perspiring and looked uncharacteristically anxious."

I purposely placed Bruno directly across from Jimmy on the table, and as hoped, he sends his underling a quick, contemptuous glance.

"I can't see how any of this implicates me in the disappearance of Mrs. Constanzo. It's all conjecture."

John leans forward, his hard-edged stare landing squarely on Bruno. "I thought as much when I first heard it until Diana found the motive for the murder." Everyone fidgets and mumbles. "You should hear her out."

"On Monday night, Clare confided in me the sad history of Joey, Rose, and Tony's mother, Maria. How she suffered from mental health issues and how cruel Joe had been to her." My gaze sweeps from Joey to Rose to Tony, and I notice them prickle at the mention of this unhappy time. "She explained how Joe had your mother committed to All Saints State Hospital, a psychiatric institution, where she subsequently died not long after. And that at Maria's funeral, Joe didn't even speak to her brother, Nino, who came all the way from Sicily for his sister's burial."

Joey, Rose, and Tony turn to their right and squint. With deep frowns knitting their foreheads, they each stare intently at Bruno's grim expression.

"But this isn't Uncle Nino," Joey says.

"No, it's not. It's your mother's younger brother, Bruno Bellassai."

"Are you kidding me?" Joey slaps his palm on the table, while Tony and Rose ogle their unknown uncle.

"I'll explain, unless you'd like to, Bruno?" With loathing in his eyes, his gaze on me doesn't falter, his mouth a grim line. "Very well then. First, the history of your mother's family. It seems there were three children in the Bellassai family. Nino and Maria, who were born close together and Bruno who came along much later. When Maria immigrated to America, she married Joe. She kept her family back home a secret because the men were part of the Sicilian mafia. She wanted her three children to be brought up without the violent ways of the past. However, she unwittingly married into the American mafia. After the domestic abuse she suffered at the hands of Joe, and when her health declined, she contacted her brothers and told them what she was going through. Before they had a chance to rescue her, she was institutionalized and died. Nino attended the funeral, but Bruno remained a ghost to the Constanzo's. No one knew he existed or what he looked like. I suspect, the brothers swore revenge for their sister but bade their time. When Nino died a year ago, Bruno who no longer had any family, decided now was the time to avenge his sister."

"It's an entertaining story, but you have no proof," Bruno says.

I wave Harrison's email in the air. "My son is a medical doctor in psychiatry and has obtained the hospital records proving Maria Bellassai was committed to All Saint State Hospital. The records also indicate that she often referred to her brothers Nino and Bruno Bellassai, who lived in Sicily and would one day come and save her."

Bruno snorts a dismissive sound.

"When my husband booked this cruise, we'd originally been allocated to cabin 430. However, when I arrived, I was allocated cabin 420. It was you, Bruno, who told me you had switched the cabins as a favor to me during my bereavement." I glare at him and he returns with a haughty look. "You switched cabins because you knew the CCTV camera in the section of deck four outside cabin 430, was faulty. You'd broken it on purpose during the last cruise and stolen the replacement camera before we embarked on this cruise. Without footage, you thought you could get away with tossing Celeste overboard." The fuzzy edge of panic frays my nerves. By now I hoped his veneer would've cracked. Even a little. But then, why would it? He's Sicilian mafia. What the hell am I doing?

"As I said, Mrs. Daniels, you've no proof to support your outrageous claims." His mocking grin riles me.

I press further. "It was you, who the deck-five wait staff saw yesterday afternoon, loitering around the 'pass.' No crew are allowed in the guest areas and yet you were seen there by two staff at that time. You poisoned one of our meals as a warning not to pursue this case."

I hesitate, stalling for time, my eyes locked on his. *Keep alert for what you've seen or heard before. The Galapagos Affair.* The Baroness and her two lovers, and the Ritters. What did Margaret Wittmer say? A closed mouth admits no flies. I need to pry open Bruno's mouth.

"You and Nino failed Maria. You know that, don't you? When she left Sicily to start a new life, you disowned her, didn't you?"

A glint of rage reflects in his dark eyes. I've hit a nerve, so I push harder. "Poor Maria traveled to America, only to fall into the clutches of Joe Constanzo. When she called Nino for help, he refused. Then she called you and you refused her, your older sister." My voice drips with judgment. "Maria asked for forgiveness, but you and Nino made her suffer. You told her it was her own fault. You and your cruel, traditional ways crushed her spirit. But that's what you intended." As a flush of rage creeps over his face, I drill deeper. "You thought that if you refused your help long enough, she'd return to Sicily. But how could she? Joe was her jailer. Finally, when she couldn't take it any longer, Maria died. Alone, unloved, and excluded from both her families." I sneer. Waving my arm in the air, I orate the last sentences with fervor. "Nino didn't come to Maria's funeral to pay his respects. He came to absolve himself of his guilt for what he'd done."

"How dare you." The accusation rumbles low and deep. "Who are you to lecture me on honor? Nino was weak. He had the chance to kill Joe after the funeral, but he didn't. But when Nino died, it fell to me to avenge my sister's death. I killed Joe Constanzo. And I killed that slut of a wife of his." No one moves. "I'm proud that I avenged my sister's death. Maria, God bless her soul, can at last, rest in peace." Like an heir apparent, Bruno places his palms on the table, raises his chin high, and waits as if to be crowned.

The energy in the Explorer Room bounces off the walls in sizzling silence.

Captain Rodriguez scrapes back his chair and stands. "As captain of the *Silver Galapagos* Expedition ship, I'm placing you, Bruno Bellassai, under ship arrest for the murder of Celeste Constanzo. Patrizio, take him to the brig."

"Yes, Captain." Patrizio marches over to Bruno, who presents his hands in front of him to be cuffed.

In his immaculate three-piece suit and exuding an almost ethereal manner, it's difficult to believe Bruno is a cold-blooded murderer. "I've avenged my sister and the Bellassai name. My work is done."

CHAPTER TWENTY-TWO

AFTER PATRIZIO ESCORTS BRUNO OUT, the Explorer Room erupts into garbled conversations. The captain raps his knuckles on the table and calls the room to order. "Congratulations, Mrs. Daniels. Excellent job." Joey grunts his disapproval. "But how did Bruno know that Mrs. Constanzo would be on board this ship for this particular cruise?"

"There were a couple of things he said in his interview, which I asked Patrizio to cross-check with company records. Bruno's worked for Silversea for some years on their Mediterranean cruises. Knowing the Sicilian mafia, he could have been using his position as cover for running drugs to various ports. A few kilos here and there on every cruise adds up to a tidy sum. It was during this time that Joe and Celeste happened to travel on one of those cruises. I suspect that when Bruno saw their names on the manifest, he wanted to dispose of them then and there, but had no opportunity. Instead he started to hatch an elaborate plan for revenge. Perhaps he convinced Celeste that she and Joe should cruise on the *Silver Galapagos* sometime in the future. He may have even included their names on the company's mailing list for this particular cruise. He then requested and received a transfer to this ship and waited, hoping that his victims, who were avid cruise travelers, would come on this cruise. A long shot, but hate is a powerful fuel. I'm sure the police will discover more during their investigation. But Bruno got sick of waiting, took matters into his own hands and killed Joe six weeks ago. Obviously, it was Bruno who gave Joe some help in falling off his building.

Then, when Bruno saw Celeste's name on the manifest for this cruise, he probably couldn't believe his luck and set his second murderous plan into action."

"Oh, my, what a horrible man." Judy's hand flutters at her throat.

"Cursed. Both sides of the family are cursed," Tony says, in a despondent voice.

"No. Not cursed. Criminal." It's time for him to face the truth.

Shouts and screams echo from outside. A siren wails and the captain's face whitens. "Man overboard."

I trade a horrified look with John.

We hightail it out onto the port side deck, where crew and passengers hang over the railing. People point and yell while spotlights rake the waters in wide sweeping arcs. I can hear the ship's engines slowing, but it's too late. Searching the faces around me, I glimpse Patrizio standing twenty meters to our left. I grab John's hand and we push through the crowds.

Patrizio looks dazed and incredulous. "He just grabbed the railing and threw himself over the side. He was so fast, so strong. I couldn't stop him."

John pats his shoulder. "It's not your fault."

"When he hit the water, he put his hands in the air and just sank, like a stone. He wanted to drown."

"He said his work was done," I say. "Bruno's got no family; he avenged his sister and the family name. He ended it his way, with honor."

The three of us watch the spotlights sweep the watery blackness, but we know it's no use. He's gone.

"Come on. We still have work to do," John says. "You need to put Joey in the brig for stealing the jewelry, and we need to get it back from the Blums."

Patrizio sighs. "I hope Joey hasn't run off somewhere."

"He hasn't. I saw Agent Sullivan slap his big paw on him when this commotion started. I doubt the agents will let him out of their sight any time soon." John claps his hands together one last time, and we follow him back inside.

★ ★ ★

FRIDAY'S EXCURSION PROVES TO BE a fitting end to the expedition cruise. The giant, age-old land tortoises at the Tortoise Ecological Reserve in the Santa Cruz Highlands are living, pre-historic proof of the fragility and uniqueness of the Galapagos Islands. Inspired by the reserve's lush green forest, I linger on the edge of one of the groups, gawking at the majestic creatures. I've seen them on television before, but the enormity of their size and the effort required of them to move, doesn't translate to the screen. Like miniature tanks, they lumber and labor, their genteel souls hidden beneath their heavy, external armor. John ambles next to me, his attention likewise captivated by the massive land-dwelling reptiles.

"Amazing." I purposely choose the same descriptor I used when I first spied the sea lions at San Cristobal wharf, wondering if he remembers.

"Isn't it?" He does.

"In the documentary, *The Galapagos Affair*, there was a myth about tortoises knowing the evil intent of a person."

"Maybe we should've brought Bruno here and let the tortoises unravel the mystery?" He laughs, and I join in. "You did really well last night. There was a moment there when I thought you were going to fold, but you didn't. What saved you?"

"My hunches. First, it was something Derek quoted me from one of Agatha Christie's mysteries, 'Keep alert for what you've seen or heard before.' This morphed into a line from *The Galapagos Affair* that Margaret Wittmer said, 'A closed mouth admits no flies.' When I put them together, it became clear. Because of Bruno's personality type and his deep devotion to family and loyalty to traditions, I knew that if I provoked him on those topics, he'd have to defend his values. Once he opened his mouth, his evil intentions escaped."

"I've got to hand it to you, all this personality-type testing and your hunches seem to work. Maybe you should come over to the Monterey police department and train us."

"No, thanks." I bend down, holding a cluster of lettuce leaves in the hope an old tortoise will see it and shamble over.

John crouches beside me. "So, has all this quenched your need for adventure?"

I face him, my hand still outstretched. "I think it's given me the taste for more. It's certainly taken my mind off being a widow." My hand jerks when a two-hundred-kilogram tortoise tugs at the lettuce leaves. His face is wise and serene, like Yoda from Star Wars.

John points to the tortoise. "It's obvious he doesn't think you've got evil intent."

"You can count on an old tortoise to know who's who." I stare into the creature's eyes and know my future will be fine.

★ ★ ★

MY SECOND DRY MARTINI ARRIVES just as Derek joins our group at the bar for pre-dinner drinks.

"I must say, you look particularly lovely this evening." He leans over and kisses me on both cheeks. While Nancy and Judy titter and John arches a suspicious brow, I blush at Derek's overt gesture.

"Thank you." Though the truth is I flung every piece of clothing out of my closet trying to find something remotely suitable for my last night on board. Unlike Celeste who had a fabulous, colorful wardrobe, I ended up with only one option—a black, sheaf velvet, V-neck evening gown. A classic style, but again, dark and unassuming.

"A spectacular necklace, similar to Celeste's jewelry, would enhance that stunning dress, don't you think?" Nancy flutters her lashes at Derek. "Set off Diana's décolletage perfectly." She kisses her fingers like a Frenchman. The crafty old dear still thinks Derek's a legitimate buyer and that I'm the one he planned on giving it to.

"Aye, it'd look bonnie." He exaggerates his Scottish brogue while his eyes linger on my bosom, sending the Blum sisters into gales of girlish laughter.

"Stop teasing them," I whisper to him.

"Maybe I'm not."

"Now you're teasing me. What would you like to drink?" I raise my martini and sip.

"I'll have one of those."

I nod to the waiter for another while John and Derek chat, and the Blum sisters make doe eyes at him. At a nearby table, I notice Rose and Angelo in stilted conversation. *No happy ending there.* Not far from them are Robert and Clare. By her body language, she doesn't seem as enamored of his advances as she had at the beginning of the cruise. Perhaps this whole affair has empowered both Rose and Clare to be stronger, independent women. I hope so.

No longer undercover, Agents Sullivan and MacKenzie perch on stools beside the piano, watching Angelo and drinking a beer each. I catch their eye and raise my glass in a silent 'cheers'. Agent Sullivan returns the gesture with a smile, while I'm certain Agent MacKenzie mouths, 'To the secret-keeper' with her salute.

With a final sweep of the room, I spot Jason sitting alone at a table and Tony at another. Both appear lonely. I want to play matchmaker but think better of it. They'll have plenty of time to sort out their issues once Emily and Jason are reunited.

Patrizio spoke to her and her lawyer in transit today. They informed him that Celeste left a letter explaining Jason's adoption details and how she hoped that, on her death, Emily would try to find her brother. Perhaps Emily and Jason have a chance. Time is known as a great healer of wounds.

I try to focus on the conversation at the bar, but my thoughts drift to Tom once more. Although he'd have thought my initial involvement in this mystery reckless, I'm sure he'd have been proud of me. A fluttering in my stomach confirms my hunch, as do the beginning strains of a familiar tune played by the pianist. The song Tom and I danced to at our wedding.

The hairs on the back of my neck leap to attention. Misty-eyed, I face the piano and let the music and nostalgia flow over me.

A hand removes my martini while a voice sings in my ear, ". . . And the way you look tonight." Derek pulls me into his arms and taking well-executed steps, waltzes me away from the bar onto the dance floor. "But to love you . . ." As he sings, the lyrics of that special song cleave open my heart.

In that moment, I forget about being married, about being widowed, about feeling guilty for being in the arms of another man. I follow Derek's lead, twirling around the dance floor, loving the way my evening gown flies out behind me. We're the only couple dancing, and I sense all eyes on us. The poise from my ballet training remerges, and I lean and lunge into the waltz, my head tilting side to side. Alive. Free. A woman in her prime. When the pianist trills the last notes, a wave of applause rushes at us and instead of dropping my head with modesty, I spin and curtsy like an Olympic skater.

Throwing my arms around Derek's neck, I laugh and cry. "Thank you. Thank you."

Wrapping his arm around my waist, he escorts me back to the bar. "Thank you. You're a remarkable woman."

I demur silently, but for the first time in my life, I think perhaps I am.

★ ★ ★

I PACK AND SHUNT MY SUITCASE into the passageway just before midnight. Overnight, the crew will transport it ashore before we disembark the ship the next morning with our hand luggage.

Still in my gown, I curl up on the bed and remove the silver box from my bedside drawer. "Oh, Tom, we had a fabulous night. Derek and I danced, and then John, Judy, and Nancy joined us for dinner. We laughed and laughed. I think you'd like them. Really, I do." My breath hitches, and I struggle to swallow the hot lump of emotion wedged in my throat. "Well, my darling, I have a promise to keep."

Fighting back tears, I slip off the bed and stroll onto my balcony. The breeze flutters my hair as the ship powers on its voyage to our final destination, Baltra. With the swell pitching and rolling, my balance shifts, but my internal equilibrium holds steadfast. I've faced my fears, physical and emotional. The time has come.

After extracting the plastic bag containing Tom's ashes, I step to the railing. For a moment, I hesitate. I sense I'm not just throwing away his ashes. I'm throwing away the life I once had. *A wonderful life.* But my gut reminds me that a future awaits. One just as wonderful. A tear trickles down my cheek. "Good-bye, my darling. See you next time."

Extending my arm, I upend the ashes over the railing. A gust of wind captures them and, spinning them into the air, scatters them into the timeless mystery of the Galapagos Islands.

THE END

DIANA DANIELS FAVORITE DRY MARTINI

INGREDIENTS:
1 Part Noilly Prat Dry Vermouth
1 Part Grey Goose Vodka
3 green Sicilian olives

METHOD:
Place ice in a martini glass and chill for five minutes.
Discard ice.
Swirl chilled glass with Noilly Prat and discard.
Fill glass with fresh ice and add Grey Goose vodka.
Skewer three olives and garnish.

AUTHOR BIOGRAPHY

Diane began her career as a schoolteacher before moving into the entertainment industry as a choreographer, director, event manager, dancer and actress, working in television and live theatre, and managing multi-million-dollar productions.

Following her onstage career, she spent many years as a stress & life skills therapist, keynote speaker and presenter, appearing on national radio and television under the pseudonym of the Goddess of Love.

For her outstanding contribution to the arts, Diane was awarded the 2019 SBAA International Women's Day Leader Award for Leadership in the Entertainment, Creative Arts and Media Industry.

She is an award-winning author of contemporary, genre-busting romance, suspense and mystery novels. Her intuitive insights into human behaviour are woven into her casts of characters, heightening the intrigue in her storytelling. Set in exotic locations, her stories are packed with emotional punch and feature empowered heroines who live life to the fullest, much like the author herself.

Connect with Diane

https://dianedemetre.com/

AWARD WINNING AUTHOR

" . . . Dare to dream bigger than ever before, dare to forge our own path no matter how hard the challenges. But most of all, dare to be you and let the chips fall where they may. We are all warrior women with gossamer wings . . . It's time to roar!

— Diane Demetre

Winner of 2019 SBAA International Women's Day Leader Award for Leadership in Entertainment, Creative Arts and/or Media Industry.

Diane was nominated as a finalist in the ARRA Awards 2018 for Favourite Romantic Suspense, for her novel *Retribution.*

In 2017 Diane won the Romance Writers of Australia Emerald Pro Award for Best Unpublished Romance Manuscript.

ALSO, BY DIANE DEMETRE

ISLAND OF SECRETS

Two love stories separated in time. Two women following their dreams. In a paradise littered with painful secrets, will love turn the tide?

1973. Cecilia "CiCi" Freemont has a restless soul and the voice of an angel. Leaving her privileged upbringing behind, she chases her dreams to the sandy beaches of an unspoiled Hawaiian paradise, Harbor Island. But life takes an unexpected turn when she falls for the island's young heir-apparent and her newfound adventure becomes too much to bear . . .

2017. Investigative journalist Tina Templeton has dedicated herself to the pursuit of truth. But when she inherits Harbor Island, her career plans take a confusing twist. Managing the sprawling island estate is tough business even with the help of aging cabaret singer, CiCi Freemont. Especially when a massive ecological disaster threatens to destroy her beautiful beaches — and the responding coast guard captain steals her heart.

As the investigation into the disaster reveals a 40-year-old mystery that could change their lives forever, will Tina find love among the secrets, or will CiCi's painful past dash her dreams on the rocks?

Island of Secrets is an epic love story. If you like generations-spanning drama, characters with hidden pasts, heart-warming romance and intrigue, then you'll love Diane Demetre's powerful novel in paradise.

~ ♥ ~

RETRIBUTION

Winner of Romance Writers of Australia Emerald Pro Award 2017.

**She's a ballerina with a dark secret.
He's a retired sniper with a tortured past.
Will they find love or fall prey to a stalker's deadly game?**

Professional ballerina Jessie Hilton wraps her battle scars in satin pointe shoes, but there's a deeper hurt that haunts her sleep. When a handsome man steps in to save her from a mugging, something about her hero makes her heavy heart leap. Though her career can't afford distractions, he may be her sole source of safety when she gains the unwanted attention of a relentless stalker.

Ex-sniper Brad Jordan survived his tour of duty, but a tragic accident cost him the lives of those closest to him. With his faithful cost him the lives of those closest to him. With his faithful border collie Whiskey by his side, Brad gets a second chance when he protects the beautiful Jessie from danger. When the ballerina's stalker grows more brazen, Brad's tactical training may be their only weapon against tragedy.

Will Jessie and Brad survive a deadly game or will the assailant destroy their chance at love?

Retribution is a stand-alone romantic suspense novel. If you like tough-as-toe-shoes heroines, second-chance romance, and page-turning plots, then you'll love Diane Demetre's heart-stopping saga.

THE STEAMY SECRETS SERIES

STAND-ALONE CONTEMPORARY ROMANCE
FEATURING STRONG HEROINES AND PAGE-TURNING
PLOTS

TEMPT ME

*One woman . . . Two men . . . Threesomes change
everything*

When Michele Johnston, a forty-two-year-old ex-dancer from the Moulin Rouge gets divorced, she leaps into her new world of singledom with unbridled passion.

Aided and abetted by three vivacious girlfriends, Michele embarks on her steamy, erotic adventures, but gets more than she expects when mysterious yacht captain Mark Miller unleashes her wanton desires.

Further complicating matters, debonair Greek businessman Nick Stavros arrives on the scene and falls madly in love with her, promising the happy-ever-after ending. But will she give up her newfound freedom? Will she choose one man over the other? Or can she continue loving them both?

Tempt Me is the first stand-alone Contemporary Erotic Romance in Diane Demetre's genre-busting series, Steamy Secrets. If you love strong heroes, hot sex, and feisty heroines, don't miss this page-turning love story with a twist.

~ ♥ ~

TEACH ME

When destiny beckons, what is a girl to do?

At twenty-four, Samantha O'Brien scores her dream job as a dancer at the famous Moulin Rouge, only to arrive in Paris to find her well-laid plans in disarray. Fortuitously, Sam is rescued by the eccentric, tarot-card reading proprietress of Hotel Hollandaise, who cautions that Paris is for lovers, but not always love.

As Sam launches into her new career, she suspects that the show's super sexy, Sicilian stage director, Tony Di Falco is more than just a creative genius and hard taskmaster, leaving her to wonder whether secrets are best shared.

Meeting Philippe Lacroix, a struggling, young artist in Montmartre saves Sam from imploding under the pressure. He introduces her to the city of love, captivating her with his angelic good looks and sensuous touch. Yet the mounting attraction intensifies between Sam and Tony, and their tense, sexually charged relationship threatens to overwhelm them. But the show must go on.

Filled with backstage bitchiness, tough rehearsals, a sprinkling of cocaine and the French addiction to cigarettes, Sam grapples with her new life. Then without warning, her destiny changes literally before her eyes, and she learns that even in the most romantic city of the world, you don't find love, love finds you.

Teach Me is the second stand-alone Contemporary Erotic Romance in Diane Demetre's genre-busting series, Steamy Secrets. If you love strong heroes, hot sex and feisty heroines, don't miss this page-turning love story with a twist.

TAKE ME

How far would you run to find love?

Aiden Bishop is a successful young lawyer hiding out in sunny Spain to escape unsavoury clients in Australia. At twenty-seven, Ace as he's known to his mates, happens upon a local flamenco club in Seville where he's befriended by Rafael Flores and beguiled by Carla Armando — a famous flamenco couple well-known for their fiery performances both on and off the stage.

With ancestral links to the famous gypsy flamenco dancer Carmen Amaya, Rafael and Carla have mysterious Romani culture coursing through their veins. Sensing Aiden's love of adventure, they invite him on a road trip from the Costa Del Sol to Granada in search of Carla's true Romani gifts. However, as the trip stretches deeper into less travelled emotional geography, long-kept secrets are exposed.

Brimming with gypsy traditions, the passion of the dance, mysterious rune readings and intrigue, Aiden realizes that he may be able to evade his clients, but he can't escape his destiny no matter how far he runs.

Take Me is the third stand-alone Contemporary Erotic Romance in Diane Demetre's genre-busting series, Steamy Secrets. If you love strong heroes, hot sex and feisty heroines, don't miss this page-turning love story with a twist.

PRAISE FOR DIANE'S WORK

An exciting and erotic read A refreshing genre-busting story of a divorced, older (I hasten to add by society's standards not mine) heroine who is determined to embrace her singledom while simultaneously casting aside her self- and societally-imposed sexual repression through casual erotic encounters. Diane Demetre offers a story that challenges our pre-conceived notions of what "women of a certain age" should or should not be doing and she does this in an empowering manner. The heroine embraces and cherishes her female friendships and though this aided in the flow of the plot, it also highlights the importance for women of having encouraging and supportive female companionship. Most importantly, we see the heroine herself allow the experiences of her new-found freedom to shape her own future thus enabling her to escape the repressive nature of her pre-divorce life. All in all, an erotic and exciting read sure to captivate and thrill readers of any age.

— AusRom Today

I really, really liked this book. The story was entertaining, but the characters absolutely made the novel engrossing. Also, I was particularly enamored with the Australian setting; especially with the country scenes, I felt like I was there.

This is a clean romance which I appreciated. Jessie and BJ are honorable, decent people trying to overcome horrors from their pasts. They have stalwart friends who support them and who are supported in return. I also loved Whiskey, BJ's pet companion. The love BJ has for Whiskey is woven intrinsically throughout every chapter. I highly recommend this suspenseful tale.

— Laurie Jenkins (GoodReads Top Reviewer)

Fantastic, emotional mystery and romance
I absolutely loved this story! I loved the characters and the way Demetre truly makes you have strong feelings for each one. This is so beautifully written with such a fantastic storyline that has you gripped right till the very end, with laughter, smiles, shrieks and tears through the emotional rollercoaster that is an Island of Secrets! . . .

— 5 STARS, Amazon

Demetre paints vividly the atmosphere of Paris and the Moulin Rouge with such detail that it adds yet another layer of intimacy to the story. A wonderful read that we highly recommend.

— AusRom Today

I bought this book and wow what a read! To every young woman it's a must! Life lessons learnt in an amazing story told! Though I had other things to do, I had to finish this amazing story! Bring on book 3!

— 5 STARS

A well-written erotic romance with its share of twists and suspense. Love the characters and the way the author describes Paris and behind the scenes of the Moulin Rouge.

— 5 STARS, Peter Brady

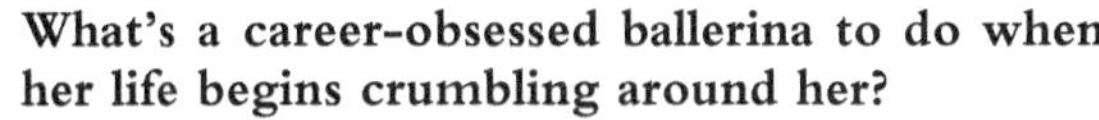

What's a career-obsessed ballerina to do when her life begins crumbling around her?

This novel had a lot going on and had no trouble grabbing and keeping my interest. Muggings, mystery stalkers, traumatic and abusive childhoods, tragic loss of family members, you name it, all revolving around a budding relationship between an ex-sniper and a rising young ballerina based in Melbourne, Australia. I love stories set in faraway places and, for me, Australia is about as far as they get!

This book is well-written and fairly fast paced with most of the action occurring within a two-week time period in December. The romance part of the story is fairly sweet and subdued but does have a bit of a sexy flare eventually. As to the stalker, I liked the use of alternating POVs that took us into his warped mind way before we learned his identity.

All in all, an enjoyable romantic suspense read with some great characters, both good and evil.
—5 STARS, Amazon, Avid Reader

I love, love, love, this book! This book was so good! It jumps over a span of about forty years. It has everything in it. From first love to first discovery. It has suspense, love lost and love gained. It also has a friendship that stood the test of time, and sibling rivalry. If you read another book this year, this is the one! I highly recommend this wonderful book!
— 5 STARS, Amazon, Tasha Thomas

DIANE DEMETRE

www.ingramcontent.com/pod-product-compliance
Lightning Source LLC
Chambersburg PA
CBHW060914190726
48286CB00002B/496
9781910397992